The *Dating* Bender

By Christina Julian

The *Dating* Bender

Copyright © 2017 by Christina Julian.
All rights reserved.
First Print Edition: August 2017

Limitless Publishing, LLC
Kailua, HI 96734
www.limitlesspublishing.com

Formatting: Limitless Publishing

ISBN-13: 978-1-64034-087-9
ISBN-10: 1-64034-087-4

Dedication

To my parents, who loved the hell out of me, even when I refused to let them. And to Candy Jackson, who taught me that anything is possible. As long as you believe.

Chapter One

Dad was tanked, which was no surprise, yet he stood eager and ready to walk me down the aisle. I peered out from the back of the church and saw no less than four hundred of my parents' friends and family. I wasn't sure if my vision was distorted due to the sweat that had seeped in, but it looked like the majority of the attendees were tipsy too. Perhaps it was my delay in getting to the church. I could have just been paranoid and projecting.

But this sizzling May day was all mine. I scratched my nose for courage, steadied my father, who looked dangerously close to toppling, and we set off down the chapel's gangplank. The cameras clicked, I smiled, and Dad gripped me for support. I felt as robotic as a Stepford wife.

Two steps in I realized why my wedding planner recommended against the full-length beaded silk organza gown. Its raised surface gave my father something to cling to when he clutched my forearm and pulled off the intricately stitched beading.

Sheldon stood side-by-side with the priest up

ahead. From far away he looked like a little boy, afraid to meet his teacher on the first day of school. My father had that effect on people.

"Are you sure you know what the hell you're doing? We've never liked Sheldon," my dad said. His boozy breath almost made me hurl. He sounded just like Grandpop, who used to snap the fridge shut and snarl every time we reached for a Ding Dong.

I stopped mid-step and contemplated. Of course I knew what I was doing. Sheldon was an escape from the craziness, and he was my best friend, which had to count for something.

We continued forward. The crowd must have heard my father's comment because everyone had hushed to silence. With each step we took, I felt my cheeks turn from rosy to firebomb red. As if Sheldon had sensed my discomfort, he caught my attention with a subtle flip of his clean-shaven chin. He motioned for me to keep walking.

As we neared the rest of the wedding party, my father almost tripped. He grabbed my shoulder to stabilize. His maneuver knocked my pale pink baby's breath veil to the side of my sweaty noggin. I arrived at the altar with a headpiece that looked as tipsy as my father.

He handed me off to my spouse-to-be, swatted me on the back, and said, "Good luck, you're gonna need it," thinking he was whispering, but he spoke loud enough for the priest and everyone in the front row to hear. His behavior made it difficult to love him, but his reign over my life would soon end.

He belched and left me there to face my destiny as "Trumpet Voluntary" hummed in the background. That song and my dad's disorderly behavior threatened to make me cry, but I resisted.

After all the years in the trenches, I was finally going to be free. In a matter of speaking. Sheldon looked pleasant in his tuxedo. What I'd call cute-subpar, but he was mine. A section of his chestnut hair flopped over one of his coffee-brown eyes. He mouthed "I love you," which made me giggle.

I tried to center myself by looking at the ground. Father Sigfried must have expected more, because he stooped down to glare at me. He pushed my chin upward, forcing me to focus on my parents' dismal church. It was dark and dank with not a bit of stained glass to be found.

An unbearable span of time passed, while he droned on and the readers spouted a multitude of ridiculous religious passages. "Love is always patient and kind," he said, a point often lost on my parents.

Thirty minutes later, he brought us to the pinnacle of the ceremony. At a glance, it seemed like half the crowd was snoozing. I looked into Father Sigfried's eyes through his large purple-framed glasses—an odd choice for the occasion. He had done a bad job at hiding his bald spot, which gave me a target to stare at.

He waddled over to Sheldon and me, joined hand in hand. Mine was thick with sweat, but my fiancé squeezed it lovingly anyway.

"Are we ready to recite the vows, folks?" he asked.

It was impossible to not laugh. First inside, then out loud.

My sister-in-law Jackie sidled up to me, grabbed my hand, and pulled me away from Sigfried.

"Sam, stop cackling. Your mom is on her way up to the altar."

I watched my mother bumble toward me.

Oh, Christ.

Suddenly, the church temperatures and my anger were climbing high. I glanced over at my bridesmaids in their hot pink cocktail dresses. They stood at attention, makeup melting off their faces. My poor tulip bouquet wilted in the humidity.

"Samantha, what do you think you're doing?" she slurred into my ear.

Somewhere between buttoning up my dress and getting to the church she'd found a moment to get smashed, rivaling only my father. What ailed these people? Just because their marriage teetered between silence and barbs, didn't seem like a justified reason to booze it up.

I wiggled my nose vehemently to instigate deep breathing. I'm not sure if it was her beady eyes or the priest's failed comb-over, but all I could do was cackle.

Dear God get it together. This is embarrassing.

"Don't make me get your father," she murmured through clenched teeth.

Between snorts, I tried to quiet her. When that failed, I pulled her out of the center of attention.

"It's bad enough you dishonored us by living out of wedlock with your man-hussy, but now you're mocking the sacrament of marriage in front of a goddamn full church. Show some respect."

Church did little to deter her tendency to curse.

4

She genuflected and stormed off the altar.

Poor Sheldon tried to settle me, the crowd, and my flailing mother. He excelled in crowd management, especially my unruly family. We Serranos were a scrappy bunch. Sheldon loved me in spite of that.

He peeled away the throng of bridesmaids as my maid of honor swathed my forehead with a lavender-scented hankie. It was supposed to be my "something new." Now not so much, since I'd soiled it with the spit of my laughter.

"Sam, you can do this," Sheldon said. "You're about to walk away from this craziness. I promise you'll never look back. That is my commitment to you."

He kissed me sweetly on the cheek. I giggled for just a moment longer, and then said I do.

***

One hour and three hundred snapshots later, the marriage was sealed. My father teetered across the grassy knoll of Annapolis State Circle. The town looked surreal with its cobblestone streets, crackerjack buildings, and lines of midshipmen walking in calculated formations. A parade of American flags waved in the background.

Dad broke up our huddle with the photographer. "Are you done yet, Samantha?" he said. "We want to get the party underway."

"Sorry to let my wedding photos get in the way of your binge drinking," I whispered.

My parents weren't full-blown alcoholics, just

weekenders, but in times of stress they drank themselves into a stupor regardless of what day of the week it was. They brought new meaning to the phrase "drinking and driving" because they not only drank and drove, they drank *while* driving. I prayed to God they might find a new coping mechanism.

My father gave me the stink-eye and then toddled toward the festivities.

Sheldon, in his first role as my husband, snatched me up into his arms and away from my father. He swung me across the lawn and ushered me into our reception. My man to the rescue.

I stood at the entrance, staring at the ornate room where we were about to make our first public appearance as man and wife. It felt like a soul-touching moment until I peered toward the dance floor. In front of everyone, my mother shouted, "Hail to the Redskins, hail victory, Braves on the war path, fight for old DC!" as she performed the equivalent of an Indian tribal dance, hobbling barefoot across the dance floor. My father trailed behind her, martini in hand, always the loyal soldier. *Martha Stewart Living* warned that serving cocktails during a party could lead to unexpected "happenings."

"Sheldon, do something. Make them stop."

"Where's your brother? Didn't he say he would take care of them tonight?"

I tore through the crowd trying to find Jimmy. He had forsaken his familial duties.

The DJ announced the father/daughter dance. The last thing I felt like doing was dancing with him, but if it put an end to my mother's chant, it was worth it. I recalled a fleeting moment of sobriety when my father and I slow danced to Sinatra the night before my fifth-grade cotillion. Today was not such a moment.

I tried to muster some love for the man who had given me life, and realized I felt nothing but annoyance. I was about to buckle, but Sheldon grabbed my hand and squeezed it gently. "Go on, Sam, you can do this," he said. "And when it's over, we can start our new life. Together."

As I looked back at him, he nodded at the precise moment I was about to flee. He gave me the courage to continue.

"The Way You Look Tonight" came on as I walked toward my father and extended my hand to him, which he needed to stay upright. I stared back at Sheldon, who wouldn't break eye contact, and knew I made the right choice. He would be my rock—my escape route out of Hell.

Chapter Two

We argued our way through Central Park in a smelly NYC yellow cab, trying to catch the Jitney bus to the Hamptons. Smashed wedding cake coated my arm, courtesy of a quick-braking cabbie—not how I'd hoped to start my one-year anniversary getaway. It seemed like a symbolic representation of the last year of dreaded bliss. Moldy smashed cake.

"Get us through the park or we're going to miss our bus," Sheldon commanded.

Wow, he could be obnoxious. They didn't warn me about spousal metamorphosis in the *Marriage for Dummies* book my parents gave us as a wedding gift.

Sheldon continued to repeat himself until the cabbie stopped short in the middle of the bustling street. Manhattan seemed impervious to road rules.

"Park no open, mister," the driver said.

I teetered between optimism and annoyance as Sheldon continued his verbal assault. At times like these, he made it difficult to love him.

We spent the next two hours waiting for another Hampton Jitney, sweating curbside on the Upper East Side, because just like the cabbie warned, the park was closed. So much for *Lonely Planet's* brilliant idea for an easy-breezy way out to the Hamptons.

***

Despite arriving in South Hampton twelve hours later than planned, I vowed to make the best of things by ignoring the fact that we had set off on our sojourn when the sun was rising, and we would catch the sunset only if we were lucky.

We arrived at the bed and breakfast and started unloading the car. With each step we took toward the front door, mosquitos descended upon my arm, biting me and the cake remnants that lingered. *Brides* magazine offered no tips for traveling with the top of your year-old wedding cake. Bite welts peppered my arm. I ignored the itching because I could see Sheldon needed his ego plumped.

"Pooh Bear, why don't we explore the town on a seaside stroll? It really is a beautiful spot you've chosen."

"Sure, anything to get some air. Bus rides give me motion sickness."

A sulking man is not attractive.

"Great, I'll get the champagne and fishy glasses we got at the wedding, and you grab a blanket," I said.

Sheldon stared at me with annoyance. Even in

our worst hours at least one of us (okay, me) tried to remain optimistic.

Why was he so damned depressed all the time? The first year of marriage is supposed to be the best time of your lives, though I felt more like newly dead than wed.

I was nothing if not tenacious, though, so I pushed us out the door, and within five minutes, as we walked hand in hand, my bites stopped throbbing and I felt a foreign sense of arousal. Maybe this trip would be a chance to reconnect.

In the months that followed our wedding, Sheldon worked nonstop in an ever-failing attempt to get his faltering rent-a-cop security company out of the red, and with every month he did not meet his goals, he took it out on me. It started with subtle jabs about my salary at the Home Shopping Network not matching his expectations. As the months dragged on, he mastered the art of verbal abuse. Just like my father, he paid special attention to critiquing my inability to complete sentences.

Shared morning coffee and canoodling fell to the wayside by month four. Dr. Phil warned about the seven-year itch but made no mention of the four-month "bitch out your bride" phase. I tried to remind myself that Sheldon loved me more than anybody ever had. He only wanted to take care of me. So what if he worked too much? There were worse offenses than wanting to succeed.

For our first anniversary celebration, the serene view of South Hampton, with its whitewashed Victorians sandwiched between cool white sand dunes, put me at ease.

"Hey, Pooh, isn't this a spectacular sunset?" I said.

"It sure is, Cubby. Shit."

And then he toppled. I dropped to the ground to help him. Blood spurted right on top of my adorable white eyelet sundress and into my sun-kissed brown locks, which had been highlighted for the occasion.

A cracked bottle of tart-apple Mad Dog lay in the wake of Sheldon's sandy tumble. At least we smelled delectable. More blood oozed out of Sheldon's foot. I screamed until I realized nobody was coming.

Men should never cry. I understand they feel pain too, but there was something disturbing about a guy whimpering like a sea lion.

"Honey, let's try to get some help. Do you think you can walk?"

"Christ, no I can't, Sam. There is a glass shard stuck up my foot. How stupid are you?"

According to my father, very.

Sheldon launched into a small rant, ending his fit by bouncing around like a clown at the circus.

I scratched my nose gently as if to wipe away his barb—an annoying habit that had only gotten worse since the wedding.

O magazine said crisis showed the strength or weaknesses of a relationship. Sheldon waved me off and called me an unrepeatable profanity. Would she count that as a sign of weakness?

Ever efficient, I got him to roll onto what supposed to be our romantic sex blanket. The flimsy, gauzy nature of the periwinkle fabric matched the shabby state of our union.

My barely ample frame struggled for the next hour as I dragged him up and over three sand dunes that were no longer beautiful to me. My father's sweating-it-to-the-oldies weight-lifting regime had built my endurance at least. It was also helpful that Sheldon wasn't the six-foot three stallion I had fantasized about marrying.

We finally made it to the side of the road. A sweet older coupled picked us up and offered us a ride to the hospital. We got into the truck despite the cow poop stink.

"It's okay, dear. Sometimes the pressure around anniversaries is counterproductive," the woman said from the passenger side through the peewee back window. "Herb and I had a disastrous first anniversary, but we've been together for fifty years!"

An adorable sentiment, but it did nothing to squelch my annoyance. I missed the days when Sheldon used to tell me he loved me before every meal and sexual encounter. Apparently, our anniversary didn't warrant a romantic reprise.

We spent seven hours in the emergency room where Sheldon cussed out two nurses, one doctor, and a small child, ending his diatribe by demanding service over the receptionist's loud speaker. After we escaped that torture, we filled our time being miserable in our four hundred dollars-a-night B&B cabin. I lied and told Sheldon I'd talked them down to one hundred and fifty bucks to get him to take the trip. My reward: he allowed me to dote on his wounded foot, which lulled at least one of us to sleep.

For our final evening, I rallied and led a toast to commemorate our nuptials over squashed year-old cake and flat champagne. I mustered the courage to seduce Sheldon by doing my version of a sexy dance. I felt like a jackass flailing my arms and caressing my non-curvaceous body. *Cosmo's* seduction boot camp blows.

The bubbly emboldened me to lean down and pleasure Sheldon orally. As I sunk into his *business,* a feeling of nausea washed over me. I vomited all over his less-than-ample apparatus. It was hard to tell by his expression if he was horrified, turned on, or irked that I woke him.

Year-old cake did not keep as well as all the bridal magazines led me to believe; or maybe it was my semi-erotic dance moves.

Sheldon left me alone on the couch of our sexless cabana. My weekend role as nursemaid to his foot was not reciprocated when it came to tending to my food poisoning.

I recuperated enough overnight to pack up our stuff as a thunderstorm boomed outside. The weather seemed fitting, considering the turbulent state of our relationship. New York could be dreary when it wanted to be, a talent Sheldon had mastered during our first year of marriage. How could I have been delusional enough to believe that a vacation in the Hamptons might melt away our problems?

***

Before ending the mess of a weekend, we stopped at my brother's house in Westchester for a visit. Jimmy and his wife Jackie were living my parents' quintessential version of life: three children, a mansion in the suburbs, and a corporate job as an investment banker where Jimmy "provided for his family," as my mother often put it. This was her passive-aggressive way of noting that Sheldon was not doing the same. Finally, a point my mother and I could agree on.

They were an attractive bunch. Jackie made soccer mom status look hip. On the outside my brother looked like every other investment banker on Wall Street, but on the weekends he morphed into someone who could easily fit within a *J. Crew* catalog. My three nieces did their part by looking far cuter than any Gap Kids model ever could. They represented the functional side of my family.

Upon arrival, I unloaded all of our crap onto the cavernous back porch because Sheldon's foot still hadn't mended. I darted around the house looking for Jackie.

Sheldon blocked me.

"Babe, can you get me some ice for my foot? It's still aching," he said, looking more pathetic than usual as he settled into the living room. I willed myself to love him more than I felt in the moment. It wasn't his fault family visits were stressful.

"Yes, give me a minute."

I scrambled around the house, room by room, until I found my sister-in-law in the third-floor playroom amid a Barbie condo complex.

"Hey there, great to see you! But if I don't get away from Sheldon, I may kill him," I said.

"What happened to you? You look hellacious,"

Jackie said. She suffered from her own form of Tourette's syndrome: the brutally honest variety.

"Well, we missed our bus, went to the beach, and spent the better part of the weekend in the ER. Oh, and I attempted to pleasure Sheldon. Let's just say I'll never have to do *that* again. Can we please get out of here?"

"Retail therapy it is," she said as she squeezed my cheeks together like a mother would do to her child. She gave me that pitiful look that happily married people often give to their not nearly as happy counterparts.

I tore down three flights of spiral stairs and tripped over my niece's Barbie doll before reaching the restaurant-caliber kitchen. Once I figured out how to work the ice machine, I bagged a bundle and slid it down the hallway to Sheldon.

"Bye, honey, be back soon," I said, already halfway out the door.

As I waited and sunk into the buttercream soft leather seats of Jackie's Jag, my marital woes slipped into the distance, as did my annoyance with Sheldon. He was a wonderful man. I just brought out the worst in him.

Thirty shopping minutes later, I found more solace in a hip pair of pink satin high-heeled sneakers. It was true what they said about shopping. The shoes managed to do what Sheldon hadn't for the duration of our trip and marital life together; they made me happy. He had tried. Just not hard enough.

I popped them on my feet, and every time I glanced down, I got a kick out of myself.

"I've still got it, right, Jackie?"

"You've got something all right, though I'm not sure what, but the sneaks are cute. This has been fun, but I have to get back to the kids."

I wondered which kids she was talking about: hers or my husband masquerading as a child.

"Sure, I guess you're right. Let me pay for these."

Trying to prolong our return home, I dallied at the register. The purse sale rack stood next to the checkout line, which gave me another opportunity to stall. I picked through every pocket of every bag on the table until Jackie glared at me and shooed me out of the shop.

Despite the forced departure, I was riding on a sneaker high as we pulled into the driveway.

I ran upstairs to the guest room and swapped my dingy sweats for a sexy nightie. Then I plucked my new pink sneakers out of their box and put them on, completing my seductive yet quirky outfit. I tried to plump up my barely-there breasts by stuffing them into a push-up bra, just like *Glamour* magazine had instructed. I looked into the full-length mirror hanging from the door and determined that my enhanced bust looked goofy given my petite frame, so I set my boobies free, convinced the shoes would suffice.

I walked into the den where Sheldon sat watching sports with his foot still propped up on a pillow.

"So, Pooh Bear, what do you think, hot and sassy, huh?"

"Sam, after all the money we blew on our

anniversary, please tell me you didn't throw our money away on a frivolous impulse purchase. I'm in enough pain."

Instead of having hot pink sneaker make-up sex, I received the cold shoulder for the rest of the night. Gone were the evenings of nude backrubs and cherry Coke floats shared through a single straw.

At breakfast, always one to stir the pot, Jackie said, "Slinky sneaks Sam bought, don't you think, Shel?"

He glared at her, then me.

"Sam, I am not amused. Something has to shift with our finances," he said.

Perhaps a real job on his part might be a start.

Jackie eyed him with disdain, and directed me to the back porch with a less-than-subtle hair flip.

"Who is he kidding? You never buy anything, *and* he's going to give you shit about a twenty-five-dollar pair of shoes? If I were you, I would get out of the marriage based on that alone, not to mention all of his other inadequacies as a man. You do realize that trying to marry yourself out of your family was a bad idea, don't you?"

Please. That was not what I was doing. Jackie could benefit from a session with Oprah on the art of being tactful. "Sheldon has always been tight with our money. That's hardly a reason to leave someone. And as my mother and the church always say, 'Divorce is not the answer!'" Maybe living unhappily ever after is.

I used the phrase "our money" loosely, since his company was tanking so *our* money translated into *my* money—not that anybody but Sheldon was counting.

People didn't give up on a marriage based on tightwad tendencies, or, at least, not this someone. What I did need to figure out was how to make the most of our disintegrating relationship. Maybe I could conjure images of our early days of high romance when he used to make me laugh. Like when he did his Lady Gaga impersonation.

When Jackie finished her tough love sermon, I fled to my nieces' tree house, where I spent the rest of the afternoon hiding out and reminding myself how happily married I was supposed to be. I also prayed to God for some direction on how to make that fantasy a reality.

The Big Guy did not hear me.

Indulging in another familial-bred tendency, I poured myself a bourbon from the stash I'd pilfered earlier from the liquor cabinet and drank it in one smooth swig. I unlaced my fabulous sneakers, climbed out of the tree house, crept barefoot to the trash can, and chucked them.

Then I walked over to the outdoor mini bar, grabbed some vodka, and sat on the patio steps. Becoming "one" with my drink, I gazed out into the starry abyss of a picture-perfect backyard that was so far from my life it could have been Pluto. The booze was not as comforting as I'd hoped.

Sitting there, looking to the sky or God or anybody who would listen, I muttered, "'Til death do us part, huh?"

Chapter Three

I tried to enjoy some much-needed alone time in our quaint sun room. The space oozed with color. Blazing yellow walls and pink trim; my attempt at painting myself happy. It didn't work. I blamed Sheldon because he refused to use air conditioning unless temperatures rose to ninety-eight degrees. Our Spanish-style *hacienda* trapped the heat like a sweatbox. Why in the hell we ever moved to St. Petersburg, Florida, I would never know. Oh, that's right—to escape my family.

Sheldon interrupted my relaxation when he clunked in and blocked my rays as he hovered behind me.

"Cubby Bear, I was presented with an opportunity to live out my life-long security dream, and I'm going to take it," he said.

"Oh, you mean you bought me that cute little Redskinette cheerleading outfit, and you want to order me around in it?" I snorted.

He repositioned himself, throwing his weight, which included the extra fifteen pounds he had packed on since the honeymoon.

"Sam, I'm being serious. Paul was offered the opportunity to run security at the Super Bowl, and he put me second-in-command. It's a killer job. This is my chance to take my ideas about security crowd management *global*."

Global, who was he kidding? It wasn't like he was helping to mitigate terrorism.

"Wow, Pooh Bear, that sounds amazing. I need to get through the push at work and then maybe we can talk about it."

"Well, it can't wait. We have to get packed for Atlanta. It's a long-term contract, serious business. I promised you financial security and this is one step in that direction."

"Honey, I can't just leave my job. Besides, this might be something we should talk through a bit before we go and uproot our lives on a whim."

I scratched my nose with one hand and started dusting plants with the other.

"I didn't mean *we* as in you and me. I meant Paul and I need to go," he said.

Clearly I missed something, because according to *Redbook* couples discussed and reached an agreement before acting. *Stand up to him, you wimp!* Quelling my tendency to curse, I decided to gather more facts before overreacting.

I moved on to dusting Sheldon's oversized boob-tube—a high-ticket purchase he made without discussing it with me first.

"So, when exactly in this scenario would I be coming out, if we were going to consider this? Hypothetically."

Sheldon stared at me.

"Sam, this is a huge chance for me, your basic no-brainer. I need to be there. Someone needs to stay back here and man the fort."

Man the fort? WTF? A year into our marriage I'm supposed to stay home and "man" a ridiculous fort while my husband jets off to Atlanta with his Peter-Pan-complex-of-a-business-partner for the next year?

Especially annoying given that just last month I begged him to let me consider a job that my mentor, Babs, had offered me. She was helping to launch a start-up that was poised to become the next generation of social networking, and she'd needed my help in Colorado.

He completely blew me off. He might have even said he needed to *stew* on it. He couldn't possibly be this thick.

I breathed in deeply, holding the exhale just like *Self* magazine advised to temper anger. It didn't work.

"Honey, you can't go off and make a unilateral decision about our life without me. Are you really not aware of the protocol in these situations?" I said.

Sheldon disliked Babs and her work ethic. He mistrusted her because, according to him, she was a has-been by-product of the sexual revolution. Her only real problem was that she never realized, with the onset of AIDS and all the other STDs, you weren't supposed to continue sexing it up randomly anymore. However, for every sexually expressive fiber in her body, Babs had equal amounts of razor-sharp business acumen. *It's fitting that you would seek out a slutty mentor.*

She became infamous for rattling up a business meeting by sliding up onto the conference room table in a micro-mini skirt to capture people's attention. The fact that she rarely wore underwear only heightened her ability to pull focus.

"Sheldon, please tell me you weren't really expecting me to stay back in this cesspool of a panhandle while you gallivant around the country without me."

I moved on to cleaning the mini-blinds and positioned my back to him, a power play from *Forbes* magazine. I peered out the window at our adorable backyard. I endured the sticky hot temps every morning to ensure we had a manicured lawn spotted with pale pink impatiens flowers, all encased in a perfect picket fence of palm trees. Unfortunately, life within the walls of our world was anything but perfect.

"Babe, I don't know what the big deal is. You'll visit me, and when I can, I'll come back here. You can keep our fort safe while I build the nest egg of our future. It's all going to work out. I want to take care of you, and this is an excellent opportunity to do that," he said.

He could be charming when he wanted to be, but still, it was a moronic idea. No sane person would take this lying down or standing up. If he thought he could just hop off to Atlanta and follow his version of the American Dream without me, then I would do the same damn thing.

I dropped my dust cloth and ran upstairs to the

bathroom to dial Babs as fast as my fingers could fly.

"It's Sam. You know that job offer you've been dangling? I'm in. When do you need me in Colorado?"

***

"Mom, I told you. Sheldon and I are not getting a divorce. Everything is fine. Our careers are temporarily leading us to work in different states. That's it. We plan to visit each other religiously, I promise. I'm going to get back to God too, like you suggested."

"Don't you dare disrespect me in an effort to hide the fact that you are making another poor lifestyle choice," she said. "It's bad enough you married him, but to live apart so you can each chase your pipe dreams is ridiculous, even for you."

I contemplated hanging up on her. Instead, I sipped more Pinot Grigio. Or "pen-wa-grego," as my mother often mispronounced it.

"Mom, seriously, social networking is not a fad. Remember Shelly? She just got engaged to a guy she met on Facebook."

"Well, your cousin has always been gullible, even more than you, which is hard to believe. What are they going to do, live together in sin on this Facetime thing?"

"It's Facebook, Mom. Seriously, this is a great opportunity."

"You really do live in a dream world. What you do with your life is your own business, but a divorce would be roadkill for our position in the church," she said. "I know you've always been a quitter, but ditching a marriage is taking it to an extreme I could never forgive. P.S., I love you. When you're not doing stupid things."

Click.

A part of me wanted to call her back and scream *get off my back you unsupportive SOB of a mother*, but instead I sipped more wine and breathed deeply. Oprah suggested using each passing day as an opportunity to practice patience.

I rationalized that, at the end of a three-month trial period, we would measure the success of each of our ventures. Depending on which job proved more lucrative, the other partner would gracefully bail out of his or her career and move to offer love and support to their spouse. That's what married people did. *Or so you'd think.*

Unfortunately, our families were not quite as placated by our plan as Sheldon was. Their response to the decision was fashioned after my Dad's favorite Sinatra song, "Send in the Clowns," but in my parents' rendition they sent in the priest.

Why did all Catholics think bringing a man of God into a relationship was a good thing? Did it really make sense to seek lifestyle advice from someone who had spent the better part of his life hiding out in a church, and according to some, fondling little boys? I'd tried to accept that consulting a priest was standard practice for my people, who preferred to pray for a better outcome instead of dealing with reality.

Sheldon's family took the decision much better

than mine. They seemed to see the brighter side of things. It was a shame they didn't school their son on the art of marital decision-making.

They honored "our" decision to temporarily separate for work, while my parents chose the tact of deny, deny, and then disown—their favorite childrearing weapon. Ever since I graduated from diapers, my family had threatened to disown me. One of their earlier attempts surfaced when I picked theater class over tennis in middle school. My father voiced his concern: "All drama people are nuts." They temporarily disowned me again when Sheldon and I moved in together, only to lift the sentence and pop a champagne cork when we got engaged. Then they learned he wasn't Catholic. At times I wished they would end the flip-flopping and make good on their threat to fire me out of the family. I wrote to Oprah for insight into why I tolerated their behavior. She never answered.

I obliged everybody by listening to their concerns over lunches, coffee meetings, and in my father's case, alcohol-bender rap sessions. At times he offered sound financial advice, usually in the morning before the cocktail slinging began. He could be helpful as long as he laid off the sauce, which was next to never.

But I knew I was doing the right thing, regardless of what everyone else thought. What sane woman would sit back and mind a frickin' fort while their husband jetted off to hobnob with some of the best football players (and cheerleaders) in the country? I would not be left behind to sift through crap jewelry, sweating my ass off and praying some lonely old fart would find my buying selections for the Home Shopping Network impressive enough to help me meet my sales numbers.

No siree. Call me pig-headed or call me independent, but I was no longer okay with being the sole breadwinner. The gravy train is over, Mr. Sheldon Milton! *Oh please, are you really this naive?*

***

I woke up groggy, having not slept that well. Or maybe it was all the wine. Bumbling out the door, I stopped off at the mailbox on my way to the beach. My mother had express-mailed another one of her silly articles. Today's installment: **Divorce Is Not the Answer!** penned by none other than the pope. She'd sent me these supposedly inspirational clippings for as long as I could remember. In my youth, they were less subtle. One of my favorites: **Celebrity Virgins—They're Not DOING IT, Why Should You?**

I glanced at the article briefly, crumpled it up, and continued down to the waterway, finally reaching Beach Drive. The waves whipped up over the bulkhead and the smell of salt sullied the air. Was I crushing my marriage, or was all of this a natural step toward rescuing it?

My Taylor Swift ringtone broke the reverie.

"Oh. Hey, Dad, what's up?"

"What the hell do you think is up?" he slurred. "I'm worried about you. I don't want you to torch your life any further than you already have. If you're really set on making this move, at least let me come out there and help you drive across the goddamn country."

It gave me hope when he showed signs of a softer side.

"Sure, Dad, that would be great. Babs wants me to start working in two weeks, so I plan to head out next Friday. Does that work for you?"

"You mean to tell me you're destroying your life and marriage to follow that lou-lou Babs? Are you nuts?"

I thought I answered him on that one already.

"No, Dad. I'm not crazy. You knew she's who I'll be working for, didn't you?"

"Shut up and hear me. I will not support your lunacy, not this time. Babs grew up with those crazy Charlie Manson kids. She's missing a right and wrong meter in that drugged-up head of hers."

The idea of traveling cross-country trapped in a car with a man notorious for lecturing me about poor life choices no longer sounded appealing. Plus, the sight of his craggy sun-starched face and barely-there gray hair would cause repeated bouts of carsickness. It was nice that he cared enough to offer, but no thanks.

"Dad, you're right. I think I need to go this one alone. If you don't mind, I need to get back to packing. I'll call you when I get there."

"I love you, Samantha, just not when you are doing ridiculous things."

At least I hung up before I started to bawl. Crying jags had become my thing lately.

The phone rang again.

"Honey, I just called to wish you well," my mother said. "I know you probably need some space from Sheldon. God knows I would have loved to temporarily ditch your father. I think *Redbook* even said it can be healthy for couples to live apart periodically. You can just fly to Atlanta whenever you're ovulating, and then the rest of the time you can be at peace not having to have 'relations.' Just remember, marriage is a forever deal."

I hung up and walked the long curvy road back home. The ocean waves settled into a peaceful calm. If only my brain could do the same.

Yes, I was doing the right thing. My father just knew I could be impulsive, so he wanted to help me avoid another disaster. He cared, just in his own way.

When I got back home, the place looked deserted. Sheldon had already gone, leaving only a brief goodbye Post-it note which he stuck to our fridge with the "forgive me, I have zinned" magnet, a remnant from our wine-soaked honeymoon. No *I love you,* just a reminder to take the trash out before I left, and a P.S. that read:

Keep a good watch over our fort.

Romantic.

A week later I packed up some of my belongings and jammed them into my VW Beetle. By the time I finished, it looked like an overstuffed clown car.

I walked back up to the house to lock down our "fort" and stood at the doorstep—the same spot that had been the threshold to our new life only fourteen months ago. My tropical dollhouse-of-a-home that was supposed to be a haven stood vacant of love. I prayed that Sheldon knew what the hell he was doing. Then I wept just like my mother without shedding a single tear, just some awkward dry heaves.

Chapter Four

"You look horrid. You need sex and sun," Babs said.

"Ha." I snorted. "It's great to know you haven't changed. The drive was brutal, but I made it. Sex is probably not the answer, but some cool mountain air might be."

Babs was exactly as I remembered her: sexually explicit and super-charged. A man-whore wrapped inside a woman's body. She had the figure of an overstuffed hourglass. Admittedly I was a tad jealous, having inherited my mother's surfboard-of-a-chest physique. But her va-va-voom bod was just the beginning. Her business savvy was as sharp as her outfits were seductive, which explained why she left HSN. She was entirely too avant-garde for that place.

"Come on, honey, let's grab lunch at the Broadmoor. They have an amazing view, and then we'll swing by the office and meet the team," she said.

The posse of hotties camped out around the

outdoor fireplace could explain why Babs considered the view to be *amazing*. For me it was more about the Rocky Mountains that dwarfed a pristine lake that showcased a stream of snow-kissed swans. The sharp, brisk air smelled like home.

"I'm so glad you're here. We're going to have so much fun together now that you're single."

"Except I'm not single. Sheldon and I are just hyper-focused on our careers right now," I said as I gnawed at my knuckle.

"I know, I know, you're not single. Whatever you need to tell yourself," she said.

"No, I'm serious. I need you to support me on this, okay?"

"Whatever, honey, don't be such a drag. You're brilliant and I've missed you so I'll take you hitched or stag."

Babs hugged me and slithered across the patio toward the pack of boys. She was unflappable. The fact that she always smelled like ganja never stopped men from soliciting her for sexual relations, or maybe they seduced her because of it.

Within five minutes, she had each of them eating out of her hands. She fed a Channing Tatum lookalike a fried artichoke nibble. Then she moved on to hand-feeding a Ryan Gosling type celery stalks with one hand as she not-so-subtly smoked something resembling a joint with the other. Could my dad have been right about her? Maybe all those times she invited people to "join the army" was nothing more than code-speak for smoking a doobie.

The serenity of the surroundings enveloped me, and I soon forgot about Babs and her antics. There was something about the snowcapped tip of Pike's Peak and the crisp air that agreed with me. I wondered if Sheldon was enjoying the sticky heat of Atlanta. Or better yet, was he missing me?

When I broke out of my haze, I noticed that Babs wasn't with the studs anymore. Maybe I'd freshen up. Anybody who had just driven across the country would look haggard.

I moved inside and walked through the marble-laced hallway of the hotel foyer down to the ladies' powder room, which reeked of fresh-picked posies. I heard some loud grunting noises that sounded like a rhino being pinned into a corner at the zoo. It got louder as I neared the restroom.

"Ahh, ahh, ahh" the rhino went. As I got closer, I realized it was a throaty woman's voice. Was somebody having a stroke in there? I dashed toward the bathroom at super-high speed and kicked the door open. Despite my eagerness to assist, I was not prepared to handle what I saw on the other side: Babs in a spread-eagle position over the granite counter, while Tatum-boy's firm naked butt wagged at me. There was close, and then there was too close for a Catholic girl's comfort. Catching your boss naked in a public bathroom having non-loving intercourse with a twenty-two-year-old stallion was the latter. Thankfully, they were the only ones in there.

"Hey, Sammy, how are you doing?" she huffed over his shoulder in between heated thrusts.

"Mmm, I'm okay, just a little tired. Can we leave

for the office soon?"

"Sure thing, Sammy. I'm almost done here. Ah, ah, ah, ooh, Channing!"

***

The Broadmoor incident caused me to have more than a moment of buyer's remorse about my decision to relocate to Colorado. *You are just now having second thoughts?* Had my father actually been right? Babs was not always the best influence, especially on a weakening marriage. Hopefully her ability to negotiate a contract would counter her negative traits.

As we stepped into the office of NetSocial, I felt the hum of greatness. The all-glass building sat nestled between the dip of the city and mountains. The view reminded me of a Swiss village.

First stop on the tour was Candy, whose demeanor screamed overachiever, but in the best possible way. She had rosy apple cheeks and a personality to match. She looked like a mid-twenty-something too—let the girl bonding begin!

"Sam, it's so great to finally meet you. We've heard so much about you," she said.

I wasn't totally sure what she meant. God knows what Babs had told her.

"Nice to meet you too. I hear you're a critical cog in the production," I said.

"Excuse me?"

"Oh, nothing. I'm just excited to be here."

Next stop was Superstar's palatial office. Apparently, he nicknamed himself that because at age twenty he was deemed to be the tech industry's equivalent to Ironman.

"Hey" was all he could mutter in my general direction as he glanced up from his gargantuan Mac monitor. Superstar's corner office was filled with black-lacquered art deco furniture that showcased a spectacular view through floor-to-ceiling windows. His office smelled liked cheap sex.

"He's busy developing a new social networking app that will revolutionize the industry. He plans to rival Facebook. His intensity is as strong as an orgasm, but hopefully more sustainable," Babs said as she felt up her own shape. "Excuse his personal skills. He has none, but he makes up for it in technical brilliance."

Wow, I'd never heard her gush so much about a man she wasn't sleeping with. *Remember, Samantha, Babs is trashy. She would gush about sewage.* I hoped she wasn't sleeping with him. Superstar was twenty years her junior, and the success of the company rested on his shoulders. Not even she would be that reckless.

No workplace would be complete without an eccentric head honcho—ours was Nate. He had the communication skills of Napoleon, but I sensed he was the perfect skipper to navigate the ship.

"Hey, Sammy, Babs swears by you. Welcome to Hell! You're in for an ass-kicking ride," he said as he punched my forearm. His crass, rude nature was sure to cement our place at the top of the tech industry heap.

"Don't worry about him," Babs said. "He never sleeps, so don't be surprised if he falls asleep on you in the middle of a meeting. Everyone has accepted his narcolepsy except him."

She led me down a buzzing corridor. Cubicles were nowhere to be found, replaced with beanbag towers. Walls were strewn with whiteboards, and tubs of free junk food dominated the see-through break rooms. This certainly was the most social work environment I had ever seen. Desks were scarce but laptops littered the floor. Ceiling murals depicted people talking and typing on their smartphones while making out with each other. Intriguing. The next generation of social networking was a world I looked forward to becoming a part of.

I was anxious to see where I would be sitting. While the beanbags looked cool in concept, they probably left people one click away from a permanent backache. We rounded the corner and stopped.

"Here's your office. It's great to have you here," Babs said, leaving me to get acquainted with my space.

My office came equipped with a perfect peek of the snow-lit streets of Colorado Springs. Sitting in my puffy pink chair—Babs knew me too well—I soaked in my surroundings. As the minutes of the day melted into hours, so did the memories of Florida and Sheldon. They drifted into the distance right along with the sun. Even though I had just arrived, I felt at peace in this building and among these people. I was home.

Chapter Five

I walked off the scorching hot runway and was immediately assaulted by the heat. All those people who blathered on about the benefits of humidity had obviously never done a day-for-day comparison of the dry, supple heat of Colorado to the stifling, sticky heat of Atlanta. The latter stunk.

But I wasn't in town for the weather, nor to see a new Super Bowl stadium in the making. My mission was to reconnect with my hubby, or, according to Babs, to get laid.

Once I cleared the sweat from my forehead and wiped down my arms and pits with a cocktail napkin, I made my way toward baggage claim. Even though I was blazing new ground at work and loving my life in Colorado, I'd been missing my man.

There was so much to fill him in on. We weren't able to talk every night on the phone like we'd planned because he was in the throes of one of his workaholic benders. This particular rendition had lasted exactly two months and still counting.

The first week we were apart we talked every night. And shockingly, we had phone sex. Babs schooled me in the art of seduction along with some tips I picked up from *Maxim*, but as the weeks wore on, so did the gaps between our conversations. It became increasingly more difficult to get him to commit to a weekend visit, but I'd done it. I surprised myself with how excited I was to see him. I was certain the distance had made our marriage stronger.

Babs sexed up my wardrobe for the occasion. I caught my own look in the mirror running through the airport, and had to admit I looked saucier than normal in my skimpy hot-pink sundress. My hair was cropped into a Posh Beckham-style bob with some extra blonde accents. *Glamour* magazine said that blonde highlights were a surefire way to keep your man from straying.

I planned to jump Sheldon at the baggage belt. *Cosmo* said these types of gestures were essential in fostering a thriving sexual relationship.

It took me over half an hour to find my bags and when I had fetched the last of them, I looked around and noticed Sheldon by the exit standing with his arms crossed while two kids played leap frog in front of him. He did not look amused, nor did he run to me and scoop me into his arms as I had envisioned.

Be bold, Babs had said, so I darted toward him while trying to do the sexy strut I'd read about. When we met, I engulfed him with a seductive bear hug, which was tricky given his ever-expanding girth.

"Hi, sex-kitten!" I said.

"Hey. We're late."

His lukewarm reception was not what I planned for after being apart for over eight weeks. How could someone be this crabby before ten a.m.?

"Aren't you excited to see me, babe? Do you like my hair and new dress?" I asked.

"Sorry, baby, stadium triage starts in two weeks and I'm swamped. I told you this was the worst possible time to come."

"I know, but we said we were going to visit each other every other weekend and we haven't seen each other once since you left," I said as I tried to blot the sweat off my face with a hankie. "I missed you. I thought you'd feel the same way."

"Of course I'm glad you're here. I'm just late for a meeting."

"Well that's too bad, bugaboo. I'm tickled to see you even if it's only for a few minutes. Maybe we can go back to the hotel and get some breakfast in bed before you have to head to work."

"Sam, you're not getting it. I can't hang out with you today. I've arranged for Ivan to meet us here so he can take you to the hotel and I can get back to my team. Remember, all of this is for us."

"Who the hell is Ivan?" I asked. *Don't swear, Samantha. You'll go to hell if you make a habit of it.*

"My intern."

"You mean you're pawning me off on some kid that's barely out of diapers when we haven't seen each other for weeks?"

"He's the Super Bowl committee chair's son who's not doing anything either, so I thought you could entertain each other."

It was hard not to read into the "not doing anything" remark as a dig for me being in the way of his security kingdom.

I smiled in an attempt to conjure a sugar-sweet voice. "Babe, if you'd like me to spend my first day with Ivan so you can tend to business, that's fine by me. You go and do whatever you need to get done, and I'll be at the hotel waiting to ravish you when you get back."

I did my rendition of the sexy eyelash bat that Babs taught me. She'd said it would guarantee sex on the spot. I must have done it incorrectly because, without as much as a blink, Sheldon was gone, and I was left waiting for the intern at baggage claim. Sitting on top of my pink leopard luggage, I felt animalistic for sure, just not in the way I imagined. Sexually frustrated was more like it. Sheldon used to always attempt to pleasure me orally even though it made me uncomfortable, but it had been months since he'd even tried.

It took Ivan, the pimple-faced geek, an hour to find me. He had such a huge stick up his ass I wondered how he was able to walk me down the street to my hotel.

***

The entire three days of my visit were spent holed up in my room or touring Atlanta and the World of Coca-Cola. The latter grew old after the third visit given my decision to shy away from Coke products when *Shape* magazine revealed that

39

cola made you bloated.

When we arrived back at the airport at the end of my visit to check my luggage, Ivan killed time by tweeting constantly, snorting after each tweet. It was hard to imagine that he or any one of his dweeb friends could be that entertaining.

Sheldon had been so busy with work while I was in town that we barely had any quality time together, unless you count brushing our teeth at the his-and-her sinks in our hotel room. God knows what he was doing all day and night that rendered him so exhausted that, by the end of each day, he couldn't muster the energy to make love with me. Not even a quickie during the entire stint of my stay.

As Ivan tweeted, I replayed the lowlights of my trip. Night one: Sheldon shuffled into my hotel room and flopped onto the bed. Following *Redbook* magazine's guidance, I took that as my cue to pounce and seduce. I mounted Sheldon and attempted to rip open his shirt purring, "Let me see those tantalizing teats!" His buttons did not fly open as effortlessly as you see in soap operas. Instead, Sheldon rolled me off of him and said, "Sam, I've got to wear that shirt tomorrow. Hands off." I pouted and he repented with, "I love you, but not tonight. I'm too stressed. I promise to make you proud one day."

The next morning, following *GQ's* advice, I tried to arouse Sheldon with a sexually charged wakeup call. He was so startled he accidentally knocked me out of bed thinking I was the alarm clock. By the time I regained my footing, he had already hightailed it to the bathroom.

What man could go without intercourse for as long as we had, then finally get his wife in the same room after weeks apart and not make a single advance? Aren't men supposed to have urges?

Of all the warnings Sheldon's friends and family gave me during our engagement, nobody mentioned that he was a camel in the sex department. Clearly, all the days of withholding intercourse in my youth were coming back to bite me.

Ivan gawked and broke up the horror film of my so-called life.

"Mrs. Milton, Mr. Milton said to tell you he was too busy to make it to your send-off, but he wishes you safe travels. He'll catch up with you on the flip side," he said.

Did he just salute me? If he was mocking me, I would knock him off his skinny little feet.

I panted for air in the terminal while getting rammed by every person who walked by. Geek-face stared at me as if he expected a tip. The only tip I had for him was to stop tweeting and start living a real life.

Instead, I said, "Thanks, Ivan."

I found solace in the fact that he was probably more uncomfortable than me.

He yelled over his shoulder, "Take care, Mrs. M., so nice to hang with you!"

The plane ride was a blip. A text from Sheldon popped up right after I landed. "Sorry about the weekend. I know this has been rough, but it will all work out, I promise." Sweet sentiment. If only I could believe it. When I got off the plane, I searched for my bags and tried to forget the whole disappointing Atlanta trip ever happened, which, when I thought about it, *it* never had.

***

"Sammy we're glad to have you back. Things have been nutty since you left. I hope you've worked out all of your marital issues and had lots of dirty sex because I need you to focus. You and Superstar are paired up on the Apple deal now, which is key for keeping our company afloat. No pressure, honey," Babs said, followed by her signature smile and eyelash bat.

She had gotten stoned and opted for a provocative purple sweater dress for our meeting. But even high, Babs commanded attention.

As Superstar sauntered into the room, I swear he smelled like sex. Maybe it was just the fact I was so pent up I was relegated to sniffing it out as a means of sexual fulfillment. It felt like I had blue bells— the female equivalent to blue balls. My loins ached.

To further my homecoming woes, in one short week Superstar had become world-renowned for his strides in the social media world. I had been forced to watch replays of his f-ing interview on *Good Morning America* while we waited for him to arrive. I watched intently trying to see the magic that everyone else saw.

His first appearance on *GMA* came when he was only fourteen and had already become one of the most sought-after hackers of his time. Government agencies hired him to crack their systems to uncover vulnerabilities. His career skyrocketed from there.

Whatever. Good for him. And me. Everyone was so busy talking about his appearance that it left little time for them to notice my lack of a marital life. Perhaps they assumed my husband was an imaginary one, since no one had ever met him.

I, unlike everybody else, was not enamored with Superstar. He was pompous, short, and had coarse hair. I'd never trusted short men. And the contrast between his choppy dark locks and pale complexion was frightful. Not to mention he was combative and tried his best to make me look inferior whenever we worked together.

I couldn't be sure if I was paranoid or clairvoyant, but it felt like he was trying to oust me from my post. That made no sense since he was supposed to be the superstar, after all. Maybe he hated to see women in positions of power. Whatever. I consoled myself by remembering I excelled at competition, despite my father's preachings to the contrary.

Superstar sat down next to me, breaking my mental standoff. Thankfully, I'd put on deodorant twice like *Teen Vogue* had suggested. His eyes lingered on mine.

"Would you two just pork each other and be done with it so we can get back to work?" Babs said.

"Shut it. I don't pork co-workers, or anybody for that matter. In case you've forgotten, I'm married. Why do I have to keep telling you people that?"

"Easy, babe, maybe it has something to do with the fact that you never talk about your husband. I'm starting to think he doesn't exist," Super-dork said.

"Well, nobody asked you. And my name is Samantha, not babe. Got it?" I snapped as I scratched my nose. "Wouldn't it be prudent to get off my personal life and back to the marketing proposal now that you've finally arrived?"

I feigned boredom by gazing out the conference room window and twiddling my hair. My non-sex-inducing highlights felt ridiculous, having failed the mission in Atlanta. At least my butt-hugging jeans and formfitting pink baby-tee looked good. My body still had *it,* even if Sheldon didn't want it.

"Sure Honey, we're all yours," Babs said.

I reeled in my last remnants of composure and sailed through the proposal. I was certain Superstar was going to jump in and take over the presentation because he typically did so, but he just sat back and listened intently.

"Great work, you two. That settles it. I'm sending you both to New York next month to present this to the investors," Babs said.

"Of course. I'll rock the meeting as always," he said.

How fitting. I finally get a career-defining opportunity, only it's with an egomaniac tech geek. I wasn't sure his big head and I would fit on the same airplane.

"Babs, I thought you were going, not me. You should really go."

With a glare like icy steel, he got up off his arrogant ass and leaned across the table, planting his elbows right in front of me. He and his coarse hair leered. I burped lightly under my breath, hoping to throw him.

"Sam, don't be an idiot. It's our brainchild, and while I hate to admit it, you showed traces of brilliance. Don't let your obvious attraction to me get in the way of business. We're hitting Manhattan together," the smug pig said.

Who the hell did he think he was? Feelings for him? Please. We were not in high school anymore. I wasn't sure of much in my life, but there was one thing I was absolutely positive about: I most certainly did not have feelings for Superstar.

Wait a minute. He thought I was brilliant?

Chapter Six

Somewhere between Pikes Peak and the Empire State Building, I had a revelation. It was not normal to fight about somebody coming to visit somebody else when those somebodies were practically still newlyweds. You were supposed to be yearning for each other so much that there would be nothing to fight about, right? If Mr. Sheldon Milton didn't have time for me, no problem. I could be just as big of a workaholic as he was. Starting immediately.

Over a very late-night, borderline-romantic dinner with Superstar the evening before our investor meeting, we sat at a primo table in the Rainbow Room. The city twinkled in the background. He leaned over, encroaching on my personal space.

"Here's how we're gonna work this. I'll engage the women with my technical prowess, and then you'll seduce the men in the room. We'll dominate as we demonstrate how our company will deliver the best marketing campaigns, which will ultimately bring the next generation of social media to the masses. In due time we will make Facebook, Instagram, and all the others of that ilk obsolete," he said.

Then he smirked at me.

I sat quietly for a moment, trying to come up with the right comeback.

"What microchip did you fall off of? You actually expect me to seduce the room? This is not the 1950s for God's sake. Has nothing changed in the battle of women in the workplace?"

"Please. I didn't mean you would bang everyone in the meeting. I was talking about seducing them figuratively by the force of the concepts we'll deliver, the way Jobs did every time he walked into a pitch," he said. "You still don't get it. We're about to change the way people relate to one another, and that makes people hot," he said as he stroked his barely-there goatee.

"Oh, well if you put it like that, I can certainly do my part." I giggled like a fifteen-year-old girl.

My attempt at staring down the legendary Manhattan skyline to deflect attention away from our supposed hotness didn't work. With New York City as the backdrop, under a certain type of lighting, Superstar could look fairly decent. Definitely not hot, but not totally repulsive.

"Good. We know our roles. So let's sit back, enjoy the food and the view, and if you could find a way somewhere within that tightly wound ass of yours to relax, I would appreciate it."

God, he was brazen. I could relax, I wasn't made of tin, and I greatly resented the insinuation.

After some stellar New York strip, a succulent

Petite Sirah, and some surprisingly okay company, Superstar dropped his armor-like shell long enough for me to learn he had been married and divorced.

He wore his divorce exactly how I imagined I would, like a badge of dishonor. He had been madly in love with his bride until he learned that, since day one of their marriage, she had been having an affair with his best friend. From the point he found them in bed together, he said his approach to life had changed. That explained his obnoxious personality.

Not that Sheldon and I would ever share a fate like Superstar's. I was too young to be a divorcée. But still, the lack of attention felt just as painful as an infidelity. In either case, we were not good enough, or worthy enough, to hold someone's attention.

Maybe he wasn't totally gross, just wounded and compensating. Perhaps it would help our working relationship if I let down my guard just a tad for this one night. *Are you really that stupid?*

***

At the onset of my first high profile investor meeting, I learned something interesting about myself. I'd spent the better part of my life being attracted to beautiful boy-toys who were tall, stunning, fabulously featured, and slightly dangerous. The type where you never cared what they said because you were too busy staring at their bodies.

Superstar was far from that type. He wasn't even in the same galaxy; however, on a blustery cold morning in New York City, he possessed one thing that those toys and Sheldon never had: a genius brain.

He had a big, fat, wildly intelligent cranium that cut through my sanity like a switchblade. The way he waved his shapely hands as he spoke about our backend interface entranced me. I felt as if he were conveying some sort of code-speak to me and only me. I understood his shorthand. Or if I wanted to be literal, longhand. His very long hands.

Somewhere in between our presentation on the intricacies of our app, and his pontificating about the future of social networking, I fell under Superstar's spell. *Undo the spell or go straight to hell!*

"And that, my friends, is how NetSocial proposes to shake up the communications continuum," he purred.

Hold on! What was wrong with me? This man-child was offensive, cocky, and repulsive on every level. You would think the fact that he was dressed up like a dork, wearing a silver silk shirt, pleated khakis, and white sneakers, would do something to deter my sexual fantasies. I gulped down a sprinkled doughnut, which only got me more revved up.

InStyle magazine advised against matching silk and cotton. There was also the fact that in the months we'd known each other, he had repeatedly tried to throw me under the bus, or in his case, the keyboard. Like that time when we were co-presenting at a client meeting and five minutes before our presentation, he took my notecards and told me to, "Wing it. We don't use crutches. We captivate. You're better than this." Granted, I zipped through the presentation without them, but his stress-inducing tactic was bonkers given the stakes.

The longer he continued to rattle off techno-geek-speak, the more I found myself melting into my chair. I took a subtle inventory of the other women in the room and they seemed equally enraptured. One particularly perky woman appeared to be salivating. The men in the room watched his every maneuver, surely hoping to poach some of his moves.

"And yes, ladies, it is that simple. A social media application that will grow and change as you do, one tap and swipe at a time," he said.

"What about Facebook?" a willowy blonde squeaked.

"Excuse the lewd comment in advance," he said. "But screw Facebook."

How in God's name could I be attracted to this goof? I was working, for Christ sake. *Get ahold of your libido, you moron.* His arrogance was legendary, even for him. Who was stupid enough to mock Facebook? Yet, instead of being appalled, I sweated beneath my undergarments.

I couldn't be certain, but it seemed, in-between all of his highfalutin geek-speak, Superstar was flirting with me. Why would God put me in this compromising situation during one of the most important meetings of my career? The erotic way he stroked his goatee upended me.

Christ, what should I do? *Stop swearing for*

starters. Ignore him? He'd eventually have to stop the advances, assuming he didn't want to botch the meeting.

I couldn't stop staring at him. Was I being influenced by the heady presentation, or was I just impaired due to a lack of sleep? Maybe it was because he forced his eyes to twinkle at me. At last, his self-imposed moniker made sense. On the most basic level, his name alone should have repelled me. What grown man-child actually nicknamed himself Superstar?

Of course, he wasn't ogling me. He knew I was married and he wasn't privy to Sheldon's resistance to visiting me. I must have been hallucinating. I just needed sex. Sorry, Mother, despite what you think, women do have needs in that department. We're not just lifeless baby-making machines.

"Samantha, is there anything else you'd like to add?" he said.

"What? Huh, excuse me?" I mumbled. "No, I'll pass."

Ha, let him take that and stuff it up his flirting ass.

"Samantha is more humble than she needs to be. What she's trying to say is that our app is going to rock the marketplace," he said, slapping his hands together, as if conjuring sex with each swipe.

After sucking in some stale recycled air in an attempt to quell the urge to regurgitate my breakfast, I spoke. "Yes, we are going to change things up; this will be a game changer."

Shut up, shut up. If you don't have a valuable contribution stop speaking, *Forbes* magazine's golden rule.

I looked at Superstar, willing him to speak. One gaze in his direction made me perspire. I channeled my mother by choosing to deny my oddly erotic feelings toward Superstar. Then I did some deep breathing like *Yoga* magazine always suggested. All that did was make me dizzy. Hopefully, it had more to do with being locked inside a sizzling hot conference room that reeked of cheap perfume than with Superstar's sexual advances. I scratched my nose and moved on to rustling and smoothing my tasteful cream crepe pencil skirt.

"Our digital social exchanges will never be the same, and you'll have NetSocial and me to thank for that. After all, I built the technology with my own bare hands,"—big hands, very big hands—he said, "and if you all don't take the offer now, somebody else will. Peace out. Sam, we're out of here," he said as he winked at me.

Finally! The Superstar I knew and hated had reentered the room, just in time to swagger out of the boardroom with me trailing behind in the dust of his brilliance.

I prayed like hell that I would make it out of New York without doing anything stupid. Well, aside from my inability to speak intelligently during the investor meeting. I one-upped myself by scratching my nose for the duration of the flight home. A fact Superstar was more than happy to point out. Pig.

***

Thankfully, God had forced the fall foliage to burst while we were gone. The aspen trees shimmered so brightly you would have thought the forest was on fire. The glimmering effect provided an ample distraction from my faltering moral compass.

Superstar and I were eating at the Blue Star, his favorite schmoozing spot, despite, or perhaps because of, the pun. Never wanting to bow to conventional norms, he demanded that we start our meal with dessert and work backward from there. We shared the Corleone ice cream ball draped in graham cracker dust and dark chocolate, oozing with honey. I didn't even know why I went out to eat with him—oh right, he forced me to join him and blamed it on an urge to confer on work matters. We were still waiting to hear from the investors we'd worked so hard to supposedly "seduce." His words, not mine.

Between bites, I tried to hide behind my dinner menu so I wouldn't have to stare at his coarse hair. However, over the tippy top of the flimsy blockade, I could see him smugly stroking his goatee. He appeared to be using my menu as a mirror to primp himself. Disgusting.

Our waif of a waitress appeared just in time to break my gaze and allow Superstar to undress her with his eyes as he continued to massage his peach-fuzzed chin. I ordered the most un-sexy entrée I could spot, buffalo chicken pasta.

As he placed his order, his phone rang. Eager for some news, I leaped across the table to answer it, but instead knocked my water all over the crotch of his ripped khakis.

He swiped the phone up into his long, lean fingers. "Talk to me," he said.

I could only assume it was one of the investors, and he was showing them who he thought was in charge. As he talked he made sexy, googly-eyed faces at me. Then he forced his eyes to twinkle in my direction. Superstar was relentless. Thank God he finally hung up, so I could regain my position of ambivalence.

"So, what's the word? Are they in?" I asked.

"How badly do you want to know, Sammy?"

"Oh, for Christ sake, stop baiting me and tell what they said or I'll kiss you. I mean, kill you."

"Now we're getting somewhere." He smirked. "They're in. For five million."

As he spoke, he curled up his tongue and lapped his own lips. Before I had a chance to inhale, he leaned across the table, grabbed my wobbling hands, and tongue-kissed me until our waitress interrupted our lip lock.

She delivered our entrees with a pissy, "Here you go." Obviously, she wished it were her and not me necking with him. Half of me felt the same way.

Horrified, with a throbbing chafed kissy face, I buttoned up my pink silk shirt all the way to the top.

I, a still-married Samantha Serrano, had just allowed a Superstar to kiss me—and God help me, I liked it.

Chapter Seven

The problem with Superstar was he was one of those natural boy wonders. Whatever he lacked in good looks he made up for with technical acumen.

This furthered Oprah's point. You were never too old to be attracted to a *new* type, and apparently intellectual geeks were mine. Not that I planned to act on the urge again. *Cosmo* always said it was okay to look as long as you didn't touch. Unless you were in an exclusive relationship, then you were allowed to touch, the more the better. But not me. No more touching.

Technically, Superstar had touched me first, so he was mainly to blame. I couldn't come up with a valid reason for why I had allowed him to kiss me, aside from the obvious: that this was what we Catholics did. We turned to self-destructive behaviors when pushed into a corner or, in my case, on a non-date with a horrible-haired dweeb. But I kept his urges at bay aside from the occasional kiss, and my hands remained off him when our lips locked.

A deal with Apple closed just before the year ended and with the good news came the promise of a thriving future, solidified by a promotion for my "ace negotiations," as Superstar dubbed my performance. I ascended from Customer Relations Manager to Director of Product Development, and the contacts I'd made were priceless in terms of securing a lucrative career. My sex life looked not nearly as promising, since it actually required my dearly beloved to sleep in the same bed with me, or for starters, be in the same state. This must be what it was like to be a man—constantly wanting sex, but unable to get it regularly.

While scribbling a sex-potential matrix on my yellow tablet, I discovered that the odds were not in my favor—especially with my long-lost husband. I considered other options. With Superstar, there would be no geographical barriers to entry.

As dusk settled in, Superstar sauntered into my office with the same force that snow poured down from the sky.

"Sam, are we ever going to talk about what's really going on between us?" he said as he cornered me in my own office.

I fumbled and flipped over my sex/no sex checklist.

"What would that be?" I shrugged.

He ignored my lame attempt at diversion and kept coming at me, closing the door and blinds behind him.

Sex in the workplace for women equaled career suicide. I needed to keep away from his sultry, pouting lips and sandpaper hair. Ick! The snow pelted the windows, splattering as the flakes met the glass. Glancing at the precipitation helped keep my libido in check. But he continued to stalk me like a hooker, so much so he landed in my lap, and then mounted me on my pink, puffy chair.

I tried to protest, but he held his hand gently over mine, and flashed those damn twinkling eyes at me while his other hand unbuttoned my blouse. As I resisted, he broke me down with each kiss. I attempted to scratch my nose, but he blocked my move with his lips.

Superstar worked me hard, ruthlessly hard. He tried to crack me like a nut, but I was unbreakable, which seemed to make him want me more.

The fact that he was a good kisser was not helping my resistance campaign. What the hell was I doing? I should have been devoutly focused on my career and virtual marriage. But instead, I sat there and allowed someone other than my spouse to straddle me.

"Sam, look at me. Really look at me. You've known all along this would happen. It's okay to give in and trust me."

Trust, my ass! I was horrible at trusting.

Okay, I take it back. He wasn't a good kisser. He was a fantabulous one. His pulsating lips sent shivers up my spine, down my pelvis, through my toes and back up again. He was one of *those* kissers, the kind that indicated he would be equally good if not better in bed.

Superstar was the type of man my mother warned me about. I now understood why. She must have been preparing me for situations like these so I would just say no. *Sex is not the answer!* If she had uttered that once, she had said it a bazillion times, none of which seemed to have any effect on me in this moment.

For an hour and counting Superstar and I did the dirty dance, balanced on the high wire, while I contemplated mixing a bit of pleasure with my work for the night. The snow pounded, the clock ticked, and nothing stirred except for us.

And "stir" we did, three times in a row. And in case anyone was asking, it's true what they say: Big hands and big brain means big…you know what.

***

I couldn't stop thinking about his engorged, throbbing penis waiting in the other room as I dove for the phone, screaming over my shoulder, "I'll get it, SexStar!"

"Hey, you, how are you? It's me, Pooh," Sheldon said.

It's me, Pooh! That was all this man had to say after all these months? Eight months of nonexistence, to be exact.

It was just like him to appear after I'd finally moved on. No doubt God was sending me a message by transporting my MIA husband to me on the day immediately following the most insane intercourse of my life.

"Sheldon, is that you?" was all I could muster.

A train filled with Catholic guilt entered the station, on target to derail my life.

"Babe, of course it's me, who else would be

calling from the border of New Mexico with a U-Haul filled with all of our stuff. Happy almost-birthday. I'm coming home, baby," he said.

I finally got the meaning of *stunned speechless.* There were so many things I wanted to scream at this man. So many questions I needed answered—so many Superstar sex stories I wanted to spit in his face. Instead, half-naked and silent with the phone stuck to my ear, I crumpled to the floor, my gaze transfixed on Superstar, who lounged buck naked on my sofa in the other room.

Sheldon prattled on while the New Mexican highway buzzed in the background. He kept repeating "happy almost birthday" as if I should present him with a dog biscuit for knowing I had aged a year without him.

"Sam, did you hear me? I'm about five hours from Colorado. I wanted to surprise you but I wasn't exactly sure where you live."

Gee, imagine that, you jackass! Maybe it was because you poofed out of my universe without a peep for months on end. He would have been in for a supersized surprise if he had dropped by unannounced last night.

Sheldon had clearly missed the unraveling of our marriage. For me, it entailed waking up in a dry-heaving sweat a couple of months ago, when I experienced what they refer to in *Cosmo* as the "breakthrough moment." In my case, the awakening led to a decision to stop fighting with my husband. There were only so many ways you could beg someone to visit you, and when they didn't, what else was there left to do short of denying the remains of your married life?

From that day forward, I tuned Sheldon out of my life. Especially last night, when I went out and had sexual relations with one man while technically being married to another. Deep down I knew Sheldon was only trying to provide for us, but he was supposed to love me enough to find a way to make our marriage work, despite everything else.

"Sam, are you okay? Maybe we have a bad connection. I said I need your address. I'm coming home, baby!"

Why did he keep calling me baby? I had never been, nor would I ever be his "baby," though the idea of falling to the ground and crying my eyes out in the fetal position until somebody picked me up and burped me sounded appealing.

This was my chance to tell him to beat it, that I'd moved on. And to drop the juicy nugget about the brilliant night of sex I had with a genius named Superstar, who had a huge penis that dwarfed his tenfold. I should have said anything to make him go back to where he came from.

Instead, I stared out at the snow-capped mountains and waited for my beautiful new life to detonate.

***

I rationalized that it wasn't *real* adultery because Sheldon and I were figuratively divorced at the moment I made my final plea for him to come out to visit me. He'd denied my request, said he was in the middle of a huge work crunch, as always. In my mind, that move ended the marriage. He didn't choose me. Maybe I'd never know if that was what drove me on top of Superstar's throbbing penis, but I had a lifetime ahead to torture myself about the mortal sin I had committed.

I should have told Sheldon to step away from the U-Haul and go back home to Florida or Atlanta or wherever the hell he had been living for the past year, but I couldn't do it. Maybe it was a way to prove to my parents that I was right and they were wrong—that Sheldon and I would be together forever. Or maybe it was just guilt.

I spent the morning dissecting my predicament while pretending like nothing was wrong as Superstar and I read the morning paper naked and swaddled in a fuzzy blanket. It worked until he got called into the office to deal with a security breach.

I ran out into the snow still swathed in my Superstar-scented blanket to fetch the mail, hoping my latest issue of *Glamour* had arrived. It would provide a much-needed dose of relationship wisdom, or at least a few stress management tips.

Instead, I was greeted with another one of my mother's clippings. This one aptly titled: ***Adultery, the Other Red Meat.*** I swear to God this woman had psychic abilities. How she knew what I'd done, I'd never know. She should quit Catholicism and become a fortune teller.

Every week she'd ask how Sheldon was doing, and I'd tell her fine, aside from never seeing him. Then she'd remind me that marriage was a forever deal. All of this, yet I still felt compelled to ring her.

"Hi Mom. Sheldon just called from the road and

he's on his way to Colorado with all of our belongings. I'm not sure if I even want him back anymore. He's never visited me once in the last year, and we have barely spoken in months," I bawled into the phone.

"Samantha, pull yourself together. You can't go on living like this. Your father and I don't approve. You're gallivanting all over town with crazy Babs and drinking to excess, I'm sure. Your husband decided to take you back. There is nothing to think about. You do it. And if you won't, don't bother coming home for Easter this year," she said.

I hadn't thought there was anybody I could hate more than Sheldon or myself until I spoke to her. Weren't parents supposed to sense when their children were in need? Weren't they supposed to forgo their own selfish desires in order to come to the aid of the child they gave birth to? Maybe Jackie was right all this time. That I had only married Sheldon to get out from under my parents. Whatever. My husband was supposed to love me no matter what—or at a minimum visit me, for Christ's sake. I wrestled with a paper towel trying to cleanse my sweaty armpits.

"I hope I've made our stance clear. P.S., I love you," she said. "P.S.S., the Easter thing still stands." She hung up.

To torture myself, after Superstar left I put my adulterous black nightie back on. I stayed like that for two hours, unable to bring myself to shower or change. I could smell him on me. His scent made me feel guilty yet mildly aroused. Perhaps dwelling on the size of his wand of flesh would help me deflect the situation. *Not even a penis is that powerful. Guilt is guilt.*

Why was it that, for Catholics, some of the most enjoyable pastimes in life would supposedly lead you straight to hell? No time to ponder that premise. My estranged husband was a mere state away, ready to wreck my universe. He would smell betrayal on me instantly due to his hack-job security training, so I'd better shower up. *Adulterer!*

Squeaky clean on the outside but still sinful on the inside, I thought about calling Babs to tell her what was going on. As the queen of sin, she would know what to do. *Walk toward the phone. Get dressed on the way. Rewash your private parts for God's sake.*

Instead, I sat mesmerized by the gingerbread-house-of-a-town I lived in. I mustered the energy to move toward my tweeting pink bejeweled iPhone— another failed attempt at coloring myself happy. Sheldon must be getting close. Or maybe he was lost. He was always lost. *Answer the god damn phone and confess your sin while you still have a shot at redemption.* I dove for it hoping it would move me one step closer to snapping back to the reality of my married life.

"Hello?"

"Hey, hot stuff. Are you still wearing that sexy black lace thing? I can't stop thinking about you in it. My cock is about to explode. I'm on my way over," Superstar said.

Oh, Christ.

Chapter Eight

As much as I wanted to be the recipient of Superstar's exploding cock, my rational side stepped in. *A little late for that, don't you think?* I told him I had to run some errands because an unexpected friend was arriving in town later. We had phone sex, which was wildly fulfilling—unlike my failed attempts to seduce Sheldon from afar. That, and the sexting that followed left me dazed on my couch for many more minutes than I had any right to enjoy. Especially with my estranged husband threatening to arrive.

I thought about cleaning up the house on Sheldon's account, but thought better of the idea. As if I were the one who needed to clean up my act—he was the deserter, not me. Instead, I binge-watched the first four seasons of *Girls*. Within minutes, I felt much better about my own life.

Then I took another shower. According to *Self*, you can never be too "clean" in this era of promiscuity. I knew they were speaking sexually, but whatever, a little cleanliness never killed anybody.

Just as I was fully lathered with Philosophy Cherry Pinwheel body wash, some buffoon pounded on the door as if the mountains were on fire and we were in the middle of an evacuation zone. A quick peek out the window confirmed that it was worse—Sheldon had arrived.

I scampered out of the shower and scurried about, on the hunt for a frumpy married-looking outfit. I landed on khakis and a button-down blouse. *Soccer mom on the outside, still slutty on the inside.* One glance in the full-length mirror almost made me hurl. Who was I kidding? It was time for Sheldon to get used to the "new" me. An independent, sexually charged, career-driven woman. Not the mousy blonde he left behind in favor of a security job.

In a fitted powder-puff pink shimmering top and ass-shaping jeggings, I opened the door.

The instant that Sheldon looked me up and down and stepped into my home, I went from fabulous to frigid. My body stiffened like one of the wooden toy soldiers my mother insisted on lugging out every Christmas.

"How are you, baby? You look amazing," he said.

More like fuckable, according to Superstar.

I kept trying to open my mouth to say something obscene or hurtful but nothing came out.

"It feels like forever since we've seen each other, Sammy."

Maybe that's because it has been, you jackass!

When he stared at me so completely clueless, my

composure went out the window, along with my dinner. Sheldon looked at me as if he expected me to clean up my own vomit. What were husbands for, anyway?

"Did you even miss me at all, Sheldon?" I said as I scrubbed puke off my window screen.

"I was so busy it sort of felt like I hardly noticed, but of course I missed you, baby."

"Who is this 'baby' person you keep yammering on about? I am not a baby anymore, Sheldon. I am in charge of an entire department at work, which you would know if you had ever bothered to call me."

My phone started chirping at turbo speeds with text message alerts. Sheldon looked at me blankly and flipped his head toward it as if granting me permission to check my own goddamn phone.

Candy: Sam, what are you doing?

Candy: Hello?

Candy: We're thinking of having a few friends over.

Candy: Are you there?

Candy: Whatever. Get over here. Lon is making his famous peach margaritas and fajitas for some of the guys, and I can't deal with the bromance for much longer.

Candy: BTW, you've been acting funny ever

since you got back from the investor meeting. What's up?

Without giving me as much as a minute to reply, she continued her rant.

Candy: Are you on your way yet?

She could be impatient at times, but in this instant I loved her too much to care. This was almost too perfect to be happening to me. I needed reinforcements to get through my reunion of unwedded-dreaded-bliss with Sheldon.

Me: Headed out. Save some tequila for me. I'm gonna need it.

***

Sheldon and I suffered through a tedious ten-minute drive to Candy's house. I ushered us in the front door where she stood waiting with a bottle of tequila in one hand and Jägermeister in the other. Unaware of the smoking-hot sex that Superstar and I had been having lately, she looked at me with the excitement only a girlfriend could conjure when her bestie is on a hot date. If only she knew the real story.

As Sheldon entered their spunky A-frame house, she mouthed behind his back, "Who's that?"

When I mouthed back asking who, her face fell and turned borderline angry.

"WTF?" she mouthed.

Not even I could explain myself, so I grabbed the bottle of Jäger from her hand and downed two shots of the deer blood. It coated my throat the way only a good cough medicine could, and it made me gag. When Sheldon made no attempt to comfort me or offer me a fucking glass of water even, I slugged back two more shots.

Lon, the consummate husband, came to my rescue with a bottle of Evian. Too bad he couldn't have schooled my long-lost spouse in the fine art of marital niceties. Sheldon proceeded to introduce himself to everybody as my "husband," and then went on to bore anybody who would listen to him. The people who knew me from work looked back and forth between us as if we had been to Mars, Venus, and finally had landed on Uranus. God knows I felt like one.

I couldn't be certain, but it looked like Candy was shaking her head at me in disapproval. All I could muster in return was a shrug and a "what are you going to do" look.

The Jäger was making me woozy, or maybe it was the sight of Sheldon trying to "work" the crowd that sickened me, but regardless of the reason, I tapped him on the shoulder, signaling it was time to go. When he failed to stop talking, I pushed him around and forced him to make eye contact with me.

"We're leaving," I said.

"I'm just getting to know everybody. This is a great bunch of guys. I can really see myself living here."

With that threat, I grabbed one more shot, and

pushed him out the door, apologizing over my back on the way out.

He drove us home because apparently I was in no condition to drive. As always, he refused to listen to my directions and got lost on the way. When we finally arrived, I ran out of the car and up to my front stoop, steadying myself as best as possible and willing myself not to vomit.

"Sam, is everything all right? Is it something I did?"

"Ya think?" I deadpanned.

With no ability to contain myself, *everything* came tumbling out. First, the Jäger-induced puke, then the angry tears. In my mind, I spewed a string of expletives that would have done my dad proud. In reality, I asked him to leave—for good.

He looked at me, confusion registering on his face.

"Are you sure?" he said.

I gave him my best puke-face death-glare. But said nothing.

And so he left.

Chapter Nine

Sheldon could be efficient when he wanted to be. In the end, it was he and not me that stepped up, took the reins, and initiated what would be the first and (I determined) last divorce of my life. *You sure as hell better hope so.*

Superstar and I had enjoyed another night of hot, steamy sex before I hopped on the plane to Florida to finalize the legal termination of my marriage. I couldn't explain why I kept porking him other than I wanted to numb my feelings of guilt, and sex seemed like as good of a tool as any. Besides, as my mother often reminded me, I was destined to end up in hell, so why not enjoy myself in the meantime?

I arrived back to my once idyllic hometown to a rainstorm of monsoon proportions, or at least it felt that way. A few minutes passed and I already hated Florida and missed Colorado. The scenes of my paltry marriage played like a poorly cut skin flick—innocence, sex, adultery, more sex, cardinal sin—closing credits—main character ends up in hell. I walked off the plane and into the terminal. My mental state disintegrated further with each plodding step. I thought I could do this. I had to do this. I owed myself, and him, that much.

Sheldon had already put our house on the market, which meant I had to return home to parse through the remains of our so-called marital life and sign the final document that would decree our marriage dead.

Steeped in sweat, I looked around the Tampa Bay terminal and saw Sheldon on the other side of the baggage claim. Perspiration plastered his shiny brown hair to his forehead. He was the only person in the airport who looked worse than me.

"Hey, Sam, hope your flight was okay."

Please, for the love of God, don't be nice to me.

"It was fine. You look tired," I said.

"Packing up our house was tougher than I expected. I still can't believe this is it for us. Are you sure? It's not too late. I never stopped loving you. I just got overwhelmed with work. I'm sorry for that."

Am I sure, for fuck's sake? Of course I'm not sure. But I had done the dastardly deed, which, in the world according to Catholicism, meant my marriage and life were over unless I went to confession. There was no way I could do that. *Pussy.*

"Thanks for clearing out the house," I said.

I tried to speak again but couldn't because tears threatened to flow.

We walked in silence through the terminal until we reached the parking lot. A walk of shame: Sheldon's shame for not caring enough until it was too late, and mine for cheating my way out of a marriage.

"All right. I guess this is it then. I put aside some things that I thought you might want," he said. "We can stop by our house and take a final look if you like?"

"That would be nice. To sort of say goodbye to our place…" I said as I choked back a tear.

"Whatever you want. You'll be okay. You know that, right? It's going to be okay."

I knew it was going to be okay. Why did he have to keep saying that? It was possible to move on after a divorce despite what the Catholic church and my parents wanted me to believe. People started over and got second chances. At least that's what Oprah was always saying.

As we drove down the once memorable Beach Drive, a flurry of memories came into focus— memories of a life that was supposed to last forever but ended before its time.

As we rounded the waterway and pulled into the driveway of the house that would soon enough belong to someone else, I scrambled out of the car. I stood, nose pressed against our spectacular bay window, an outsider looking in on my own life. All the peach walls, white picket fences, and palm trees couldn't put Samantha and Sheldon back together again.

He got out of the car, and like a nurturing, devoted old husband, he walked me into our home for the last time. The house was barren and void of any form of happiness, empty except for a lone box that was labeled **Cubby Bear** in bold letters, with a sad face drawn underneath.

I ran over to it and picked through an assortment of knickknacks that Sheldon had set aside for me. A hand-sewn snowman ornament, my favorite. A squishy "I heart you" keychain, his first gift to me. And the "forgive me, I have zinned," magnet, which was hard not to take personally. This was what he chose to save for me as a reflection of the best parts of our time together?

A lonely tear slipped down my cheek. I prayed to God Almighty to prevent me from breaking down, but the big guy let me down. I sat hunched over my **Cubby Bear** box, holding it like it was my baby, while I cried just like one.

Sheldon walked up to me, held me and rocked me into a more settled state.

"Samantha, it is going to be okay."

At least one of us was sure of that.

Chapter Ten

The visit to what was once my marital home was heartbreaking. Sheldon was my best friend, but even he couldn't deliver me from evil. I had loved him to the best of my abilities, which were limited given my upbringing. Our friendship changed my life and without it, it was hard to know who I would be anymore, other than a divorcée responsible for the dissolution of a marriage. And a sinner.

After hours spent at the airport diluting my guilt with booze the way only a Serrano could, I decided I was free to move on with my life. As I swigged down the last of my Bloody Mary, waiting for my plane to board, I sent Superstar a racy email to anoint my freedom.

It had been a couple of days. Surely he would be yearning for me as badly as I was for him, or at least I hoped so. People couldn't have such wanton sex and not miss each other, right? I reviewed my sent message and confirmed that it still seemed sexy and mysterious without—as *Elle* magazine advised—being too forward or needy.

I got up and wandered around the terminal for an hour to burn some time and then stopped off at the restroom. It was still bloody hot, even though it was 10 o'clock at night. Florida sucked as badly as I looked. Having a husband appear many months too late to reclaim your love took a toll. I had massive bags under my eyes. Sorry, *Self* magazine, cooled cucumber slices can only do so much.

Superstar must have been rubbing off on me because email and Facebook calmed my nerves. The departure board showed that my flight was delayed another hour, so I found a wine bar and ordered a spicy Cabernet to match my sure-to-be sweltering sex life.

I fired up the nifty NetSocial app on my iPad, which we were beta testing before the official launch. Superstar had recently enhanced the interface to spark more social engagements. Hopefully, my seductive message would engage *him*. Hmm, it was odd that he hadn't responded to my previous email yet. He was always online. How could he go offline in my time of need? I could tell that he had read the message but for some reason, hadn't responded. Bad social netiquette if you asked me.

I was fairly certain my note was cute and witty while being sexy at the same time. What more did he want? I had just ended my marriage. He should know that I needed to erase my past by flinging myself forward, sexually, as soon as possible.

I thought about my mother's best defense: *Wine makes everything better*. It *almost* saved Christ, so why not me? I shot down the remains of my vino. It burned and coated my throat all at once. *You're going to need a lot more than wine to save your soul.*

Another stomach-twisting hour passed. The airport temperatures climbed, as did the raucous behavior at the wine bar. There was lots of pounding on the bar, and suits swatting each other on the back with one too many attaboys for my taste.

Amped up on cheap wine, I may have serial texted Superstar and every person in my contact list followed by a Twitter bender aimed at Mr. Twinkle Eyes himself. The PA system stopped the frenzy by announcing my flight was beginning to board. I stuffed my iPad into my cow print pink purse and sprinted to the gate.

"I'm headed your way!"

***

"Ms., please return your seat to the full upright position and stow your tray table. We're about to land," the pissy flight attendant said as she tapped my hand.

Christ, had I passed out? I had a horrible dream where I went on a social media bender. No, it was fine, everything would be okay, just like Sheldon said.

My head throbbed to an evil airport rendition of elevator music. Superstar's penis inside me would remedy that. *Marie Claire* said sex could be an instant cure for a hangover.

As I wobbled off the gangplank to the greeting

gate at Denver International Airport, I looked for Superstar. It was hard to tell where he might have been hiding. Didn't he say he would meet me at the airport? He was probably waiting downstairs at the baggage claim.

I flicked on my phone certain he'd have texted to tell me where he was in the terminal, but there was nothing. Surveying the area with the precision of a Navy Seal, I still couldn't find him. After fetching my bag, I walked with purpose all the way to the next terminal. Still no Superstar. Was this God's way of punishing me because I had committed multiple acts of adultery?

I fumbled with the iPad trying to get the damn thing to chirp with its magical new message ding, but nothing. I shut it off and then back on and waited for it to reboot. After one too many seconds the bitten apple appeared, reminding me that we all make mistakes. Even Eve ate the apple for God's sake.

Still not a single message from Boy Wonder. Had I ever sent him my note? I double-checked my sent folder. Yep, eight messages ought to have covered it. Perhaps the last that read ***ASSHOLE*** might have been one step too far. Oprah was always saying never to use all caps, as it could be inflammatory. She had a point. Not only was I divorced and disowned, but also too free with flapping fingers. But really, could anyone be held accountable for messages sent under the influence? That was the whole point of Twitter; it's the Millennials' answer to drunk dialing.

I rang Babs to see if she had been in contact with

Superstar. Maybe he had dropped his phone in the john while trying to pee and control that gargantuan penis of his.

"Hey, I'm back. Have you heard from Superstar? I'm not getting any new messages from him," I said.

"Hey, sweetie, welcome home. I'm glad you're back. Hopefully you can start to focus more at work. The whole divorce thing has been getting in the way of your performance, and yes, I just got a text from him a second ago. Relax and meet me for a drink. I miss you!"

"Babs, I'll call you right back."

I tried to calm myself by massaging my nose. It didn't help. I lugged my stuff to the curb and hailed a cab. The jumping up and down, as if I were on a pogo stick, attracted a cabbie, but drew scared looks from passersby.

"Hey, where are you? I'm desperate for a cocktail," I said to Babs, who I dialed as soon as I'd settled into the backseat of the cab.

"Phantom Canyon, honey. I can't wait to see you. There are tons of cuties out tonight. Now that you're single again, we can party. I just dropped some E," she said, and hung up.

Perfect, Superstar's favorite hangout. He was always there trying to seduce the crowd like he did at client meetings. Connectivity was often patchy there given the bar's proximity to Pikes Peak, which could also explain his lack of response. Or maybe the amazing sex we had before I left was not as good for him as it was for me?

As I pulled into the parking lot, I felt a sense of

peace from the familiar surroundings. Tasteful brew bars with thoughtful food always calmed me. The NetSocial team had spent many nights here. Plus, the food and beer were so good, it would distract attention away from my rumpled outfit and airplane hair.

As I walked through the entrance, a glorious view of the mountains assaulted my senses as the whiz of bar banter engulfed me. So did the prospect of a new life. Divorce would not define me despite what the church and my family chanted relentlessly.

The scent of sweet potato tots filled the air and reminded me of home. My mom favored the tater tot variety as opposed to this spiced up version, but still. Maybe she would find a way to support my decision to divorce.

I pushed past the throngs of people and headed upstairs, where I spotted Babs seducing the sexy bartender while making eyes at a pair of underaged guys across the room. She was hard to miss in her plunging crimson tube top and miniskirt. The fact that it was still winter didn't seem to matter. She often coached me to "flaunt the flesh" regardless of the time of year.

I caught her eye and she motioned for me to join her.

"Hey, honey! Welcome home. You look awful. You need a man sandwich," she said as she grazed a twentysomething's buttocks with her manicured fingertips to indicate I should sit on his lap.

"Good to see you too. I've missed…"

I choked on my words when I looked past Babs to the pool tables. Superstar sat on the corner of one, cupping someone's chin as he kissed her. What the hell? Blatant public displays should be banned except for has-been episodes of *Jersey Shore*, when it's hilarious.

"Honey, is everything okay?" Babs said.

Clearly the E was talking. Of course I wasn't okay. Instead of Superstar greeting me with a welcome-home bouquet of tulips, he was engaged in a lip tango with some other woman.

Not only hadn't he answered my emails and texts, but he appeared to be on something that resembled a date, or worse yet, in the throes of a hook-up. There had to be a reasonable explanation that I couldn't wait to hear. Maybe he was in the midst of one of his client-wooing sessions…although kissing a client could be considered a conflict of interest, not that he seemed too concerned about it.

I catapulted myself to the other end of the bar and stood before them, arms folded, like an angry mother. The girl looked barely legal. Babs followed.

When Superstar did not ditch the dame and envelop me in one of his luscious kisses, I thought I'd provoke him into an embrace.

"So, hey, how are you? I tried to get your attention. Did you see me waving at you?"

"Yeah, I caught that. Would you step aside, doll? You're in the middle of our game."

"Are you serious?" I said. "I've been gone for a week and all you have to say is I'm interrupting your game?"

"Well, you are," he said as he wagged his hips and lined up the cue stick.

Who did he think he was? His nakedness was still fresh in *my* mind, yet he stood fondling somebody else's cheek with a rod.

"You're in the way. Beat it," he said.

When did he turn back into the arrogant and cocky bastard I met that first day on the job? And when exactly did he find the time to seduce a Betty Boop wannabe?

"Didn't you get any of my emails and texts?"

He laughed and stroked his peach fuzz.

"Oh yeah, I got the first one, the second one, and the trail that followed, it was mildly entertaining."

I stared at him trying to make sense of his behavior. I waited for him to recant his statement, or at least attempt to ravish me on top of the pool table, but he remained focused on the dame and his game.

I grabbed the Slippery Nipple shooter from Babs' hand and flipped it right on top of Superstar's coarse head of hair.

"*Asshole*. You complete and total *asshole*!"

Chapter Eleven

In the months that followed the A-hole incident, Superstar never spoke a single word to me except for work-related matters, which went from hot and sexy to stilted. He was no longer interested in having me in his bed or in the boardroom. Not only did he dump me after my insidious scene at Phantom Canyon, he attempted to squeeze me out of my job.

Newlywed, divorced, dated, and dumped. I had developed quite a name for myself. *Why not simplify the monikers and just go with sinner instead?* How could somebody so brilliant and geeky turn out to be such an asshole? I mean, bad person. Given the fallout, the "A" word had been stricken from my vocabulary.

My first failed post-divorce liaison felt like a sinner's payback from the devil himself. If only I had been sent to hell. Instead, I was stuck working with the tech geek every damn day. What was I thinking? *Apparently nothing. As usual.*

I fought hard and worked crazy-long hours to

retain a place of importance at the company—penance for my infidelity. Superstar "rocked the tech stratosphere" (his words) as he continued to pork his way through the workplace.

Following the demise of our relationship, the company, unlike my love life, took off like a speedboat. NetSocial went from five employees to over two hundred in less than a year.

I worked at such an insane pace it left little time to pine over my divorce—or Superstar. For his part, he remained an asshole in lamb's clothing, aside from the coarse sheep's hair.

Many new faces inhabited NetSocial's headquarters. These "expats," as I liked to call them, were charged with whipping the company out of start-up mode and into a corporate powerhouse as soon as possible. As one of the company's initial employees, I found the strategy offensive—especially when our bean-bag towers were replaced with institutional-looking cubicles and soundproofed offices.

Babs was pushed off the management team and replaced by a new regime of Superstar wannabes who lacked her verve and social networking know-how. Among the more annoying new hires was a caustic Italian Catholic who called himself Frankie Frank, and Carson, a nose-picking "suit" who Candy promptly nicknamed Boogie.

There came a time in one's life when visible boogers should not be a problem you're faced with. Boogie, at thirty-one, had not reached such an age. How hard would it be to do a double-take in the mirror before leaving the bathroom, and if necessary, blowing those things out of your nose? Especially before heading into the boardroom.

"Hi Boog—sorry, Carson. How's it hanging?" I asked.

From what I could see, far too low.

"Well, Sam, now that you ask, things aren't going so well. I was charged with putting a financial schema together, mapping a plan for longevity and growth, and yet nobody has followed my recommendations," Boogie said as he entered the conference room, clipboard in hand.

Clearly, he had forgotten what decade we were in. Boogie conducted himself with the arrogance of a Wall Street suit minus the fat wallet and sharp looks. The fact that he wore actual suits to the office worked against him almost as much as his poor nasal hygiene habits.

"Sam and I did that three months ago, which is why we shouldn't waste company money to redo it. Catch up!" Candy said as she flicked a faux nose pick at his back.

"Oh. I wouldn't have bothered had I known that," he said.

"No problem. You may want to hit the little boy's room before the meeting starts," Candy said, miming a tissue dab to her rosy nose.

"I hate to break up the hen party, but the meeting should have started at 0800 hours, so you're all late," Frankie said, standing at attention behind the podium.

He looked like an idiot up there at his makeshift pulpit. He was way too formal for our company. Plus, it looked like he attempted to wear an outfit that coordinated with the wall color of the conference room. Sea green was not a good look on anybody.

"Sam, cut it out, stop staring," Candy whispered.

"What?"

"He's a bozo. Please," she said.

"*I* obviously know how to captivate clients, having attended the best colleges on military scholarship and scoring top of my class. You all could benefit from learning even one-half of the sales strategies I have to offer, so focus," Frankie said.

I scribbled to Candy:

Who cares. Why does he always spit out his credentials?

He was so *not* NetSocial material. We weren't corporate. We were cool. Plus, he had a receding hairline and wore sweater-vests with pleated khakis as a uniform. Nobody wore sweater-vests anymore and no man should ever wear pleated pants, especially to work. Pleats made it impossible to ascertain if the wearer of said pants had a boner, or if the bulge in the britches was just a bad cut of the fabric. Either way, did you really want people pondering that premise whenever you walked into a room?

"I would like to kick off today's session with a PowerPoint presentation," he said. Then he adjusted—his pleats.

This man knew no other way. PowerPoint was antiquated. I couldn't wait for Superstar and Frankie to have an ego showdown. Superstar would cackle at this display.

Despite his arcane audio-visual preferences, Frankie's business acumen shined through as he talked about the top-secret ways our app would change the meaning of social networking. Superstar would be threatened by Frankie's Ivy League education since he never even finished high school.

I peered over at Candy. By slide number five, she already had a glazed-over look on her face as she twisted her long black hair and daydreamed out the window. Admittedly, the mountains were extra attractive today. Snow still capped the top of Pikes Peak even though it was the dead of summer.

Boogie looked totally entranced by Frankie's presentation, further cementing his position as the resident brownnoser.

"I'm here to make your life easier. Use me when you need me. Call on me at any time and I'll be there," Frankie babbled.

He sounded like a cross between a telemarketer and an insurance salesman.

"And that, my tribe, is how we shake up the social media stratosphere."

He adjusted his pleats, for the fifth time in the last hour. Candy had started a tally sheet. He saluted us as he walked out of the room.

"Please fire me now," she said. "I can't take it. He's clueless."

"Isn't he brilliant?" Boogie said.

Boogie frequently mentioned that he would one day take over the company. Perhaps he should start with a simple hankie swipe. There was only so far you could climb with balled-up boogers getting in the way of your career trajectory.

"Oh yeah, he's brilliant all right," I said.

It was impressive that I managed to make it through the meeting without hurling. Between Frankie's speech, a hangover, and Boogie's boogers, that was no small feat. I excused myself from the meeting and made my way back to my office in hopes of grabbing a quick nap.

Instead of shuteye, though, Frankie greeted me at the door looking like a poorly dressed prepster.

"Sam, can we talk?"

That was all this guy ever did. *He's your boss. Show some respect. He served our country, which is more than you've ever done.*

"Sure, what's up?"

"At ease, soldier," he said. "I realize we haven't totally connected, but I think we could help each other if you're willing to work with me."

That would be just like a man. Come kick me when I'm hungover and don't have the energy to resist.

"Okay," I said, hoping to get him to leave before he busted out another PowerPoint presentation.

"That's great news, Sam. There are two camps residing in this mess tent: those who have been following Superstar's lead, and those who are looking for more, how shall I put this, more skilled and scholarly leadership. While he was our beginning, I feel quite confident that he's not our future. Wouldn't you agree?"

"Frankie, you've got my attention. What did you have in mind?"

"The social networking conference Dreamforce is fast approaching. This is where I want us to make our move and launch the app—without Superstar. We, and not he, should be leading the troops. This San Francisco event will put us in a position to do just that. I'm not interested in being your boss…I want to be your partner," he said as he power-shook my hand.

Aw shucks, what could a gal say to a proposition like that? In that moment, Frankie moved from foe to friend.

Chapter Twelve

In a couple months' time, Frankie and I were entrenched in a synergistic relationship as boss and semi-subordinate. Despite his pleated pants and PowerPoint preference, Frankie and I had become allies. My personal life also flourished with a colleague named Ryan, who fast became a best bud. Ryan and I spent hours hanging out in that wonderful no-pressure friend-zone, often on the ski slopes. After the back-to-back fiascoes with Superstar and the divorce, friendship felt like the only way to go.

The cool thing about life in Colorado was that you could start skiing as early as October, which is what Ryan and I did. One November weekend, as we rode the Arapahoe Basin ski lift up the mountain, laughing at silly knock-knock jokes, Ryan popped my earmuffs off when he leaned in to kiss me. What a surprise! The power of his pucker almost knocked me right off the lift. It was unexpected and surprisingly sensual, like a scene from *Girls*.

Ryan met the criteria that *Glamour* magazine had outlined in their article on procuring a man with "relationship potential" at the workplace. Tall and fit with tousled brownish-black hair, he had mastered the super sexy fresh-off-the-sheets look. He was also single and available. After that passionate kiss we shared and the nurturing way he treated me, I decided it would be okay for me to explore the possibility of a deeper connection with him. I got up the courage to invite him over to watch the relationship classic, *When Harry Met Sally,* hoping he would glean the larger meaning of the film.

He tickled me on my satin rose-print couch, sliding us all over the place with each smooch.

"Ryan, you're bad. If you don't stop, we will never get to watch the movie and learn why women and men can never be *just friends.*"

He looked at me sternly and then curled up his tongue and touched his nose with it as he crossed his eyes. Then he kissed me. I found his blend of goofball seduction oddly erotic.

"Ryan, stop, you're making me giggle," I cooed.

"Cutie, would you still like me if my face stayed this way?" he said, still cross-eyed.

I wondered if my striped pink walls were causing his peeps to cross or if it was part of his seductive plot. He smelled like vanilla which made me want him even more.

"Of course I would. It's just if you don't leave soon, Frankie and I are never going to get our presentation done in time for the conference."

I had strategically invited Ryan over on a night

when we wouldn't have enough time to get too intimate. Even I had boundaries. Plus, no matter how much the world twirled and the dating road rules evolved, playing hard to get was still and would always be the most prudent tactic in securing a long-term relationship, according to *Marie Claire*.

"Okay, okay, you're right. One of us has to save the company," he said, "I'll let you get to work. But this is to be continued."

He smooched me one last time and did that sensual trick with his tongue and nose and walked out my front door. Damn, he was so sweet, and not in that annoying way, just adoringly respectful. As much as I hated to see him go, the could-be budding romance would have to wait. There was work to do. I slipped on my comfy hot pink Uggs and set off to Jack Quinn's to meet Frankie.

***

Frankie had a thing for booming Irish pubs. He claimed they inspired greatness; I thought they just stunk, aside from this one, which was borderline snazzy for a watering hole. I obliged his Irish urge because he had become my mentor, and the pretzel kabobs rocked. In return, I was a keen listener— mostly when it came to hearing his marital sob stories.

After three hours of reviewing PowerPoint in a bar, anybody would need a respite. Mine included daydreaming about Ryan over a glass of Jameson Irish Whiskey, straight up. I coughed every time I took a sip, but I liked the feeling as it burned its way down my throat. Let Frankie overthink our strategy for the trade show—I'd had enough. I sipped and coughed and pretended to listen to him.

"We met in high school and it all seemed so promising. Especially when we won prom king and queen. That was a highlight," he said.

The whiskey almost made me laugh, but I held it inside. If powder blue tuxedos and puffy satin dresses were a high point, I felt sorrier for him than for myself. It looked like Frankie was about to cry. Good God, man up.

"Then Sherry got pregnant right out of high school, which ruined all our plans. But like good soldiers, we carried on, got married, and tried to build a life together. I don't think Sherry ever forgave me for impregnating her too soon."

"Wow, that's too bad. But you guys have beautiful children. That's what really matters."

Why was it that married people always wanted to talk to their single friends about their troubles? It didn't make sense. If we had all the answers, we wouldn't be single.

"Well, it's probably just a bump. Everybody has them. I'm sure you and Sherry will be fine. Dr. Phil always has good insights into this kind of stuff. You should check him out."

"Do you really think so?"

"Yes, his advice is outstanding."

"No. I meant about Sherry and I."

"Oh sure, sorry. I'm sure everything will work itself out," I said.

Or so I hoped. I hated to see men, other than Superstar, suffer.

Frankie, placated enough to complete our presentation, rewarded me with another shot of whiskey. It was funny how he had predicted that we would become allies in the war against Superstar. We were kind of like brother and sister twins, the yin to each other's yang. See, Harry and Sally? Men and women could be just friends.

Chapter Thirteen

"Sweetie, I'm gonna miss you this weekend. You and Frankie spend more time together than we do," Ryan said.

"Pookie, you have nothing to worry about. Frankie is my work husband, and you are my boyfriend," I said as I ravished him on top of my fuzzy fuchsia rocking chair.

Ryan and the chair made me dizzy. Having a relationship was effortless with him, which made me *really* like him.

After an abbreviated make-out session I sent him off on a mission to hit every bump on the ski slopes, but not before dropping me off at the airport.

When we got there, we smooched a little bit longer, which was tricky in Ryan's vintage burgundy Beetle. Cramped but cute! He gave me one last peck, unloaded my suitcase curbside, and pushed me on my way so I wouldn't miss the flight. All of the necking had put me behind schedule. Thankfully, the Colorado Springs airport was pint-sized, so I swiftly checked my luggage and boarded the plane just in time.

Airplane flights had turned into therapy sessions for Frankie and me. At takeoff, our topic du jour turned once again to his marital discord. Midway through the flight, though, our usual roles reversed, and by the time we landed in San Francisco, I had unloaded the unabridged version of the Sheldon saga on him. It was the first time I had talked about my divorce out loud to a real person. I felt cleansed. *Maybe try going to church to cleanse your soul.*

As we waited for our luggage at the turnstile, Frankie resumed yammering.

"Sam, I never realized you had been through all of that. You seem so strong," he said.

"Well, I guess I fooled everybody, including myself. I was taught that when trouble strikes, you pretend like nothing has happened, which I guess is what I did during the end of my marriage. It just seemed easier. But eventually you have to pass through the anger and grief to get to the other side."

"Yeah, I hope you're right."

How could I get him to stop talking? Maybe I should burp lightly to throw him. His intensity was starting to make me uncomfortable. Denial, that was the answer. I looked past his sweater-vested shoulder in hopes of spotting our luggage.

"Sam I never realized how much we have in common. I blame the Catholic Church." He chuckled.

"So do I, man, so do I."

I looked into his eyes and he grabbed my hand.

It was impossible to break his gaze. He had a point. We were simpatico because of our upbringing. He understood me, the real me, like nobody had until now. *Oh Christ, here we go.*

***

At the conference, people flocked around our booth. Apparently, all of Frankie's PowerPoint presentations had made an impression because the press couldn't get enough of us. By the second day of the conference, we had been dubbed the "wunderkinds of the social networking world." Take that and stuff it up your keyboard, Mark Zuckerberg and all your fake Facebook "friends." I counted six different quotes in four global newspapers. My favorites: "NetSocial—Beyond Friending" and "NetSocial's Serrano and Frank Fly Company to Social Media's Next Stratosphere."

Beyoncé's "Run the World" ringtone interrupted my visions of grandeur, which included Frankie and me on the cover of *Wired*, he as Superman, I as Wonder Woman. I pushed off my satin pink sleep mask to grab the screaming device, but not before knocking my white noise machine to the floor. I prayed that someday soon the love and snuggles of Ryan would replace my need for electronics to lull me to sleep.

"You two were fucking brilliant!

"Hey, Nate, morning," I said.

"I just got off the phone with Apple. We're taking our company public thanks to you and Frankie. Welcome to your new post of VP of Marketing. You've earned it," he said.

There was only one person I wanted to revel in

the excitement with. I dialed without hesitation.

"Hey, I have some amazing news. Hang onto your boxers. I got promoted to VP. Can you believe it?"

"Sam, you more than anyone deserve this. Your time has come," Frankie said.

"Wait, you mean you knew about this and you let me rattle on about my divorcée woes all night? You bastard," I said.

"Nate wanted to wake you up with the news. He made me promise to hold off on telling you."

"Yeah, wow, this has been crazy. Too bad we have to go back home today, I feel like celebrating."

***

Left with no other alternative, Frankie and I got sauced on the flight back home. The adrenaline and booze buzzes ran as high as the sky.

"I blame my family. I needed out of that house and Sheldon was my ticket. He was my best friend, but I'm not so sure I would have married him if my parents hadn't been on my back about getting serious with my life. With each beer my father swilled, he reminded me that I was not living up to my potential. Then he would burp at me between curses."

"Sam, he sounds like a bad role model."

"My mother forced me to go to church and confession every Sunday as if I were the only sinner in the house. Afterwards, we would share a caustic family meal and my father would remind me that I needed to get a job or a husband. He would not respect me until I did. I just wanted out from under them, so marriage seemed like the easiest way."

"Don't be so hard on yourself. You did what you needed to do to free yourself from that toxic situation. You're doing just fine. Excellent, actually, Ms. Vice President," he said, bowing his head as if I were royalty.

"Thanks, Frankie. Nobody has ever really seen the good in me until you came along. I think I may be bound for greatness, or at least goodness. I feel so fortunate to have you as a boss, and a friend," I said, toasting him with my plastic cup.

The leggy flight attendant looked down her nose at me as she passed our row. Not even her snotty attitude would curtail my happiness. No one could. I looked out the window as we flew above the marshmallow clouds, comforted by the thought that Frankie hadn't judged me for marrying young and divorcing myself out of a bad relationship.

"Since we're being airplane-honest, Sherry and I were best friends too, but I don't think we were ever *in love*," Frankie said. "I've stayed with her all these years because of the kids. And like the Catholics always say, divorce is never an option."

He tilted his head and gazed at me so intently I felt my ears sizzle.

Turbulence broke his stare. A wobbly-voiced co-captain warned us to brace for a rocky ride. Seatbelts clicked on in unison as our flying boat ricocheted between the clouds that went from cotton-puff white to gun-metal gray.

This was not the way I wanted to die, having poured out my sad life story on a plane for anybody within earshot to hear.

I gripped my seat and the barf bag, trying to calm my tousled body. That last glass of bubbly may have been a bad idea.

Frankie looked more terrified than I felt. When he grabbed my arm for support, all I could think about was the fact that I was about to die on a plane seated next to a pleated-pants-and-sweater-vest guy. It would paint an uncool picture in the *Denver Post*. After all I had endured, was this God's fate for me?

Thankfully, after a few more minutes of threatening turbulence, the plane leveled out, though the cabin remained in a silent stupor for the duration of the flight. It was only when we slid onto the snow-covered runway that I began to feel safe.

Disembarking, I realized that Frankie was still holding my hand, which seemed odd, so I intentionally dropped my Coach knock-off purse so I'd be forced to unlock my hand from his. While I picked up my lip glosses that had tumbled out, I realized that not once during the bouncy flight had I thought about Ryan. I may have actually experienced a stomach flip for Frankie, and it wasn't an airsick tic. It was the thing your tummy did when you met somebody who you thought might be *the one.* It must have been a near-death fluke because Frankie was someone else's *one* and technically so was I, for that matter.

Thankfully after he helped me collect the rest of my belongings he picked at his pleats all the way off the airplane—a big turn off, or at least it should have been.

We didn't utter a word as we drove away from

the airport. Frankie's thick fingers looked nice on the black leather steering wheel of his Volvo station wagon, the quintessential family mobile. The threat of nausea bubbled. Probably post-traumatic airsick disorder, or I still couldn't handle booze with the same stamina as my parents. My mind drifted, right along with the falling snow, as a slew of thoughts boomed in my brain.

As we pulled up to the office parking lot, we skidded in the snow that had accumulated during our ride and bumped to a stop against the curb. Frankie unloaded my belongings. As I awkwardly shuffled about, Frankie caught my eye and leaned in toward me.

Chapter Fourteen

'Tis the season to be jolly! *Keep telling yourself that, dear.* I'd been going bonkers ever since the San Francisco trip until I decided it was best to ignore the memory of Frankie's glistening eyes and bizarre lean-in. Odd behavior was to be expected when people survived what felt like a near-death experience.

Meanwhile, I buzzed along at work, and things were going better than ever with Ryan. In a month's time, we had successfully transitioned from best friends to a full-on exclusive relationship. To avoid awkwardness, I orchestrated my interactions with Frankie so that we were never alone together. Ryan made me ecstatic, yet I was still riddled with anxiety.

To temper the angst, I resurrected a tradition from my marital past—a Christmas shindig. Ever since Sheldon and I wed, I had stopped feeling the Yule, but this year felt different. One e-vite later, and I had reawakened a glimmering part of my former life.

Candy and I bonded in the break room during lunch. As I sank my teeth into a gooey salt bagel, she said, "Sam, I know I don't say it enough, but I'm really proud of you. You've really turned your life around. You've advanced your career and your personal life. Bravo to you."

"Yeah, I guess you're right. Things are fantabulous. I just hope I don't do something to muck it all up."

"Oh, shut it. You have to stop torturing yourself. Your parents have killed your self-esteem, but it's time to get over it. You're in a responsible relationship, which will stabilize the rest of your life."

I considered that maybe I should trust that Candy knew what she was talking about. She and her husband had been together since high school. Sure, I'd taken my knocks along the way, but maybe it was possible for a kitty to change her spots.

At the end of the day, I charged out of my office to head home for party prepping. Frankie appeared and blocked my way. His eyes glistened.

Oh Christ, what now?

"Is everything all right between us? I feel distant from you ever since our trip."

I fumbled for the right words and channeled my mother by avoiding all eye contact and fixating on the bird that sat on the ledge of my window. He tried to force me into direct eye contact, but I remained in a glare-down with Tweetie until he gave up.

"We'll be at your party tonight. Looking forward

to it," he said.

"Okay. Feel the Yule!" I breezed past him and out of my office toward the elevator.

I felt flushed. Was it possible to have hot flashes at my age? That would make me a gynecological rarity since I wasn't even old yet. No, no, it was probably just the erratic heating system in the building.

***

Back at my house, I whipped up my favorite winter party treat—eggnog, a feel-good serum— especially when laced with spiced rum as my mother always made it.

Snow flurries dropped, Nat King Cole hummed, and the house smelled like sugar cookies. The party spread would have made my granny proud. As I twirled around my gingerbread-style home to Christmas carols, my eggnog high was interrupted by Ryan's "You're the One That I Love" ringtone.

"Coming, Snookie," I screamed. "Are you feeling the Yule, baby?"

"Hey, Sammy, I hate to break this to you right before everybody shows up, but I don't think I'm going to get out of this client meeting anytime soon. Superstar is insisting that we hit the tit-bars with the clients. Boobs are the way to our future. His words, not mine. Your boobs are the best."

"Are you serious? Can't you learn to say no to him? He knows my party is tonight. Just bring the clients here," I said.

As much as I wanted Ryan at the party, I knew

that intimate soirées were not the way to lock down a deal with power players. Damn Superstar.

"I'm sorry, sweetie. I promise I'll make it up to you," he said.

As much as Ryan was a dreamboat, I wished he'd grow some cajones.

"No worries, I'll lead the holiday festivities, alone. Enjoy the tits!"

I tried not to sound too bitchy. At least the booze had given *me* some cojones.

As I laid out the last cookie, the doorbell rang.

"Coming!"

This was so exciting. My very first post-divorce holiday extravaganza! The house was decorated to the extreme with three mini-Christmas trees and an elaborate snowman village. All of my trees were short and fat, which was exactly how I loved them. Sheldon hated plump squat trees.

The entire NetSocial team stood at my stoop singing "We Wish You a Merry Christmas" wearing Santa caps. Yes, it was a smidge goofy, but the schmaltzy sentimentality brought me to tears.

"Aw, guys! You are too much. Thanks for making it. Come on in, eggnog awaits."

Candy led the pack of cheer-givers wearing a stylish Santa-style minidress, black fishnets, and lace-up boots. This explained how she and her husband kept the love alive. She continued to sex things up, just like *Glamour* suggested.

I ran around the house like a dog in a meat shop serving up food, eggnog, and cider, and then pouring champagne for a toast.

"I just want to take a moment and thank you all

for sharing this special occasion with me," I said. "It's been a rocky year, but I can honestly say I finally feel like I'm home. Okay, I'll shut up. Wait, thanks to the Internet gods for blessing us with a date to take our company public!"

"Oh, Sammy, get over here before you get the cookies soggy with your boohooing," Candy said. "Where's Frankie? It's strange he's not here since you guys put the whole deal together."

"I don't know. I saw him right before I left the office and supposedly he and Sherry were coming. Something must have come up."

I was relieved. I'd been feeling progressively uncomfortable around Frankie. I knew there was no reason for it, but I still felt awkward in his presence.

After several more rounds of cider and cookies and one too many work stories, we gathered around the piano to sing Christmas carols. The crowd didn't dismantle until midnight.

It was a fantastic night. I would have a huge headache in the morning, but it was worth it. I had officially ended the reign of Sheldon McScrooge.

The team headed out in the same way they had arrived, singing. They were corny, yes, but they were people to call my own.

After months of post-Superstar drama, my professional life was thriving and I'd garnered an amazing circle of friends. Even Boogie had been pleasant enough. Someone must have finally spoken to him because his nostrils were almost booger-free at the party. That was the thing about the holidays: they really did bring people together. As I bustled about cleaning up the remains of good cheer, my doorbell rang. Yay! Ryan must have escaped the tits.

I popped on the hot pink Santa hat that Candy brought for me and slipped out of my clothes into a skimpy rose-colored robe.

"I'll be right there, Snookie," I said.

On my way to the door, I tripped over a pile of presents. "I'm feeling the Yule, baby," I said as I opened the door.

"Hey, Sam."

Horrified, standing in my doorway half-naked, I stammered, "Wow, F-Frankie I-I wasn't expecting—you. I thought it was, well, I don't normally come to the door this way."

What in the hell was Frankie doing here in the middle of the night with a big bottle of champagne and a bundt cake?

"Make yourself comfortable," I stalled. "I'll be right back."

He must have expected everybody to still be celebrating. That would explain his antler headpiece...but who brought bundt cake to a party? It wasn't 1950. And he still donned his stupid glassy-eyed stare.

I had to pull myself together. This was not the time to get paranoid. I had just hosted a smashing soirée.

I ran upstairs and changed into a non-sexy college sweatshirt and baggy cargos. I peeked in the bathroom mirror to make sure I looked presentable yet frumpy. I rubbed my nose abruptly before heading downstairs to try to get rid of Frankie.

Instead of making a graceful reentrance, I

tumbled to the bottom of the staircase. Being clumsy at all the wrong moments was another trait I'd inherited from my mother. Frankie ran over to help me off the plush mauve carpet. Thankfully, I had purchased the more expensive padding, so it broke my fall.

Frankie's hand lingered on mine.

I smoothed my pant pockets and hair, willing my face to return to its normal shade of pale. It rebelled by remaining firebomb red. My cheeks could've burnt toast.

"So, what brings you over this late without your wife?" I said, striving to counter my mother's inability to give straight answers by being overly direct in my questioning.

"I wanted to salute our success on the IPO. In the craze of the last week, we never got a chance to celebrate together," he said, ignoring the significant part of my question.

Perhaps the lack of partying had something to do with the fact that he's married.

Ignoring my awkward pause, he blundered on.

"I come bearing good news," he said.

"Oh, really? I can't imagine what in the world there could be left to celebrate because we have been celebrating all night long. To be honest, I'm pretty pooped," I said as I tried to shoo him out of my home as quickly as he had arrived.

"Trust me, Sam, this is one thing you didn't celebrate."

"Oh. Well, who am I to stand in the way of a new cause to celebrate? What, did Nate finally decide to fire Boogie?" I asked as I fumbled with the tip of my nose.

"No. I asked Sherry for a separation."

I scratched my beak more feverishly than ever, causing a small droplet of blood to trickle off and onto my sweatshirt. Thank God I'd changed out of my sexy robe.

"How nice for you. Could I get you a sugar cookie and some eggnog?"

Before he could answer, I ran into the kitchen. After all these years, I understood the method behind my mother's food-offering madness. Suggesting edibles in the midst of an awkward situation gave you a justified reason to flee.

When I returned, Frankie shared his plans to move out of his buckling marital home. Half of him looked like he was going to skip to the rooftop with glee to join Santa and his reindeer. The other part appeared to be crying. I was not prepared to handle either. I paced and began cleaning up the party wreckage. I attempted to guide him toward the front door with my rum-soaked dishcloth. He ignored my histrionics.

Giving up, I headed back to the kitchen and said, "Frankie, I'm going to get myself a slice of your cake. It looks amazing. Can I grab you a piece while I'm at it?"

I fumbled in the drawer for cutlery and fished out the biggest knife I owned. I cut the sugary delight with a surgeon's precision and flipped it onto a plate as Frankie walked into the kitchen. I waited for him to adjust his pleats, but he just assaulted me with one of his ridiculous glassy-eyed stares.

He stopped moving when he was a few inches

from my butcher's knife. I stabbed into the cake to cut another piece. He placed his hand on mine and directed it to the countertop, causing me to release my weapon. He turned me away from the sink and pulled me into his personal space. Then he stared at me, his full lips puffing in my presence. Did he bite them when I wasn't looking?

I suddenly understood why my mother never made eye contact in times of crisis: denial. I tried to put her signature move to good use by looking out the window and focusing on the gigantic snowflakes. They seemed almost as huge as Frankie's lips.

"Samantha, did you hear what I said? I just told you I left my wife and kids and all you can think about is bundt cake. What's wrong with you?"

Sweat ran down my back. It became near-impossible not to hurl in the stench of my own BO, or maybe it was Frankie's declaration that was making my stomach sick.

"Well, you brought the dumb cake. It would be rude not to offer. Martha Stewart always says when people bring food to a party you serve it on the spot."

Countless glasses of champagne and eggnog later, Frankie had confessed the unabridged story of the disintegration of his marriage.

I should have kicked him out before his waterworks flood started. If you ask me, coming over and crying got the rude prize regardless of what Martha said. I should have been the one bawling, not him.

He ended his depressing tale by telling me he

loved me. Then *I* cried, inside.

What kind of married person pranced around a single girl's home wearing antlers while dropping the "I love you" bomb? It was just wrong. *You're just now grasping this?* People shouldn't be allowed to blurt out crap like that. According to *Fortune* magazine, when uttered by a boss or colleague, it might even be considered sexual harassment.

I no longer felt the Yule and had to wonder if I would ever feel it again. I'd have to stop throwing Christmas parties if this is what I could expect as a closer.

As Frankie continued to unveil inappropriate intimate details, I nodded a lot and threw in a bunch of you-don't-says. *Kick this man out of your life, or at least your home.*

Instead of listening intently, I realized that I should have said something more along the lines of: "This is completely inappropriate, you married bastard, please leave." Instead, I said nothing.

"We just haven't been connecting ever since little Frankie was born," he droned on. "I tried to leave so many times but couldn't muster the courage, until now. You inspired me."

Oh please. I tuned him out while he continued to whine and even managed to maintain a pleasant state of concerned detachment. Mom would have been proud that I never made eye contact, not even once. I cleaned the coffee table where I had accidently spit out my eggnog when he made his absurd declaration.

"Sam, I have never met anybody like you. You're the strongest woman I know. In fact, you glow."

Glowing, wow, I'd never heard that one before, only read about it in *Allure* magazine. They spoke in terms of cheeks, so not totally applicable.

"No matter how much I love my children, I'm not doing them any favors by staying with a woman I don't love. I don't expect you to act on, or even respond, to what I'm saying. I just had to tell you how I felt."

Kick him out now!

"You are my hope and my destiny. Even if you never return my feelings, I will go on being a better person having known you. Well, I guess I ought to let you get some sleep. You look tired."

He came closer, hesitating to adjust his pant pleats. When he was done with all that rustling he looked at me with another glassy-eyed stare and said, "Thank you, Samantha Serrano, for being this kind of woman. Goodnight."

He walked out, closing the door gently, though not hard enough for it to shut completely. I sat in the entryway staring out into a front yard covered in virgin snow. The same flakes that had stopped falling the moment that Frankie left. The lawn remained pristine except for a lonesome trail of prints left by a preppy pair of loafers.

Finally, I mustered the strength to shut the door, and while the wind stopped biting, a wave of something else replaced it: the feeling you got when you realized for the first time in your life that someone saw the good in you that had gone unnoticed until now.

I vomited all over my kitchen floor, which was

where I spent the remainder of the night cowered in the fetal position. Somebody finally loved me, only it was the wrong guy.

***

I went to church the next morning to pray for God's forgiveness for allowing Frankie to spew his sinful confessions all over my home. The Catholic Church and my parental teachings were finally getting put to good use. But then I did what we Serranos always eventually do: I denied the events of the prior night. I lit a holy candle and wished for the disappearance of all of the touching sentiments that Frankie's puffy lips spouted.

Due to the epic amounts of champagne we had consumed, I assumed (or at least hoped) that Frankie wouldn't remember anything. Men always seem to forget when they tell someone they love them—a fact that typically perturbed me, but in this instance, I prayed for it.

To distract myself from my troubles, I planned how I would pounce into the open and available arms of my loving boyfriend on my lunch break. I hoped Ryan had cut off that overgrown beard like he promised. It wasn't helping matters. The mountain man look didn't work for him or for me. The forest of whiskers made it hard to find his lips when kissing time came around. If only Frankie would grow one. Facial hair aside, it was Ryan and not Frankie that was the man for me. Of that, I was certain.

Talking to God within the confines of church did

nothing to allay my panic, so I decided to go into work early. My drive to the office taxed me mentally despite my attempts at singing myself happy. "I Will Survive" and "Dancing Queen" could only get me so far out of the rabbit hole.

I snuck in the back entryway hoping to avoid our receptionist, Perky Pam, who for unknown reasons arrived hours before everyone else—likely to tweet meaningless drivel to her countless followers. Candy arrived at my office door before I had a chance to sit down. What was *she* in so early for?

She loomed, trying to force eye contact. When I didn't cave, she entered. I sunk into my chair and began tapping on my keyboard pretending to be focused on an urgent email.

She tilted my monitor to the side so she could glare at me without obstruction. I could tell by her expression that she knew I was not typing a real message. Perhaps it was the string of expletives that gave me away. E-cursing comforted me.

"Sam, did you drink too much last night? You look green. Is there anything I should know about?"

How this chipper clairvoyant was so perceptive, I would never know.

"Yeah, I'm not feeling so hot. And, well, technically it wasn't me that did the 'something.' It was someone else. Never mind. I resumed church services."

She looked at me blankly.

I rambled, willing myself to shut up.

"Frankie made it to the party."

She forced me out of my chair and into the center of my own office. She turned me in circles as she looked me over.

"Holy crap, you're in love with him, aren't you?"

This time *I* stared blankly.

"He was supposed to be our nemesis. Reel in your hormones already. And what about Ryan?" she said.

"I know. You're right. You're always right. Ryan is my soul mate, not Frankie. How could I be in love with someone who owns fifty pairs of pleated pants and picks at them constantly?"

"Holy Christ! You *are* in love with him. I was half-kidding. You need to cease and desist all personal contact with him," she said as she wagged her finger at me. "No late-night meetings, no Irish bars. Convene only in groups of three or more, and avoid direct eye contact with him. If you follow my instructions, everything will be okay. Okay?"

Her words hung in an attempt to convince both of us that what she said was true.

***

I tried to ignore Frankie the best I could for the next week. He was the only one in the office who looked worse than I did. On Friday afternoon, he ambushed me in the breakroom and ushered me into his office like a drill sergeant.

"I just thought you should know I served Sherry divorce papers yesterday," he said as he fumbled with his pleats.

I wondered if this was a guilt-ridden tick of his and not a crotch adjustment as I had previously thought.

While I was sorry to hear his news, it perturbed me. It had nothing to do with business and therefore was not my concern.

Luckily, Boogie interrupted by knocking on Frankie's door. His nose was unkempt as usual. I tried to skirt out of the room but wasn't quite quick enough. Then I tried to adjust my own pleats. Impossible, since I was wearing a turtleneck sweater dress, my attempt at dressing myself dowdy.

While I straightened my non-existent hemline to avoid eye contact, Frankie said, "Right after the holidays we're headed to New York to lock down our next round of funding."

This was clearly another one of his ploys to get me alone and profess his undying love for me in a new city. I would not fall prey to his seduction. I wasn't a moron. *Well, that's debatable.*

"Frankie, I don't think I'm going to be able to make it. I've not been feeling well, female problems. You know how it is."

"Well, actually, I don't. What I do know is, unless you're about to get admitted into the hospital, you're coming with me. Our IPO has been delayed and we need to get it back on track. The company's future depends on it," he said.

Likely story. It was hard to place stock in words uttered during a pleated-pant-pick.

"Wow, that sounds super serious. Maybe Ryan should go. He is a much more accomplished presenter than I am. Plus, he's a man. I've heard that financial types respond better to men. I think

Wired just ran a story about it."

"Be that as it may, you're still going. Here is your ticket. We fly out on the fifth of January."

He had certainly turned out to be a bossy bleeding-heart desperately separated sad sack of a man.

Chapter Fifteen

New York had a reputation for being a romantic cesspool of deception, but I would not get trapped in its web. I went to church before leaving and called the airlines to move my seat seven rows apart from Frankie. Seven was my lucky number, which would hopefully work in my favor to ward off any unwelcome romantic inclinations.

I didn't sleep the night before our flight to ensure that I looked haggard. How sexy could Frankie find me in a brown corduroy jumper and scuffed Mary Janes?

We shared a cab from JFK to our hotel, but I sat in the front seat with the cabbie to maintain a safe distance. He and the driver droned on in man-speak while I stared out the window, waiting for the cityscape to come into view. When it did, despite all the chaos, it lulled me into a state of calm.

Until we got out of the cab and Frankie stared at me lovingly.

I caught a glimpse of myself in an ornate mirror that hung near the lobby in the Plaza Hotel. The face looking back at me was painted with guilt. I couldn't tell if it was because of my piss-poor looks or the fact that I had offered my hand in friendship to a married man who recently told me that he loved me.

"This hotel is spectacular, isn't it?" I gushed. "I don't think I've ever been anywhere so stunning. It's a bit spendy for a pseudo-start-up, don't you think? Not that I'm complaining, it just seems like a lot of money when we're here trying to raise money. I mean, you'd think the company might have resorted to having us share a room to save funds if we were going to stay here, not that that would be a good idea. I'm just saying…"

Stop babbling, you moron.

"Sam, take it easy. How about we get checked in and then we can take a walk? It's a magnificent afternoon. We should enjoy it now, since work will take over later."

The smart thing to do in this situation would have been to counter Frankie's invitation with a polite yet firm, *No, thank you. I need to call my boyfriend, have phone sex, and then go to sleep.* Instead, I stood silent and frozen, like the picturesque statue perched out in front of the hotel.

"I'll check us in and you can wait here," he said. "I'll be back in five so we can take that walk." Wink.

Oh, for the love of God, I wished he'd stop twinkling his eyes at me. It was just wrong.

Lucky for us, it was still light outside. Nothing ever happened to people in daylight. When he finished checking us in, he pushed me outside, only adjusting his pleats once.

"There's nothing like a brisk sunset walk in Central Park, wouldn't you agree?"

Say something, Samantha. Good girls don't take strolls in Central Park with taken men. Despite my attempts at speaking, nothing came out.

The next thing I knew I was in the midst of a romantic stroll with a married man-whore. The leaves crackled underfoot, yet the park remained peaceful. Damn Giuliani for making it safe so many years ago.

Frankie's eyes became glassier with each step. I should have been freezing but my thumping libido warmed me on the inside.

Minutes into our walk, I discovered we were holding hands. Good God! How had that happened? Friends and colleagues didn't hold hands. That would be unprofessional. But there we were, boss and subordinate, married and unmarried, walking hand in hand through Strawberry Fields. Damn him, how did he know the thought of John Lennon would ignite me?

He sang the song "All You Need is Love," completely out of tune as he stopped at a bench.

I felt his soft and supple lips on mine. He had stealthily swept me up on the bench with him.

In my head, I went tearing out of the park. In reality, I kissed him back. *Step away from the lips. They're married to someone else.* I engaged in a hot and passionate lip tango with my boss. John Lennon beamed down on us.

It's true what they say about Italian men: they really did know how to make use of their assets,

Frankie's being sensual lips and a huge penis. Okay, the latter was speculation based on the size of his feet, his very big feet.

His apparatus stayed safely tucked within his stupid khakis, but his tongue worked wonders on mine. I was in way too deep.

Damn you, New York City, for luring me into your luscious world of love and deception.

***

I wish I could say that I avoided him for the rest of the trip, but it was impossible. Instead, we wined and dined the investors relentlessly. Thankfully, my guilt-ridden alter-ego stepped in and prevented further loose-lip action in the after hours.

I told myself the kiss was a fluke, never to be repeated or talked about again. If my mom were present she would have offered us bagels and cream cheese to encourage the denial. Instead, in tribute to her, I drank a lot of red hot schnapps and passed out in my hotel room every night. Manhattan had swiftly become fuel for my flailing moral code. Good thing we were leaving.

I must have awakened as my mother because I made no eye contact with Frankie for the entire cab ride to the airport. I kept my peepers plastered out the window as the skyline melted out of sight.

It was fitting we flew out of Newark, an ugly, stinking airport, which helped to squelch any romantic inclinations I might have been tempted to have.

As we entered the terminal, I acted quickly.

"I have to pee."

I made a move toward the ladies' room, and when Frankie wasn't looking, diverted my route toward the check-in counter. There was no way I was going to sit next to him for the entire flight. I would cease and desist with all personal contact, just like Candy had instructed.

Luckily, God was on my side and I got my seat moved far away from Frankie. So what if I would be sitting right next to the pint-sized plane potty? *A fitting place for a stinky sewage girl like you.*

The flight would grant me some time to think, and to conjure up a delicate way to tell Ryan about my lip-smacking indiscretion. Hopefully, he would understand and forgive me.

I had three vodka tonics and dozed off.

Four hours later, we banged onto the runway, waking me from a peaceful slumber, the type of sleep where men and women and bosses and subordinates could just be friends and not inappropriately kiss one another in Central Park.

Thank God we were home. *You're going to need a lot more than God's help to get you out of this mess.*

Frankie and his smoking hot lips waited for me at the gate. He gazed into my eyes, placed a note in my sweaty palm, and folded my fingers around it.

I thought about opening it, contemplated giving it back to him, but settled on sprinting down the airport corridor.

When I stopped for a water break, I stuffed the note into the breast pocket of my sensible pink oxford shirt, which I buttoned up to the top while making a personal vow to God and myself never to read the letter. I made my way outside, where I waved my arms at a cabbie. It started to hail yet I stood there getting pelted, immobilized by my deceitful behavior in New York.

"Get in the frickin' car, lady, or I'm moving on," the fat, cranky driver said through his barely cracked window.

That New York attitude had followed me home.

"Can you hand me one of those paper towels? I'm covered in sleet. Your behavior is deplorable for someone in the service industry," I said.

It felt better reprimanding him than admitting my own bad behavior. He repeatedly clicked the automatic door button to rattle me. I one-upped him by pulling out a notepad and pretending to write down his license plate, but he locked the car door, again.

"If you don't open up your door, you oversized goof, I will call your superiors."

I banged so fiercely on the windows that he finally acquiesced and unlocked the door. I slipped into the back seat and spit on him. I forgot about the Plexiglas partition, so technically, I spat on myself. The driver failed to notice any of it.

Once I came down off the adrenaline high of my outburst, I softened my inner voice just long enough to convince myself to open Frankie's letter.

Samantha, I knew from the moment I saw you in our first staff meeting that you were the one for me even though it defied all of the rules. Over the last several months, out of respect for you and my children, I have stayed away. I kept my distance. But after the moment we shared in New York, I can no longer do it. I cannot look back. I can only focus forward. I know that I asked for nothing from you, but now that is not so. I know you feel the same way. I know it is not appropriate, and it makes no sense at all, other than when something feels so right, there is no way it can be all wrong. I have done my part by proceeding with a divorce and leaving my family. By choosing a chance at living with the woman of my dreams. I have already given up all that I know, and all that I ask for in return is you. I am asking you to give me your heart. I promise to hold it gently, and forever, right next to mine.

Love, Frankie.

Shit!

I read and reread that letter trying to find the evil, trying to find the reasons to tear it up and go running to my boyfriend. I tried to block the kiss and note out of my mind. It was the most love-filled thing I had ever received, the only downer being the iffy marital status of its sender.

I spent the entire weekend in bed with the note lodged under my pillow, praying for God to strike me down or fill me with some sanity. I prayed for Him to give me the strength to bail myself out of my slutty situation and to grant me the courage to recognize right from wrong.

God did not answer my prayers, or maybe it was me who would not allow Him to help. The romantic side of my brain grappled with the idea that nothing else mattered because Frankie was the soul mate I had been waiting for. Two wounded, divorced souls, connecting despite the marital boundary between them. Each prepared to love so completely and unconditionally it would melt away everything else that stood in the way. Or at least that was the fairytale ending I prayed for.

Chapter Sixteen

Despite my loose lip action in New York, Ryan and I maintained our status quo in the relationship for a couple of weeks. This was easy enough given he had no idea what had gone down. The same could not be said for Frankie who pulled me into his office. He looked at me softly. I thought he might cry.

"Samantha," he said, trying to make eye contact with me. "Out of respect, I decided to leave you alone until my divorce became final, which it has. And, because you are the caliber of woman that you are, I know proof is necessary. Here are the final papers," he said as he pushed a sheaf of legal nonsense at me.

I never looked at him directly, not even once. My mother would have applauded my lack of eye contact. I prayed for him to adjust his pleats, break the moment, un-pout his lips—none of which he did—so I cut the tension by staring out at the dropping snow as I babbled.

I dry heaved. And just like my mother, I

muttered incomprehensibly, and ended with, "You know what I mean, don't you?"

"Well, not exactly," he said.

I glanced at the papers in relief. Now I could love Frankie, legitimately, and not go to hell.

"All righty then," I said, and ran out of his office. Despite my best intentions, I was not equipped to deal with him or his divorce papers.

***

Later that night, staring at my heart-shaped bathroom mirror, only one word could describe my look: sinful. I prayed that Candy would telepathically know I needed her help and come running, but she never did.

Looking eye to eye with myself in the reflection, I practiced telling Ryan that I had shared an illicit makeout moment with Frankie. In my mind, Ryan looked back at me with one of those *I expected better of you* looks. I had rehearsed the speech many times over the past couple days, but had yet to deliver it. There was no way I could break his heart in person so I dragged my body into the kitchen, picked up my retro rotary phone, and dialed. Not even the heart-filled wallpaper that surrounded me would make this any easier.

"Hey, sweetie, how are you? Exactly the girl I was hoping to hear from. Are we on for skiing this weekend?" Ryan said.

"Well, I don't know if that's a good idea."

"Why not?" he asked.

"I'm not quite sure how to say this." I burped to

buy myself more time.

"I don't think we should hang out for a while," I said as I scratched my nose until I felt warm drops of blood fall onto my lip.

I couldn't tell if the droplets came as a result of my gross habit or if it was God's not-so-gentle reminder of the perils of cheating. Christ suffered on the cross, so should I.

"That's okay, sweetie. I get burnt out on skiing too. We can just hang and watch movies or something," he said.

"I don't think you understand. I'm not sure this whole dating thing is good for us, since we work together and all. Maybe we'd be better off as friends."

Silence.

I disgusted myself. I scratched my nose even harder. It felt like his silent treatment was my penance for being such a pussy to break up with him over the phone and then lie about the reason.

"Okay," he said, and then hung up.

I willed him to call me back, to not let me go, to beg me to stay, to draw me into his life, and more than anything, I prayed for him to save me from myself. But he never did.

With one swift phone call, I had ended a perfectly good relationship for no valid reason. Except Frankie. Whatever, Ryan hadn't even bothered to fight for me.

Using Oprah's positive self-talk techniques, I pulled it together and peeled myself off the buckling tiles of my cold kitchen floor. I felt bad, but it didn't squelch my feelings for Frankie.

He understood me better than anyone I had ever met. The fact that he was married when our love began no longer mattered.

***

Frankie moved into the attic of a dumpy, barn-like house. In order to visit, I walked up three flights of rickety wooden steps that hugged the side of the house. Once inside the makeshift apartment, I had to crouch over so as not to hit my head on the beams of the barely vaulted ceiling. His kids would probably like the stunted roof given their pint size, but they had yet to visit what his ex-wife had dubbed the "apartment of sin."

Frankie and I cried as we hugged hello. It was strange since we'd mutually agreed via text, that neither of us had ever felt happier. Despite our dysfunctional beginnings, we had been granted an opportunity for true love. I reminded myself that such an occasion called for celebrating, not sobbing.

"I'm sorry to get your blouse wet Samantha. I'm just so happy to see you. Come here, my love. We just need a sexual release and everything will be all right."

"Yeah. That's what *Cosmo* always says. Passionate, loving intercourse makes everything better."

With Ryan, I had vowed to hold sex until marriage, but with Frankie, none of those Catholic trappings seemed relevant. He swept me into his arms and kissed away my tears as he used my silk sleeve to wipe away his. I tried hard not to care. In one smooth motion, he pushed me over to his tattered couch and pulled off my clothes with purpose.

I fumbled with his zipper until he came to my rescue by undressing himself for me. My nerves had gotten the better of my seduction strategy.

Frankie's penis bobbed before me. I looked at it lovingly but I, unlike it, remained frozen like a statue. When he stopped jiggling the thing, it reminded me of Michelangelo's *David.* Frankie's apparatus looked equally if not more endowed.

Our moment of penetration came quick, as did I. For the remainder of the night, he held me tightly. I cried silent drops of joy until the sun rose the next morning. With the light of day, I felt as if I might have made the biggest mistake of my life.

Then I denied it.

Chapter Seventeen

For the next few weeks, Frankie and I were stricken with alternating bouts of hot sex, guilt, happiness, and sadness. I felt guilty for being a home-wrecker, and Frankie was melancholy because his children were in turmoil over the breakup of their family.

Despite these distractions, in our love bubble it seemed as if we could spend the rest of our lives together. I ruminated over the idea of becoming a second mother to his children, and it made me full inside.

His wife was not nearly as taken by the idea.

On a particularly dreary, rain-soaked Monday morning, I was summoned to a meeting with Ryan and Frankie. When the session adjourned, I tried to go over and say hello to Ryan. He never uttered a single word, just radiated disgust.

It struck me after he walked away that I might have killed the one healthy and pure romance of my adult life for a married man with three children who happened to be my boss. *Let's do the math. Bad,*

bad, and bad!

Ryan never bothered to call me out directly on the affair with Frankie, but I suspected he knew. There was no mistaking Frankie and his glistening, lovelorn eyes—eyes that he seemed incapable of controlling at work, especially in meetings. I often wondered if they were glassy because he was so fond of me, or if they got that way from all the crying we did.

Candy, over the duration of our friendship, had developed the perception of an FBI agent. She cornered me right after the meeting and forced me to agree to dinner with her as soon as we finished work. One too many hours later, we met in the semicircular loading area outside of our office compound. She mandated that I sit in her pearly blue Mustang convertible and shut up for the entire ten-minute trip to The Loop. I complied because she'd been sporting a *don't mess with me* look all day.

The funky little Mexican joint appeared to be hunkered down into the cracks of the mountain, and fittingly, its décor looked equally craggy. Without waiting for the hostess to seat us, Candy led us to our regular table and motioned for me to sit down. She ordered us the usual.

We sat in uncomfortable silence for five minutes before our food arrived. I assumed I was allowed to open my mouth wide enough to feed myself.

Without waiting for permission, I bit into a fish taco. It was a savory little sucker. The lime juice stung as it squirted me in the eye.

"Are you having an affair?" she blurted out.

"Am I allowed to talk yet?" I asked.

"Oh my God! You *are* having an affair! I wasn't sure but hoped you wouldn't be that stupid. Holy shit, please tell me it's not with Frankie?"

I tried to speak, but started crying instead.

"Christ. At least tell me the sex was worth it," she said as she poked at her shrimp quesadilla.

"It's the best I've ever had. Sort of like this taco."

I stopped eating and looked at a has-been piñata hanging from the ceiling, along with some random nappy if not colorful bras.

"Well good for you, I guess," she said as she switched *her* gaze to the bras.

I wondered which one of them was hers. She claimed to have ditched her brassiere here last week during a date night with her husband. Maybe that kind of racy behavior was why they were still together. That, and her gigantic melons.

She focused back on me with a look of disgust. She always told me that frivolous sex was healthy, yet now that I'd done it, she was judging me over a paper-mâché pig pepper shaker. I opened my mouth to interject, but she shushed me and flagged down the waiter.

"We need a pitcher of pineapple margaritas with two straws."

We sat in silence until the pitcher arrived. Then she gestured for me to slurp down a hefty dose of the fluorescent drink. After my first suck and the brain freeze that followed, she continued with her interrogation.

"Oh, my God! Are you in love with him?"

I started to answer, but she shut me up again.

"What could you possibly be thinking? You're not supposed to fall in love with your boss. Who is married with three children. With all those estrogen-fueled mag rags you read, you'd think you would've learned that by now."

People started to stare as she yelled at me as if I were a tween.

"Well, I didn't mean to…it just happened. And don't mock my magazines. They provide a great source of solace."

I waited for her to laugh but her face remained stony, so I continued to slurp away the silence.

"If you could've seen this letter he wrote me," I said, "you would understand. It's kismet."

I grinded my nose and sucked on the striped straw with equal abandon. The more I sipped, the heavier my head felt.

"Oh shit, is this why you broke up with Ryan? You've really lost it. Frankie isn't even divorced yet."

I chugged the remains of the pint-sized pitcher.

"No, he's divorced, I saw the papers. I would've never had relations with him otherwise. How stupid do you think I am?"

I scratched at my boobs in an attempt to distract her from answering.

"How can you be so intelligent at work, yet so clueless about love? He's not divorced. He was droning on about it this afternoon. He served Sherry the papers multiple times but she hasn't signed them yet. Apparently, she's refusing to go through with it. What papers were you looking at?"

My stomach gurgled. I tried to tell her that I had only glanced at the contract long enough to see the word divorce, but nausea prevented me from speaking. *Redbook* never mentioned that signature verification was required in these types of situations.

The margarita threatened to repeat itself.

I sat in a taco-tequila haze. This could not be happening. I was in no way meant to be dating and falling in love with a married man. This was not what I signed up for. I fought to hold back the urge to hurl.

"Shut up. Just because your boobies are bigger than mine doesn't mean you can treat me this way," I shouted as I pounded the table with the pitcher.

I got up, ran to her side of the table, and flaunted my flat chest in front of her face.

"These are worthy. And so am I."

The people at the table next to us hid behind their menus. Christ. My tirade reminded me of past Serrano family dinner nights, most of which ended with my father reaming somebody out for no reason. My tantrum knocked down one of the dangling bras from its perch above our table. Or maybe Candy flicking her fork to settle me down had something to do with it. Whatever the cause, a dirty, dusty D cup landed on my head and ended the outburst.

"Sam, you need to face facts. He's married, and he's likely going to stay that way. Get out of this train wreck of a relationship as soon as possible, before you cause any more damage."

I hated her. Where was she when I needed

someone to talk me out of dumping Ryan and sleeping with Frankie?

"This is the real deal. You don't understand," I whined, struggling to disentangle myself from the monstrous cups. "He even made these romantic plans for Valentine's Day. He orchestrated a big night out to cement our relationship for the world to see."

No sooner had I freed my face from the grody tit sling than Candy bolted up from her seat, grabbed me by the neck, and pulled me into her more than ample, hundred percent natural C-cup bosoms.

She defied my family's typical reaction by giving me what I needed most: a boob to cry on. I loved her again.

"Pay attention," she commanded as I burrowed my cheek deeper in her comforting cleavage. "Tomorrow night, you're going to put on a fabulous dress, blow out your hair, and go enjoy a fantastic evening. You can deal with the rest of it later. Use a condom."

I un-nestled my face from her tit.

"So you think everything is going to be okay?" I asked.

"It has to be."

Chapter Eighteen

Ginormous heart-shaped pellets of hail flew out of the sky, but even the weather could not bring me down. Instead, I took it as a sign: God was sprinkling a little bit of heaven down on me and my soul mate for Valentine's Day.

Despite my cheery disposition, by the time the precipitation stopped, I was crunched up on the couch barfing my guts out. It must have been the month-old Pop-Tarts and sour milk I had for breakfast.

For a moment, I thought about canceling on Frankie, but my inner martyr prevailed. I blamed the Church since I had started attending again right after I broke up with Ryan.

I tested my stomach's strength by going to pick up the mail, and was pleased that I did so without vomiting. Yet that small victory was short-lived since I noticed my mother had sent me a new clipping, ***God Will Love You Even if No One Else Can.***

Enough dallying. I had to get ready for my hot

date. I leaned up on my elbows, recited one Hail Mary, and flopped off the couch. Once I powered through the sick feeling in my tummy and endured a few minutes of disorienting ceiling spins, I pulled myself off the shabby pink shag rug and waddled to the bathroom to get ready. The sight of my dirty bathroom steeped in hairballs almost made me hurl again. My tendencies toward keeping a clean home had moved to the wayside, right along with my relationship with Ryan. So what if I was sloppy now? Frankie still loved me. I fell into the tub and soaked away my sickness with the hope that some of my sins would wash away too.

I made it in to the restaurant, but despite my best efforts, still felt and looked like hell, which was fitting given my sinning of late would likely send me straight there. Frankie employed all the right moves you'd expect from a cheating husband.

"You look beautiful, honey. I can't wait to get you into the hotel room. Have I told you lately that I love you?" he sang, literally, a tad embarrassing.

Frankie knew exactly how to cut through my inner pain, guilt, and insecurity. The hours of our special night at an obscure and hidden wine bistro flew by as smoothly as the jazz trio whirred in the background. The tunes lulled me and my stomach to a state of peace. Everything in the world stopped rumbling, including my guilt-ridden imagination— aside from the odd pang between cheese courses. With each bite, I melted more deeply into the music and our love zone.

So what if we had to drive all the way to Denver to eat without being spotted by anyone who knew us? He assured me it had nothing to do with hiding out and everything to do with the restaurant's intoxicating pasta dishes.

His rose-colored shirt blended in with the dramatic décor and made it look like he was naked, except for the ruby velvet drape behind him that ensconced his body. I was enamored with someone who loved me back with abandon. There was no way God could think this was sinful.

Frankie, the perfect gentleman, propped me upright at all the right moments to prevent my nausea from returning. He enveloped me with his eye-sparkling stare throughout the duration of the meal, which I tried hard not to regurgitate. Was he worried for my health, or mesmerized by my beauty?

Sweat slid down my cheeks and nose. Frankie soaked up my perspiration with a heart-shaped cocktail napkin as he whispered in my ear.

"Samantha Serrano, I love you more than my own life." He repeated this to the point of nausea. It was hard to tell if it was because of the heady conversation or my upset stomach. I turned freakishly red; half because overt declarations of love embarrassed me, and half because I felt I might hurl at any moment.

As we made our way back to the hotel, Frankie continued to murmur sweet nothings at me. Despite my feelings of uncertainty and illness, I had never felt happier.

We navigated the tight hallways of our hotel and made it to our room just in time for Frankie to rip our clothes off. As we stepped inside, he tore off my lacy briefs and stuffed his erect penis inside me. We had dirty sex right up against the hotel door as it and my legs remained partially open. Normally, this would have embarrassed me, but not tonight. We did it again a mere seven minutes later on the dingy mustard carpet—fulfilling and dizzying, yet disgusting all at once.

I couldn't be certain if we did it anymore, since I passed out for the remainder of our special night. In the morning, I realized that Frankie had carried me off of the smelly floor and onto a butter-soft down comforter—the consummate gentleman.

I lounged in bed like a queen bee until I realized that instead of spooning Frankie, I was wrapped around an oblong, suede throw pillow. He must have slipped out of bed to get us breakfast, instinctively knowing that our lovemaking in the night sucked away my sickness and replaced it with cravings for complex carbohydrates.

Stark winter sunlight beamed through the picturesque bay window, reminding me of our passionate night. Frankie broke up my daydream when he entered and hovered over me anxiously like a hound dog, signaling it was time to leave. Not necessarily the wake-up call I'd hoped for after fornicating all over the place last night.

I prayed that his urgent need to vacate the hotel room had something to do with hunting down his wife to finalize the divorce papers. He thrust my overnight bag into my hand with the same force he had pushed his penis into me. In the light of day, it did not feel nearly as romantic.

He hurried me through the packing process, and

without a drop of coffee or a single good morning kiss, we checked out and were on our way. We barely spoke and didn't even hold hands. He dropped me off at home and could not have sped out of my driveway fast enough.

The rest of the day passed into night without a single call from Frankie. I fantasized about him breaking into my kitchen window, ripping off my Strawberry Shortcake underwear, and mounting me on my new butcher-block countertop. I convinced myself it didn't matter that he never came over, because my va-ja-jay needed to recoup from all the action it had on Valentine's Day.

* * *

I awoke the next day thankful that my weekend bout of nausea had disappeared almost as quickly as Frankie had the day before. I was exhausted though. Dirty sex could do that to a girl. My early a.m. shower did little to jumpstart my day. But the voicemail that arrived while I bathed woke me right up.

"Samantha, I'm on my way over with a proposal that needs an overhaul. You'll need to work on it from home for the next couple of weeks. And by the way, Sherry and I are back together."

I replayed it over and over until I vomited all over the bathroom floor. I thought about cleaning it up but couldn't.

To think the last personal words Frankie uttered to me were, *Do me, do me, baby, I am so rock-hard looking at you. If you don't do me now, I will*

140

explode my love all over this hotel room.

Not so charming when he arrived at my doorstep ringing the bell from hell, sopping wet with soggy papers in hand. He walked inside and thrust the mess at me.

"I've marked up the document with all the changes that need to be made. Basically, rework the entire thing. I expect better from you." He started for the door without as much as a look in my direction. I repositioned myself in front of it.

He'd busted into my home before my coffee even had the chance to percolate—bad form in the eyes of *Good Housekeeping,* as was his notable lack of eye contact. My mother would have loved him. Aside from his marital status.

I waited for a proper greeting as he spat out random contract points.

Not a peep about our torrid weekend. Not even a simple g*ood morning.* He just fumbled and grinded on his pant pleats with a vengeance I'd never seen before, while pacing around my home in a silent stupor. He wrestled with the pleats with the anger of a jilted Real Housewife of Orange County.

"Frankie, look at me. Don't you have anything else to say beyond the comments on this ridiculous proposal?"

He looked away. Then *I* started pacing, followed by a vigorous eyebrow rub with one hand as I collected outdated women's magazines off the floor with the other. I paused and waited for him to answer me.

"Why in God's name did you pursue me if you never had any intention of divorcing your wife?

Candy told me she never even signed the papers. WTF?"

He clicked away on his dumbass Droid, not bothering to look up.

"I was doing perfectly fine on my own—in fact, I was doing better than fine, I was fantabulous—and now I'm just fucked!"

I scraped my nose with one of the pink heart-painted fingernails I'd manicured for Valentine's Day. The sight of them sickened me, or maybe it was Frankie.

Like a skilled surgeon with absolutely no bedside manner, Frankie stared at me blankly and did a two-sided pleated pant-pick—as if his dick was so large that it required a double shake. I'd seen the package and it definitely wasn't *that* big. *Did you ever stop and think maybe you shouldn't know what a married man's package looks like in the first place?*

"I'm sorry you feel this way, Samantha. I know you had certain expectations, and I did not live up to them. It's time for you to accept that I am no longer available to you. The sooner you're able to move on with your life, the better off you'll be."

Thank you, Dr. Kevorkian, just rip my heart out and sell it on the black market.

"For the love of God, would you stop grabbing at your pants?" I shrieked. "It's gross. Do you have crabs or something? Oh Christ, you probably do. That would be some kind of Valentine's gift. But with the way you're acting, maybe all of the dirty sex we had on the stinky hotel floor was a dream."

My rants fell on deaf ears. The good doctor

clinically handed over the remains of the paperwork and walked out my front door. The rain fell in epic, global warming, proportions. I prayed that the combo of the huge drops and pig manure I had used to fertilize my lawn would cause Frankie and his dorky pants to slip. No such luck.

I opened the door and screamed at his receding form as I stripped off my clothes, desperate to get his attention.

"Don't you miss me? Don't you miss my body, and my heart, and my flat boobs?"

He stood in the pouring rain, his face registering only pity. A silent rage stirred inside me; my body quivered. I spotted the Valentine's card and box of chocolates he had presented me just hours before. Running around my lawn—stark raving mad and scantily clad—I hurled chocolates at him one at a time, finally gaining a small sense of satisfaction by knocking him in the eye with a dark chocolate sea salt caramel. Unable to stop myself, I flung the hideous heart-shaped box at him.

"You dirty, cheating, pleated pants, sweater-vest-wearing bastard!"

Because the candy box was such an obnoxiously oversized monstrosity, it split open the skin just above his eye. *Success!* I chanted under my breath.

As I stood on my landing step naked with tears streaming, Frankie stood across from me, chocolate splattered all over his face as blood oozed from his left eyebrow.

It was hard to know who I hated more: him or me, but it was no longer relevant. I was done.

***

In the months that followed, right in line with the demise of my fleeting affair with Frankie, our company tanked too.

We did not go public as planned. Nate made the ill-fated decision, during a no-sleep bender, to delay our initial public offering for what was to be one week, but morphed suddenly into never.

In the world of social media, much like in the land of love, one day could change everything. In NetSocial's case, the delay was just long enough for our competitor to pull a Slick Willy and beat us to the IPO punch. Our rival went public and poached most of our staff. Soon enough the rest of us were downsized right out of a job. The day Nate walked into the office eating yogurt instead of munching on Cheetos, wearing a suit instead of his typical uniform of jeans and a backward-turned baseball cap, he didn't need to say a word. His put-together look and abrupt switch to health food said it all.

The wave of destruction flashed before me. I had succeeded in messing up every aspect of my life. Maybe it was time to get out of town and on with my life...or maybe just die in the process of trying.

Chapter Nineteen

It's been said, that Catholic people at times—okay, always—engage in masochistic behaviors of the non-sexual variety. This, however, was not one of those times. Moving back in with my parents was temporary. My lack of a job dictated it. At college graduation, I had vowed to never become a needy sponger, yet here I was, on the verge.

I drove into the neighborhood of my childhood. It looked exactly as I left it so many years ago, aside from the maple trees, which had continued to sprout long after I stopped. To the outside world, our street and home might appear innocent and unassuming. It was anything but.

The peewee U-haul that carried the remains of my so-called married and then divorced life dragged behind my car, an ugly reminder of my sinful past. It was a wonder the thing could make it out of Colorado with the physical and mental load it carried. Perhaps that was why it broke down twice before getting out of the state. Or maybe U-haul just sucked.

I looped around the block twice before turning the truck into my parents' driveway, where I felt tempted to run over my father when I spotted him. He had lawn-mowed his way through my teenage years, yet the yard still always looked unkempt. Mowing under the influence could do that to a lawn—and a person. Amid the yo-yo levels of grass were signs of a lighter hand, like the geraniums that formed a perimeter around the house—my mother's touch.

"You still can't drive," my father bellowed from the side of the driveway. "Don't step under our roof unless you're prepared to go to church often. Every god damn day."

I rolled up the window and peeled down the rest of the long, potholed driveway. I almost flipped him the bird and u-turned right out of there, but knowing my limited options, I parked and walked into their home. In my mind, I held my head up high. In reality, I sulked into the musty foyer.

The outside of the house showed such promise with its A-frame structure and natural wood finish, but the inside carried an air of staleness along with the slight stink of booze. We used to be a happy young family before all the drinking—or at least I thought we were. There were happy times like when my dad took us to Kings Dominion and rode the roller coasters with us incessantly. No matter how many times we asked, he obliged.

"Sweetheart, get the hell up here. There is a bagel waiting for you," my mother said.

Her version of hello. This woman served bagels regardless of what time of day it was. Afternoon felt too late for breakfast carbs in my cookbook, but it was one of her kinder gestures. Martha Stewart, however, would call my mother's homecoming menu a flop.

I climbed up the stairs and entered my parents' seventies-style wood-paneled kitchen to enjoy my burnt bagel in peace. After fifty-five years, my mother still hadn't mastered the art of toasting. The paneling indicated she hadn't learned to decorate yet either. The taste of charred bread conjured images of what it might be like to burn in hell for your sins—not the least bit savory. Reconnecting with my faith, after a landslide of indiscretions, might not be a bad idea.

My mother tumbled into the room, interrupting my redemption fantasy. I couldn't be certain if she was drunk already or just clumsy.

"Samantha, here's a copy of the *Pennysaver*. I highlighted some jobs for you to consider. As long as you're living under our roof, your father wants to make it clear that you will be responsible for paying for your keep."

"Of course, Mommy."

"It's insulting we even had to ask. You should have offered. We will not support you until you get a church annulment. Then you'll be allowed to stay here with free food and board, but until then, you can drop your daily fees here."

Oprah always said it was good to set boundaries.

"Seriously, Mom, a coffee can? Is this really necessary?"

Her look indicated that it was. "I promise, as soon as I get my first unemployment check, I'll pay you."

She glared, picked up the rock hard remnants of my bagel, and pushed the can in front of me. For this food and treatment, I had to pay?

"We're leaving for church in ten minutes. You might consider changing. I left out your prairie skirt and ruffled blouse. I'm not sure why you left it here when you moved out."

"Sure, Mommy, I'll get changed."

My father shuffled around outside, still in his ratty bathrobe and slippers, presumably drunk before sunset as always. His getup didn't seem like an appropriate church frock or physical state, yet my mother failed to notice. It always annoyed me that even though my father professed to be an upstanding Catholic, he never managed to actually make it to church himself.

I changed into my outdated ensemble and bumped into my father by the stinky downstairs bathroom. That man pooped more than any person I knew. Buckets of beer did that to a man. He toted a burnt bagel in one hand and his loyal pooch, Penelope, in the other. A mangy pair. Maybe he slipped her booze regularly, which would explain why she always looked so homely. Or perhaps living under "his roof" caused even a dog to deteriorate. I tried to remember the positive affirmation technique that *Self* magazine had taught me. *I love my father. He loves me. We are a loving family.*

After five minutes of attempting this mental meditation, I gave up and asked him about his presence at church while he was eating so he couldn't easily respond.

"Just because you never see me inside doesn't mean I'm not always there," he said, exposing the half-chewed bit he gnawed on with aplomb. "And mind your own business."

He pushed me upstairs and dropped his plate in my hand, signaling his work with me was done. Then he burped. That was the real sin. His breath smelled rank.

As I walked his dish to the kitchen, I could feel my food threatening to repeat itself. The last time I'd gone to their church was at my wedding. Maybe if I had attended services more frequently, I wouldn't have ended up back home.

"Dear, why don't you wait for me in the car? You've upset your father again."

Sitting behind the wheel in the same Ford Fairmont station wagon that my father had taught me to drive in, I felt like I was sixteen all over again. Maybe it had something to do with the fact that I sported the same outfit my mother made me wear to my teenage confirmation ceremony. She was more nostalgic than I gave her credit for—or maybe it was a passive-aggressive form of torture.

She eventually appeared, donning her signature look that consisted of a red floral top and black slacks that weren't quite capris and not long enough to be full-length pants. She completed her fashion statement with a knock-off Gucci purse and scuffed penny loafers.

Mom gestured for me to scoot over into the passenger seat so she could drive. Then she told me to pray for forgiveness on our way to church, and said that she would do the same. For me. I placated her by bowing my head and murmuring gibberish for the entire length of the trip. Thankfully, it was a short one.

When we arrived, she ushered me out of the car with an imaginary broomstick and pointed me down the path to her view of salvation. Despite the fact that it felt arctic outside, I sweated just like I had right before I bumbled down the aisle with Sheldon.

I used a stress management breathing technique from *Yoga* magazine to stop the flood of tears from busting through my dam of self-control. The tears broke through anyway. Just as I suspected, yoga was pointless.

"What? Stop staring at me," I said.

"Now you listen to me. You will show me respect in the parking lot of the Lord or I swear to God I'll bop you straight on the head," she said. "No need to cry yet. We're not actually going to church. I made an appointment with Father Sigfried to discuss your annulment."

I should have known it was a strange hour to go to church. And by the way, who in the hell would keep the name Sigfried once they entered the monastery? It sounded like a bad joke. Nobody wanted to put their religious fate in the hands of a man who looked like George Costanza and was named after a lion tamer.

"I'm not ready for that," I said. "I'm not even sure I want one. The whole thing doesn't make sense. I can't in good conscience denounce a marriage that four hundred people witnessed."

"You have a lot of nerve bringing up good

conscience. You lost yours when you got divorced," she ranted as her arms flailed like a freefalling bird.

"Well, it's stupid. But if it'll make you feel better, we can go in and listen. I'm just telling you I'm not going through with anything," I said.

Father Sigfried appeared before my mother had a chance to spew an expletive at me.

"We're so ecstatic to be here, aren't we, Samantha?" she said to Mr. Holy.

"Well, actually Father…"

She interrupted me by shooting a look that felt as if it came straight from Satan's eyes.

Father Sigfried took this as his cue to lead us inside the rectory—into the same room where Sheldon and I did our Pre-Canna course study. It was just like the Catholics to set up a training course for marriage. I must not have been listening hard enough during the *Thou shalt not commit adultery* section.

I did pay attention to some of the stupider stuff like sex for procreation being the only reason for intercourse. And that the only acceptable form of birth control was abstinence. And the rhythm method, my favorite. The classes might have been more effective if the instructor was a relationship expert, instead of a priest who hadn't had sex, possibly for decades. Listening to Sigfried talk about how the "woman" in the relationship is supposed to monitor her menstrual cycle to ensure that no "relations" happened during "non-childbearing" days was beyond uncomfortable.

Revisiting the scene of our marriage boot camp course reminded me of a point of promise in my life—or at least it felt like it at the time. Until Sheldon almost popped one of his temple veins when Sigfried explained that by choosing to marry a Catholic, he was bound by church law to raise his kids Catholic—I had conveniently failed to mention to him I had already agreed to that as a tactic to get my parents to attend our nuptials.

"You can't force us to raise our children that way if we don't want to," he had said.

Ah, the good old days. *You mean the days when you laid the foundation for ruining your life by marrying outside of your religion?*

"So, does that sound good, Samantha?" Father Sigfried said, ending the onslaught of memories.

"What? Sorry, Father, when I've got a migraine my head throbs and it's hard for me to concentrate. And my mind wanders. What was that last bit?"

"That's not all that wanders with her, Father, which points to the larger problem at hand," my mother said.

"As I mentioned, an annulment is a simple agreement that states the marriage never happened," Sigfried said.

He appeared to be such a sane man—aside from the part where he suggested that I denounce a marriage that he officiated.

Unable to listen to the drivel any longer, I ran out of the rectory, blaming my headache. My mother eventually followed while apologizing over her shoulder. I enjoyed the uncomfortable silence during the ride home. She drove two miles over the speed limit for the entire trip, a sure sign that she was miffed at me. Aside from binge drinking, she never broke the rules—until today, when she gunned it through our neighborhood and down the driveway. To annoy me, she repeatedly stopped short on the brakes, her passive-aggressive way of f'ing with me.

She parked the car on the lawn and waited. Then she got out and walked into the house swearing to the sky, or was it God? I straggled behind hoping the icy temps would freeze me out of my misery. By the time I reached the front door, my father and Penelope were waiting to greet us with boozy breath and wet paws.

My mother reappeared in the doorway and stuffed her fake Gucci between me and the door in an attempt to block me from entering.

"Samantha, I would like you to explain to your father why you refused to get an annulment," she said.

How could I put this into terms these drunkards could understand?

"Well, Daddy, it's just, you can't wave a wand over something and pretend it didn't happen when people witnessed it. I also don't think, as a non-Catholic, Sheldon would appreciate the whole annulment process."

My bout with candor drove my father inside and into his rendition of exercise—pacing around our living room. And not your mainstream pace. He preferred a bob and weave style, reminiscent of Rocky Balboa in my father's favorite flick, *Rocky*. Unlike the Italian Stallion, my pop's moves were more about beer buzz than boxing. It amazed me how much he staggered after only his first few

Miller Lites. This man had put down at least 10 a day for as long as I could remember. You would think he might have built up a tolerance.

"Well, that's his own damn problem. Nothing you've told me has done anything to explain why you won't correct your mistake. How can anybody possibly be this stupid? Let me correct myself, choose to be this stupid," he said.

Then he dragged poor Penelope up on his lap. He petted her as if she were a sateen treasure. The fact that she was a matted mangy terrier did not seem to bother him. She was the only thing I had ever seen him cherish besides his corduroy OP shorts—birthed back in the Reagan era.

Like the dad I knew and often disliked, he was completely unaware that spit flew in my face as he ranted—the consummate sloppy speaker. He headed toward the kitchen, likely to get Penelope a treat. It wasn't long before his boozy state caused him to stumble to the ground. He just missed squishing her. She seemed unfazed, always the loyal soldier. I wished her no harm.

"See what you do to me?" he said as he pulled himself upright and waved my mother and me toward the kitchen.

Mom tried to divert attention away from my father by clacking around stuffing pots into the pantry. I used the disruption as a means of escape to the den. Sitting on the worn denim couch, I swatted at dust mites and prayed the jolt from my dad's tumble would prevent the next tirade.

My dad had turned into his father, who used to bark and growl every time we opened the fridge, but instead of being worried we were snagging one too many Ding Dongs, I suspected my father was more worried about his booze stash.

Pops defied the odds by maintaining a silent stare, refusing to blink. Until he made me cry.

"Oh, Christ, what now?" he said. "Do you see this, Susan? Our full-grown baby is crying. What kind of game do you think you're playing, anyway? Are we supposed to believe that you actually feel bad about this whole ordeal? Please, give us some credit."

He fixed his combover that had un-overed itself when he fell. He steadied himself enough to walk back into the kitchen to crack open another beer as though nothing had happened. Happy hour started early at the Serrano pad. On his way back into the den, just to torment me, Dad burped loudly. Then he stopped short, lingering in my personal space and staring at me as if he expected some sort of explanation for the waterworks.

I said nothing. I tried to stop crying but failed.

"Why do you refuse to make this god damn divorce deal right with the church?" he said.

I tried to channel my mother by not making eye contact. Always one to outdo me, he continued to drink and not speak to me for the next fifteen minutes. Then he loosened the belt that held up his ratty OP shorts. This, his signature move, indicated a lecture would soon follow.

"You're a misfit of a daughter, you'll never be anything more. The state of your life makes me want to curse."

As if he needed a reason.

I tried to come up with something to make him stop. I contemplated socking the arm of his tattered plaid La-Z-Boy, just to rattle him, but couldn't bring myself to do it.

"She's a lost cause, dear, just forget about her and get over here…my feet ache and need some attention," my mother said.

"Oh, Jesus Christ, rub your own damn toes, Susan. They stink," he said. Then he turned back to me. "We've wasted a lifetime on you. Either go to church tomorrow and get the annulment, or start packing your bags. I swear I will lock the god damn doors for good this time."

Spoken like a true Catholic.

He wrinkled up his reddish-purple face, which made it look like he might erupt at any moment. I couldn't tell if his freakish tone was because of all the booze or that he was dangerously close to having a heart attack. I felt like I should say something, run away, or better yet, confront him. Instead, just like a battered wife, I sat there and took it.

Three hours and hundreds of barbs later, somebody had to stop the verbal abuse.

"Daddy, I'm going to bed."

In my mind, I spat in his face before I walked downstairs, but in reality, I crept into my childhood bedroom and crawled under the pink Strawberry Shortcake canopy of my old bed and tried to dismiss all of the hateful things my father had spewed at me. It was probably just the booze talking, but still.

After a few minutes of contemplation, as the

ever-sweet Ms. Shortcake stared down on me with her goodness, I packed a small duffle bag with a few must-have essentials and peeked out of my room to confirm the exit route was clear.

I panned my room one last time as a tapestry of memories, none of which were pleasant, came into focus. I grabbed my bag and snuck out the back door. In the pitch black of night, I crept along the long driveway of shame, and then hoofed it down the street with the speed of an Olympic racer, running on foot from everything and everyone.

I wasn't sure where I was running to, but I was quite clear on what I was running from.

Chapter Twenty

I chose the Peter Pan bus as my transport out of hell and into what I hoped would be anything but. When I stepped into the chariot, though, I had a moment of buyer's remorse about the decision. I've never understood why buses felt seedy, but they did. It seemed as if everybody onboard was hiding out or running away from something or someone, so I'd probably fit right in.

The rainstorm that followed me from Maryland to New York felt fitting—and since my stint back home brought me back to an almost infantile state, so did wearing the red floral romper I had stitched during my days with the 4-H Club. It was one of the few outfits I could find in my haste to get out from under my father's roof. At least this abrupt departure didn't involve a marriage. I prayed that New York would be everything that Frank Sinatra belted it could be. So what if he was my father's favorite crooner.

To forget my monsoon-like experience at home, I got chummy with my seatmate, Jan, who knew a friend who had another friend who needed to sublet an apartment. She made it sound fab. Then her sister, Janey, sitting across the aisle, thrust her phone in my face to show me pictures of the building, which looked nice enough. I had nowhere else to go, so I agreed to rent it for the month. Anything would be better than living with my parents.

I spent the rest of the ride fixated on the dismal weather. The rain turned to hail, reminding me that nothing stays the same, except for my parents. And my inability to cut them out of my life. I still hadn't figured out why I had continued to allow them to reign over me.

Those days would soon be over. By the time we crossed into New York City, I had reached some conclusions. First, sitting by the bathroom on a five-hour bus ride was not an ideal position for someone prone to barfing. Second, I had no life plan. But at least I had a place to live. Hopefully, it wasn't a hole.

The bus pulled into Penn Station and I felt as if I were on another planet. The chaotic pace refreshed me—an opportunity to be amid everyone else's mayhem instead of my own. I used my lone leopard duffle bag to flag down a friendly cabbie who charged forty dollars to get to the Lower Eastside. He should have paid me to ride in his taxi because his body odor smelled like nothing I had ever sniffed before. He overcharged me, but it was worth it since I realized, stepping out of the cab, that I was finally free.

Some of the excitement wore off when I peered

inside my new dwelling. The tiny abode elevated the meaning of the words "studio apartment" to new or lower levels, depending on how you looked at things. I wasn't totally convinced that it was legal to call a closet-free three-hundred-square-foot room an apartment, but it would have to do for the short-term. *New York* magazine was right: Two thousand dollars didn't buy much in this town. I needed a job and fast.

At least the pad had a bathroom, which counted for something; I'd heard some places charged extra for such perks. On the downside, only a stick-thin person could fit inside of it, because when you opened the door more than six inches, it hit the sink. Did I miss the *Good Housekeeping* issue that said pint-sized potty rooms were the new pink?

Sitting in my windowless one-room apartment, a mantra materialized in my mind: *new* city, *new* rules. I had gotten way too serious in the relationship department—with disastrous results. I would take Candy's advice and have meaningless sex with younger men who I would ditch before they had a chance to break up with me. Light and loose, that was how I would roll.

Janey texted me later that night. I had only talked to her briefly on the bus when she and her sister were doing the hard sell on the apartment. She went as far as promising me friendship if I took the place. I needed a gal pal in the city almost more than I needed a place to live, so I agreed.

When I didn't respond to her text immediately, she rang.

"Sam, where are you?"

"I'm at the apartment trying to make it feel like a home. I bought some flowers at the bodega downstairs. I'm painting myself happy!"

"Oh dear God. What are you still doing there? Nobody ever stays home in Manhattan. The annual fireman's bash under the Brooklyn Bridge is tomorrow night. You're going with me. Jan warned me about you and your family problems, but no worries. Nobody is more bitter than me. Alcohol and men make everything better."

Surveying my one-room pad, I understood why nobody stayed in. I guess scantily clad firemen wouldn't be a bad way to get to know the city.

"That sounds like fun. What should I wear?"

"Something tasteful, short, and skimpy," she said.

I wasn't sure how one didn't contradict the other, but whatever, I'd pull something together. The more I talked to her, the more I liked Janey. She sounded like the consummate city girl—bawdy and boy crazy. Nothing at all like Candy, who I was desperately missing. But maybe if I was lucky Janey could be a stand in.

I flopped onto the air mattress that I'd scored at the CVS down the block and disappeared into the buzz of the city with taxicabs and street talk busting through the paper-thin walls. The raucous undertones lulled me to sleep, much like my parents' bickering always had.

I didn't wake up until two p.m. the next day. I guess the weight of my trip—or maybe the last year of my life—had taken more out of me than I thought. I pulled on my old fuzzy pink tracksuit so I could roam the building and introduce myself to some of my neighbors.

That took all of five minutes. Not a welcoming bunch. Not a single one of the eight doors I knocked on opened. I did hear an obscene word or two. The mildewed ceilings and brown, faded wallpaper matched the lackluster welcome. But at least the hallway had windows so I could see that a sun-filled day awaited.

I spent the rest of the afternoon running around my neighborhood getting familiar with the surroundings—which, beyond the bodega, included a pizza shop across the street and a bagel store two streets away—eats on the cheap. My kind of town. The East Village seemed to be on the cusp of another re-gentrification process, much like the makeover I had in mind for my own life.

I started with a new outfit I found at a thrift store around the block: sensible leopard pumps, a stretchy robin-egg blue mini-tee, and denim capris. Perfect for an outdoor party. I got back home just in time to change and zoom down to the subway to meet Janey at the Brooklyn Bridge stop.

The rain that followed me to New York had retreated and revealed a scorching spring evening. Despite all the sewage that supposedly ran rampant in Manhattan, I smelled lilacs and gyro meat.

The subway was good for a quick ride, and apparently so were city boys, per Janey. As I stepped off the train, I saw her, arms waving almost as high as her skirt crawled up her thighs. She looked slightly more trampy than she did on the bus. When did tube tops and micro minis with

162

spiked heels come back in fashion? Maybe they never went out, given the catcalls that followed us off the subway and out onto the streets.

"Most of the guys at this party will be firemen, need I say more?" she snorted as she plumped her oversized boobs. I couldn't be certain if they were real or not, but in either case, they threatened to topple her.

"Cool," I said.

"I look forward to this party like every year because it's like a surefire way to get laid. The men are hot and wasted. What could be better?"

"Wow, how nice," I said, thinking I had escaped such boozy behavior when I left my parents.

"I never wear underwear to this thing. I hope you didn't either. It makes for easy access," she said.

I think boy crazy for Janey meant crazy slut on heels. No judgment. *You are the company you keep.* This was uncharted territory. I didn't know about most New Yorkers, but I kept my underwear on in public places. Anything less could be construed as classless, not to mention a bacterial nightmare. Sitting commando on a subway seat that God knows what or who went down on? Gross.

We walked for fifteen minutes through a maze of cobbled streets and tenement buildings to the edge of the waterline, where, as if by magic, the Brooklyn Bridge appeared before us. It was a view I had seen in so many movies, none of which did any justice to the sight in real life. Its stance at the tip of Manhattan brought an air of bravado, which matched the throngs of muscled firefighters peppering the pavement.

163

I fished for my compact to primp one last time. When I finished I looked up for Janey. She was gone, and I doubted it was to get up close and personal with the bridge.

After ten minutes passed, I realized that she might not be coming back. I would have felt self-conscious about being at the party alone, but the drunk crowd seemed to barely notice my solo status. *Cosmo* encouraged us girls to find power in our solitary moments, so I popped open a Bud and took in the view.

The minutes flew like seconds, especially after four beers. Armed with liquid courage, I set out to, as Janey had put it, "troll for men," which might explain her disappearance. The city sweltered, even though it was only May. The heat rising off the pavement matched the smoking-hot firemen. At least, I hoped they were as hot as I thought. Beer goggles could be deceiving.

I slurped down the last of my brew and took in the sights. A Long John Silver type babe-o-licious man strutted toward me. He had to be at least six-foot-four, topped with platinum blonde perfectly tousled bedhead hair and the looks and pecs of a soap star. I pinched myself to make sure I wasn't hallucinating. Nope. He stood practically naked before me, flexing those beautifully sculpted muscles, shirtless. And to think he fought fire and crime in the city. How sexy and hot was that? Did all men romp around topless here, or was that just a fireman thing? Not that I was complaining. I calmed my anxiousness with a quick nose scratch and vowed to make the most of my surroundings.

My phone rang. I answered hoping it was Janey calling to tell me where she was hiding.

"Hey," I said.

"Where are you, dear? Hopefully at church taking care of your annulment. I have a clipping set aside for you when you get back, entitled **Being Single is Not So Fabulous."**

"Mom, I'm not at church, and like I said before I left, I'm not getting an annulment."

"You said no such thing. Don't come home until you do it. P.S. I still love you. But not until you get the annulment."

She hung up before I got to mention I was never coming back. Had they still not figured out I had left for good?

The lure of my surroundings called me back to Long John as he sidled in closer. I couldn't be certain, but he appeared to be winking at me. I scanned over my shoulder to see if there was a tall blonde bimbo behind me, but it was mainly firemen. Was it possible that this beefcake had aimed his eyes at me? Maybe New York could be my playground after all.

His shiny pecs throbbed in my direction as he moved them effortlessly. It made me flush and giggle.

It turned out Long John was not NYFD, but he did play a firefighter on *Days of Our Lives* while sidelining as a construction worker. Fine by me.

"Would you mind, just for fun, pretending you're a fireman?" I purred in my sexiest voice.

"Sure, babe, I'll be whoever you want because I'm an actor," he said. Bravado seemed to ooze out of his biceps.

I melted into his gaze. My days with course-haired tech geeks and married men were behind me. Long John could be just the type of guy to break me into the NYC hookup scene. Light and loose! Candy would be proud.

"Would I recognize anything else you've been in?" I asked.

He leaned in toward me, potentially for a kiss, but stopped short as Janey appeared behind him.

"What the hell do you think you're doing, bitch?" she shrilled.

"Hey, Janey, where have you been," I said. "Thanks for joining the party."

"I saw him first. I've been eyeing him all night," she said as she charged toward me.

"What are you talking about? I haven't seen you once since we got here. It's not like you even know him. Where have you been this whole time, anyway?" I asked.

"So what if I don't know him? Now I'll never get the chance since you stole him from me. I was working up the courage to talk to him after Vin left me in the bathroom earlier," she said.

"Oh. Sorry to hear that."

When I probed further, I learned that Janey had picked up, and then had sex with, a random guy in a Port-a-Pot latrine. Brilliantly slutty!

"Are you serious? Not to nitpick, but *you* left *me*. I had to find someone to talk to. Lucky for me, John swept in and rescued me," I said as I sent a subtle, sexy wink his way. "If anybody should be mad, it's me."

"Yeah, right on, babe," Long John added.

God, he was hot. I couldn't be sure if he was interested in me or looking for someone better, but who cared as long as I got to gawk at him for a few more moments. I waxed ecstatic over the potential size of the bulge in his britches.

As I pondered, Janey turned on me as quickly as she had befriended me. Her arms flipped around like a seal as she screamed, "You man-stealing bitch! I should've known by the way you exited the subway you would go after all the guys. This, after everything I've done for you? Go to hell."

Yes, we agree that's where she and you belong.

She turned to Long John in a fury.

"You dickless asshole. I gave you everything I had at the keg (apparently a boob flash) and you treat me like this?"

Without as much as a breath, Long John grabbed me and threw me over his shoulder.

"Let's get out of here, babe, I don't live too far away," he said as he galloped out of the party with me over his shoulder, fireman style.

I didn't know if it was the sultry air, his manly maneuvers, or just my need to escape psycho girl, but I went with it. A mile into our mission he put me down in an alleyway of a desolate street in Brooklyn and planted a tongue-kiss that was so erotic it made me tingle.

Long John continued to thrust his sculpted body into mine. I couldn't be certain, but I may have had an orgasm right on the street corner because of that kiss. My mini-tee stuck to me, steeped in sweat—a blend of his and mine. Things like this didn't typically happen to me. *Of course they don't because it's trashy behavior, even from a two-timing adulterous divorcée!* Or maybe they did and I'd just been missing out on this kind of action because I spent too much time feeling guilty about not praying enough for God's forgiveness.

The tanned, godly creature spoke, resuscitating me from the kiss. "Should we head back to my place, babe?"

Babe wasn't usually a term of endearment that worked for me, but because of the sexy way it rolled off his luscious long tongue, I let it slide.

"Sure," I squealed without a pause.

I knew I'd regret this in the morning, but with Manhattan glowing in the background, I couldn't think of anything better than being petted by a stallion. My decision solidified when I spotted his pee-wee stick throbbing right through his cargo shorts. Good God, it was the longest thing I'd ever seen.

***

NYC fling number one—the hottest pick-up ever. Because tequila was involved, I wasn't totally clear on what did and didn't happen, but I suspected there was no penetration since my undies were still on.

While *my* underwear was on, the same could not be said for his. A point that was confirmed when his alarm clocked blared "Highway to Hell" at 5 a.m., jolting him off the futon but failing to wake him from his slumber. The fall did expose his more than ample apparatus. I couldn't help myself. I leered for way too long.

I would have remembered having sex with that. Also, based on the size of his apparatus, it would have knocked something loose inside of me, and I saw no evidence of a rough ride, other than an empty bottle of tequila and some dirty tube socks.

He sprung up.

"Shit, babe. I'm late."

He pulled on some camo cutoffs and ended my fantasy. His apartment was littered with towers of scripts and wallpapered with posters of chicks in swimsuits.

"I hate to cut out without banging you first but I got to get to the site."

"No worries, really."

He readied for work while I tried to make my bedhead relax down to a respectable level. He reappeared with a Pop-Tart and fed it to me. Even his fingers were sexy.

When we finished eating, he pulled me into his arms and thrashed his tongue into mine as he pushed me out the door and to the curb. He stopped groping me only long enough to hail us a cab. Having him sitting shirtless next to me all but erased my hangover.

He stared intensely. I sweated profusely.

"Babe, you were bad. You were so bad you were actually good. Wow, the control you've got. I don't got that. My cock is going to break off in this cab if we don't have sex right now."

The driver glanced back nervously. I smiled politely and continued to perspire and rub my nose discreetly. Meanwhile, Long John slid his hand down my pants and not-so-gently massaged my private parts.

"If we don't fuck soon, I might explode. Are you gonna make me wait forever?" he said.

Confirmed. We did not have sex. Thank God.

Shit. What was wrong with me? I should have bedded this hunk when I had the chance. He broke my obsessive thinking by sweeping his long, luscious fingers through the neck hole of my t-shirt and pinching my nipples. The cabbie leered at us through his rearview mirror and turned up the radio. Nothing fazed these drivers.

Long John continued to "pet" me all the way over the Brooklyn Bridge. *You've ensured a one-way ticket to hell, dear.*

He fondled my buttocks as he twirled his tongue in my ear. I thought about letting his penis enter me as we rounded the corner of 14th Street and Broadway, but it felt too crowded for such behavior with the cab driver less than a foot away.

"Hey, John, as much as I'm turned on right now, I just can't. It seems unsanitary. I hope you know it's not for a lack of wanting you, believe me."

He stared right through me. I looked down, trying to avoid his gaze and wished for his nuts to stop throbbing beneath his shorts. Or was that him playing with his own balls?

"Babe, you're killing me. You're so hot. Wanna go camping next weekend?"

I would've agreed to bear his children if he'd asked. He crashed his lips into mine until I answered him.

"Sure, I love camping!"

A total lie, but being stranded in the middle of the wilderness with a stud of his magnitude seemed worth a little roughing it. I got a quick flash-fantasy of him ravishing me on a bed of leaves. It would be okay to have sex with him in the woods with nobody watching, but not here.

As we pulled up to the construction site, my modern-day white knight leaned in, kissed me on the cheek, and slipped the cabbie a fifty as he commanded the driver to take me wherever I wanted to go. He winked at me and then he and his bulge swaggered away. Before I had the chance to digest the events of my "ride," Long John turned around, pounded on the roof of the cab, and tongue-kissed me through the open window one last time before sprinting down the block. I remained breathless and the cab driver speechless for the remainder of the ride.

If these were the kind of nights I could expect in Manhattan, my single life was sure to soar. When I got home, I peeked in the bathroom mirror to verify that it was me looking back. Had an alien pod absconded with my body? Near sexual liaisons with studs was not normally my thing.

A tawdry version of myself stared back. As I examined my reflection more closely, I noticed I had a neck full of hickeys. They formed a pattern that resembled leopard print. *Cheap hussy, harlot going to hell and back.* I had twenty-six minutes to get myself covered up, dressed up, and to Times Square to start my new job as a production intern at Sure Shot, a position I had secured upon arrival via a job posting on Mandy.com. One brief interview over stale coffee and I was in. Apparently, they loved my start-up stories, and my experience from NetSocial enough to hire me.

I wondered how well I'd fit in with the other twenty-somethings at the office, many of whom probably had real sex the night before. I was a disgrace to my age bracket. But, more importantly, I wondered, could I actually go camping merely to have sex with a wannabe soap star/fireman? For trampy singles everywhere, I sure as hell hoped so.

Chapter Twenty-One

A couple of weeks into my gig at Sure Shot, which I liked to think placed me at the heart of New York's entertainment scene, it became obvious that living in Manhattan was going to be much more expensive than I had planned. This observation was worsened by the fact that my paltry NetSocial severance had dwindled quickly. But I reassured myself that the decision to ditch technology in favor of a creative career would be so worth it. Like Oprah always said, you couldn't put a price on discovering your bliss. So what if I had to take a non-paying gig that relegated me to doing meaningless tasks like logging film stock and ordering stamps for the office? If that was what I had to do to break into the movie biz, so be it.

But then I received my landlord's hate mail, reminding me that my second month's rent was due. Or as she put it, "Pay up now or get out." She furthered her point with six exclamation points. Clearly, she was out of touch; nobody uses exclamation points anymore. It was emoji all the way baby.

Two hours, countless emails, and three homemade martinis later, I landed a phone interview. Oh, how I loved Craigslist, my go-to guide for all of life's conundrums. The posting made it sound like a dream job, working part-time for a communications mogul named Molly from the Upper East Side. She traveled the globe coaching some of the most renowned on-air talents in the world. A martini-induced sound sleep would ensure I aced the interview tomorrow.

After an easy-breezy meeting, Molly hired me part-time to work out of her home office. The way she explained it I would be doing light marketing.

By day two on the job, I realized that "light marketing" meant instilling a heavy-duty overhaul on her day-to-day personal life. She was a bit of a head case, yes, but she paid well, so I'd vowed to stick it out. The flexible schedule also granted me enough time to still swing the internship.

When I told my brother about the new job, he agreed to brief my parents on the career shift over the phone to avoid another full-scale meltdown. They still hadn't forgiven me for skirting the annulment, so this new bit of intel would likely fuel their annoyance with me.

Despite Jimmy's smooth investment banker talk, the news apparently broke them, especially when he explained how I willingly left the traditional work world in favor of "nutball entertainment," as my father had put it.

My mother connected her own dots and assumed I turned to a life of porn on the streets that surrounded Times Square. She told Jimmy to remind me that porn and divorce were mortal sins and I still couldn't come home until I got an annulment and went to confession. PS, she still loved me, but not until I paid penance for my past.

After one week in Molly's office, it became clear why she paid me such a hefty sum. She was impossible to work with. I suspected she was heavily medicated, but the drugs did little to quell her rampant mood swings—most of which she directed at me. Her office reminded me of home.

One minute, we'd be having a perfectly normal discussion on work or dating. The next, she was throwing CDs and pencils at my head and screaming about how nobody could ever do anything right, blaming "the change" for her erratic behavior. After one of her manic episodes, she threw a keyboard at me for not saying "It's a wonderful day" at the end of a phone call.

Fridays were especially bad. I prayed that today would be different.

"Sam, I'm heading to my shrink. You better not botch anything up while I am gone," she said. "Sorry, honey, I didn't mean that."

"Wow, she's a little intense, don't you think?" I whispered to her cleaning lady who stared at me with knowing eyes.

While Molly was gone from the office, I tried to get as much work done as possible. I tidied up her pit of a home, my attempt at organizing Her Highness happy.

A few hours later, she bounded into the living room of her ornate, tacky apartment. While she was tastefully dressed each day, her home was not.

"Sammy, I'm back, my dear. How are you, sweetie?" she sang. She must've forgotten about this morning's outburst. If I didn't know better, I'd swear she was related to my mother, Queen of Denial. She entered the spare bedroom-cum-conference room of the apartment where I sat, carrying an obnoxious, overstuffed bouquet of calla lilies.

"Here you go, my sweet! Oh, I love my girls. Do you know how lucky I am to have you?"

The housekeeper and I knew exactly how lucky she was to have us. Nobody else was fool enough to put up with her lunacy. I reminded myself I needed the money.

Thank God I finally caved and agreed to go camping with Long John. Whenever Crazy Molly rode me hard about my lack of attention to details, I thought about him riding me hard all night long in an assortment of positions throughout the wilderness. After a few tedious phone calls I realized he was dumber than I remembered, but so what? It was the biceps that mattered most in this instance.

I just needed to make it through the day and I would be free from Molly the nutjob and ready to let loose in the forest. By midday, I wondered if I would ever get out of her lily-lined prison.

When I could stand it no more, I said, "Molly, I've got an overnight date set for this weekend. Do you mind if I cut out now? I still have to pack and I have no idea what to bring."

"Something sexy, sweetheart. Skin is still in.

And take the flowers. Some men still need an aphrodisiac to get the engine started."

I doubted that John needed anything to get in the mood, but I obliged anyway to avoid any possibility of her becoming upset.

"Thanks, Molly, you're the best."

"I know, dear. Enjoy."

Thank God I got out of work early because I never imagined how tricky it would be to pack sexy, camping-friendly underwear and attire. After an hour of attempts, I found myself surrounded by a tower of Victoria's Secret teddies and thongs, cargo shorts, tanks, and a multitude of bug repellants. My cell jolted me out of the stress cycle.

"Sam, would you be interested in working on a production crew on weekends for our documentary, *Life in the Hamptons*?" Marjorie, my other nutjob boss, asked.

"We'll be out there shooting for the rest of the summer. And there is pay involved in the form of free travel in and out of the city on the Jitney and a free place to crash."

I had nothing better to do, and it would move me one step closer to actualizing my dream of a creative career.

"Sure, Marjorie, that sounds great, when do you need me?"

"Immediately."

She hung up and sent me a terse text message with all the logistics. Since merely packing for my camping trip caused me to break out in hives, an honest excuse to cancel felt like a blessing from God. I called Long John.

"Yo, babe, I was just masturbating thinking about you," he said.

How charming.

"Wow, you don't say. John, I really hate to do this, but I got called into work this weekend, so I'm not going to be able to make it."

"Babe, you are so good at playing with me. Yeah, I can't go neither, huh, huh, huh."

"No, seriously, I really can't go," I said.

"Babe, stop it. I just came all over my futon thinking about it. You can stop messing with me now, I'm finished. What time should I pick you up tomorrow?"

How stupid could one hunk be?

"John, listen to me. I'm not coming onto you or encouraging you to pleasure yourself. I can't go camping. Do you understand?"

"Damn, babe, I'm getting hard all over again. Imagine how hot we'll be, boinking in the woods."

Even more charming. By the time we got through the tough-to-follow parts of the conversation, I was horny too. Beyond all his stupidity was a voice that oozed of sex.

"Babe, get your ass over here right now and fuck me. You're totally killing me, man."

As appealing as that sounded, I needed to be on the Jitney super early in the morning. He continued to moan on the phone, which made me even hornier. I broke down and had phone sex, which was not nearly as fulfilling as I'd hoped. Without having his buff body as a distraction or a physical gesture to stop him from talking, his dumber than dirt tendencies outweighed his hotness by phone. In reality, it felt like a torturous form of safe sex. My mother would have been proud.

"John, that was amazing. But I really do have to get off the phone. Thanks, though. It was great. Maybe I'll see you around the city sometime."

"No problem-o, babe. I leave for LA in a week. That's why I wanted to hook up this weekend."

Not even smart enough to lie. But I realized I was no better. I was incapable of finding a suitable fling.

Chapter Twenty-Two

Standing on the corner of 40th Street waiting for the Jitney, I vowed to enjoy the ride and my upcoming stint at the beach. I looked forward to replacing the hideous memories from my one-year anniversary romp to the Hamptons with something more pleasant.

The welcoming green-and-white Jitney bus pulled up to the curb. It looked much classier than the Peter Pan Bus. I slipped into my seat and pulled out *Glamour* for a relaxing read. Unfortunately, someone sat down beside me—she looked nice enough, but after all the phone sex, I had no energy left for idle chit-chat. Also, ever since the Janey incident, I was gun-shy when it came to befriending the women of Manhattan, so I looked out the window to discourage conversation.

Once you got out of the hub of the city, cruising down the Long Island Expressway via bus granted magnificent views. Rolling hills, glimpses of the ocean, gigantic maple trees, and the sweet smell of serenity beamed through the tinted windows. *Travel and Leisure* magazine had dubbed the Hamptons the "must-see" destination of summer. I overheard the barista at Starbucks say the only way to survive the swelter this time of year was to escape the city. Then he charged me six bucks for a triple-shot latte.

Despite my attempts at repelling people, I soon let down my guard and found myself bonding with my seatmate, a native New Yorker named Shannon, who was also of Irish-Catholic descent, and single. The perfect travel companion. We could commiserate about being on the brink of thirty. How did this happen? Oh yeah, marriage, divorce, binge dating, moving home, boom.

The conversation flowed along as smoothly as the rolling countryside. I felt a connection with her that I hadn't felt since I left Candy back in Colorado. And she seemed sane, at least so far. I hoped it stayed that way.

"Sam, you should totally join a share house. It's the only way to experience the Hamptons."

A foreign concept at first, but she soon made sense of it.

"Think of it as summer camp for adults. A bunch of single people rent a gargantuan-sized house to play in for the weekend, all summer long."

"Sounds fun. Is it crazy expensive?"

"Not our house. Plus, you can do a half or quarter share if money is tight. You'd still get to come out every other, or every few weekends. It's a blast."

Sounded like an ingenious way to extend college camaraderie, but with class and style.

"I'll think about it for sure."

We both got off the bus at the Sag Harbor stop. It wasn't nearly as muggy as in the city. Instead, a refreshing sea breeze cut through the heat and my new wispy-banged haircut.

"There are even a few spots left in my house. You should check it out. We're having our annual deck party in a couple of weeks. Stop by."

"Thanks, it sounds cool. I do have a place to stay with my job, but the party sounds fun. I'll try to come."

"Just text me. It'd be cool to see you there."

***

Two weeks into the shoot, I had yet to see how ordering ice and stamps constituted an "on-set" job. My role was more about sitting in an un-airconditioned hovel of an office for twelve hours a day than working on the actual production set.

The fact that my workspace dwarfed even my apartment was remarkable. It was just big enough to contain an archaic wall phone, a yellow tablet, and an empty soup can filled with gnawed pencils. I spent Thursdays through Sundays manning base-camp, as Marjorie liked to call it. Then she'd remind me I was getting the "production experience of a lifetime," a point she repeated no less than three times a day. These entertainment people knew how to sell the dream.

In reality, I worked for free and lived like a small mouse without the cheese. My job duties consisted of fielding frantic calls from Marjorie, who was lucky enough to be working on the real film set.

Just when I started to fear death by boredom, it would be time to head back to the city to work with Crazy Molly. Perhaps I needed to analyze why I surrounded myself with crazies, or maybe it was me who was the whack job?

A day in the life of an intern meant duty called at 5:30 a.m., by which time I'd entered my closet of a workspace to answer the phone with a screaming person on the other end.

"Sam, the ship is sinking! We're going down. We are not on schedule—and we need ice, can you go get it?" was a typical Marjorie rant. Then she'd remember she couldn't release her prisoner and say, "Wait, who would watch the phone? Stand by, I'll call you back."

Cell phone, anyone? Then I would hear all the film action and bustle in the background, which only cemented my pissy attitude. I feared that listening to the director shout "cut" through the phone line would be as close as I'd ever get to being part of the production.

Marjorie suffered from a Napoleon complex. She was short, overly bossy, and had a bad mustache. The fact that she was a woman did not preclude her from this categorization.

When midday boredom set in, I'd perform my "make the phone ring" dance. Once in the throes of a moon-walk maneuver, I bumped into my milk-crate-tower-of-a-desk, toppled it, and broke two half-eaten pencils with my butt on the way down. I still worried about lead poisoning.

My phone trilled to Michael Jackson's "Beat It," a retro ringtone I had selected specifically for

Marjorie, who tempted me to use the one-line zinger every time she called. It was a sanity-saving technique I snagged from *O* magazine. Oprah had recommended a more meditative song, but for me, the throwback tune centered me enough to answer the phone in a pleasant way.

"Samantha, where is the goddamn ice? I asked you to get it two hours ago. Where the hell are you?"

"Um, you told me not to get it yet, to wait until you called back with orders," I said.

I could hear her breathing heavily and knew I needed to act fast.

"I would love to get you ice, just tell me where the set is and I'll get it to you ASAP."

"Oh right, never mind. Just stay where you are. You've got work to do. You better not be mocking me. This is the job of a lifetime. Don't ever lose sight of that."

I sat and stared at the corked walls for another three hours and reflected on my summer social plans until I realized I didn't have any. Then, an hour before the end of my shift, I had a brain burst: tonight was Shannon's deck party.

While my days at the office had yet to morph into the career-defining event I'd hoped for, the party could cement my social life for the summer. I rang up Shannon on the bat phone.

"Hey there, it's Sam. I'd love to go to the party if the offer is still open."

"Totally. I can't wait for you to meet everyone. You're gonna love it. Why don't you come over early and get ready with us? I'll text you the address."

"Thanks, that would be great."

This was a bonus considering my internship quarters were nothing more than a tent by the beach with limited access to running water. Not even close to the idea of glamping as depicted in *Glamour* magazine.

It turned out my office was a fifteen-minute bike ride away from Shannon's. I tried not to get too sweaty, but since temps had climbed to ninety-five degrees and one hundred percent humidity, I was drenched by the time I arrived. No worries, I told myself: this would give me ample cause to shed my pink polo shirt and replace it with my cotton jersey candy-striped tank dress—light and loose, without being trampy.

I skidded into Shannon's driveway and assessed the property. The grounds were just short of enchanting, and conjured images of a Ralph Lauren-styled polo match, complete with a field of tightly cut grass and manicured bushes. Ancient oak trees lined the perimeter of what turned out to be an otherwise drab-looking mega-house.

Shannon had mentioned that she stayed in the cottage behind the main house, so I pedaled until I hit the back of the property and parked my wheels under the apple tree. I freshened up my look by flitting my bangs back and forth while spritzing them with water (a tip from *Elle* magazine), and lapped up my sweat with the back of my backpack. Shannon opened the door.

"Sam, you look adorable. Good for you getting in some exercise before all the cocktailing."

185

"Thanks again for inviting me."

As she talked, I wondered about a could-be future with a potential new best friend. She would make a perfect wing woman—fun, down to earth, and we looked nothing alike so hopefully we wouldn't attract the same guys. Shannon's flowing dark brown locks softened her ivory complexion and sizable height. And best of all, no signs of neurotic behavior so far.

"No problem. Trust me, you'll never want to leave. I'll take you on a tour of The Mansion," she said.

She led me up to the main house. It was a mansion, albeit a dumpy one. It had seven bedrooms varying in size and appointment, furnished with mainly bunks and cots and squishy, soggy Astro-Turf-like carpet in each of the bathrooms. The living room wasn't much better with three futons and a card table. More than a whiff of mildew bounced off the walls. The cottage seemed much more appealing as it sat across from the sprawling pool and lounge area.

Shannon made introductions along the way. The men were a bit older, in their late-thirties—your typical Peter Pan types, except they lacked one important criterion—smoking-hot good looks.

"Oh, don't worry about them, they're completely harmless. They're like brothers, but sweeter."

After we finished the rounds, she led the way back to the cottage. On the outside, the structure reminded me of the childhood lake house where my extended family and I spent our summers—some of the more pleasant memories of my youth. It was an adorable blue and white A-frame with a loft area where Shannon stayed.

"Hey, if there's still room in the house, count me in," I said. "My workplace housing turned out to be a little more 'roughing it' than I had envisioned."

"That's so exciting. We have an opening in the cottage. We'll have so much fun," Shannon assured me.

We spent the next hour getting primped and ready to go. Shannon even helped me fix my hair and make-up, which were in dire need of an extreme makeover.

"Let's hit the deck party. The men await!"

The scene was beachfront bliss with ripples of beautiful boys poised in front of the crashing summer surf.

Shannon caught my stare.

"Yeah, I know. Unbelievable, right?" she said.

"That's the understatement of the summer."

A few minutes into the party, I locked eyes with a stud perched on the railing of the deck. With one glimpse at his beyond-buff body, I knew I could be headed for trouble with this crowd. A fling was mine to be had.

Buff Boy, as Shannon nicknamed him, was not exactly age appropriate at thirty-nine, and the sun had not been kind to his face, but his body was built like a stallion right on up to his long sturdy mane of Jared Leto-like ombre hair. And the way he moved—his swaggering hips reminded me of Justin Timberlake shaking his thang. Buff Boy was every bit as "equipped," minus the mouse ears of course. And the sexy Long Island accent was an added bonus. I couldn't stop my cheeks from blushing. The fact that he flirted with every girl in The Mansion did not squelch the embers of my fantasy.

"Hey, Shannon, what's his story?"

"Well, he's a fixture in the Hamptons. Everybody loves him. That hair is something, isn't it? Since he and his brother grew up here, they've mastered the art of the summer fling. They're also our neighbors," she said. "Everyone has tried to bag him. A few were lucky or unlucky enough to have succeeded. Poor Leslie over there," Shannon tossed her chin toward a mousy blonde waif, "turned borderline stalker after their brief liaison last summer."

"Oh my God, she looks as crazed as this girl I met when I first moved here, frightening."

"And just so you know, there's a lot more where he came from. The beach is swarming with manly delights," she said as she poured me a glass of sparkling rosé.

I would pace myself. I had all summer. Sometimes you had to be patient and practical to get what you wanted. At least that's what *Marie Claire* always said. Hooking up with a soon-to-be neighbor might not be the best idea. I vowed to enjoy his biceps from afar. *Showing restraint, that would be a first.*

Shannon introduced me to one of her friends, Evie, a younger girl who apparently liked to let her cleavage do the talking when it came to conversing with men. She had a great, albeit risqué, fashion sense. After a brief chat, she left us to get another cocktail.

188

"She's super nice and fun once you get past her need to be the center of everyone's attention," Shannon explained. "Her ability to reel in men with her near-perfect boobs never fails."

Evie soon returned with a watermelon mojito in hand. I observed how she used her position as an investment banker to her advantage, balancing high-level financial discussions with flirty looks and a low-cut dress. Despite the revealing nature of her outfit, she got annoyed when three different guys made googly eyes at her chest as she chatted them up about mergers and acquisitions. Though her outfits suggested otherwise, men weren't supposed to gawk at what she dubbed "the kittens."

Evie could be the sex factor of our trio. It would be impossible to try and compete with her plunging peacock-blue sundress, so I might as well befriend her. She completed her look with an oversized brimmed sun hat and coordinated sunglasses. The Audrey Hepburn of the Millennial generation.

Mojito make-out moments ran rampant around me, so I settled into a wicker rocking chair and noticed the unfamiliar sound of chirping birds, something I'd missed since my move to the concrete jungle. The blue jays were almost as engaging as the boys romping around on the croquet field. Men in Oxford shirts and madras shorts, accented with chiseled chins and gorgeous tans, were sights I could get used to here in the Hamptons.

Though my professional life had staggered, things were heating up on the social front. I pledged to redirect one-quarter of the time spent on work matters into my dating life just as *Elle* magazine suggested.

I tried to look relaxed as Buff Boy sauntered toward me. His sexy tresses danced in the breeze, as did his exposed pecs. He had managed to slip off his shirt on the way over. It was hard not to gawk at his Usher-like abs. His butt-hugging jeans were equally alluring. His sensual moves put him back on the top of my fling wish list. Hubba, hubba.

By the time his tanned bare feet hit the deck planks, five party girls surrounded him and clung to him like a wet suit. Bagging him might be more challenging than I thought. Not that I was interested. *How charming, Samantha. You've left a marriage to mingle with a man-child.* Pleated khakis and sweater vests begone!

He eventually settled against a pillar across from me. I switched my focus back to the birdies because the intensity of his gaze frightened me. Was he flirting, or did I have something stuck between my teeth? I prayed for the former.

I sipped my drink slowly in an attempt to seduce him with my slurp. Shannon and Evie bantered about last year's deck party in between vodka shots. By the time I'd polished off my drink, Buff Boy had flipped his steely gaze in my direction until Serena, a fiery redhead, lurched up behind him and tickled his chin. A bit forward in my book. Was she a scorned hook-up from last summer, still pining a year later? Note to self: do not become this girl.

I repositioned myself, boobs forward per Evie's instruction. I needed to look open and available for Buff Boy. Not that I planned to give in to my urges—nor would he ever be interested in a recovering Catholic like me.

I played it coy all night, close but detached. Then a highly intoxicated Evie sashayed over to me. She sizzled with each step. I could learn a lot from her.

"Sam, you can't sit there being passive. If you want to make something happen, take charge!" she said as she accidentally grazed my elbow with her left boob. Her tits began their assault on Buff Boy.

She dragged me over to him. "I would like to introduce you to my Midwestern friend, Samantha," she said. As a native New Yorker, she considered anybody not from the island of Manhattan to be a Midwesterner.

"Midwest, eh? Nice," he said in that silky Long Island accent.

His dark brown eyes twinkled down on me. And down they went, since he was so damn tall. He had the physique of a body builder and lifeguard rolled into one. My life as a production intern was looking up.

Chapter Twenty-Three

According to Shannon, The Mansion was split between a younger and older crowd. Since we fell into the former group we were written off by the latter as nothing more than boy-crazy party hounds. Considering last night's no-sleep kamikaze bender, they weren't totally off base.

The party was still buzzing at 5:30 a.m., a fact that crystalized when I realized I was going to be late for work. I covered my crazy hair with someone's ratty baseball cap, tripped over a pair of distressed underwear on my way to find my bike, and bumped into Shannon and Evie along the way.

"Bye, guys, see you later. This was a blast, but I've got a movie to make!"

The only thing more important than getting to work at that moment was making a pit stop at SagTown coffee, just barely within biking distance. It would make me even later, but I was desperate.

As I waited in line with the two ginormous open-mouthed lion statues glaring at me, I realized two things. The first being that I'd forgotten to change out of my party dress from the night before. The second was that Buff Boy stood at the front of the line. I attempted to hide behind one of the snarling monsters, but ended up knocking into a tray of low-carb bran muffins.

I tried to act cool, but when he smiled at me, I dropped my work bag. Packs of condoms and Jelly Bellies poured onto the floor. Marjorie had demanded that I keep a stash of both in case the director needed a quick fix. Scampering to stop the candy from rolling in his direction, I prayed for composure. *Prayers are lost on you at this stage of your life.* Sweat slid down my face as Buff Boy walked toward me.

I hoped he wouldn't notice that I had on the same outfit from last night and would pardon me for being such a spastic klutz. My face glistened with a red undertone as he strutted out of the coffee shop. Excellent—I had managed to make a fool of myself in yet another ZIP code.

I stunk of booze, my head pounded, and I was late for work. My summer was off to a smashing start.

During my ride to work, I tried to convince myself that my tawdry look could be construed as a good thing. It conveyed my status as a free and confident woman.

When I entered the internship office (shack), an answering machine, of all things, blinked incessantly at me. Before I had a chance to check messages, my cell and the wall phone barked at me in unison.

By arriving a half-hour late, I had missed

fourteen calls from calm Marjorie, terse Marjorie, belligerent Marjorie, and finally, Marjorie firing me on the answering machine's final message. She went from perky, to perturbed, to hell-bitch, and monster Marjorie over the course of a painful, eight-minute long message. I wanted to call her back and scream, "Get a real phone with voicemail, nobody uses answering machines anymore," but didn't.

It was official. I'd been sacked from my first job. I had to wonder if it mattered when you were working for free. The upside was, I could go home, shower, and sleep off my hangover.

By the time I got back, most of the older crowd from our house had left for their morning ritual: a marathon jog to the beach. They were a lively bunch.

I made my way back to the cottage and climbed the stairs to the loft, which was sweltering hot, but I needed sleep so I stripped down to my underwear. I felt up the bunk beds for a free spot. It was like summer camp—who knew what you were going to find in there.

One night in and I already loved the place…except when Evie pranced around topless in her g-string panties. She was a little too free if you asked me. I felt a lump on the bottom bunk, probably Shannon passed out. Halfway up my climb to the top, Evie bounded into the room.

"I am so horny. Oh, Sammy, you look dreadful. I hope you at least got some action last night. The bags under your eyes are horrific. For me, everything went fuzzy after that last round of

194

shooters."

I paused to come up with a way of telling her I had been fired from my internship, but it was too late. She had already lost interest and moved onto her own problems.

My energy waned, so I let her rattle on while I pondered the tough questions of the hour. Was it appropriate to get fired on a voicemail, an answering machine, in a text, and then in a confirmation email? Overkill if you asked me, but according to *Forbes*, in this age of instant information, you had to cover all your bases.

Shannon peeked out from under the dated floral bedcover.

"Sammy, so proud of you nice…" and she was out.

Fired, divorced, floozy, cursed—at least my new friends loved me flaws and all. *Don't count on it, dear.*

***

I anesthetized myself with booze on the weekends and retreated back to Manhattan and Crazy Molly's work dungeon on the weekdays, for that I was grateful. Oprah was all about gratitude journaling. Aside from Molly's manic personality and volatile mood swings, she paid me, which was more than I could say for the internship— correction, former internship.

On weekends, I played sex-free cat and mouse with Buff Boy—flirty, yet distant—my attempt at remaining mysterious just like *Cosmo* suggested. It was unclear what type of effect, if any, this was having on him, but what I did know was it made me want *him* more.

While being carefree wasn't my strong suit, it was for Shannon. Despite our common Catholic upbringing, she rolled guilt-free through her hookups with Irishmen and firefighters. I longed to be like her.

Only a couple months of summer remained. If I wanted to make tracks, I needed to conjure up a situation where I could make a subtle move on Buff Boy. Tomorrow's midsummer bash might be my best chance to pounce.

Evie be-bopped out of the bathroom, topless and shaving. No female could possibly have this much body hair.

"Sam, you need to plot your manhandling strategy now. The other women are closing in. You need to play seriously hard to get."

That showed what I knew. Here I thought it would be a good time to switch to a more straightforward approach. Lucky for me, Evie volunteered to manage my social life for the rest of the summer.

"We're going to happy hour before the party, just us cottage girls. This way, when you run into him, you'll appear more open and available with sparkling eyes from all the booze. Follow my advice and you'll wind up bopping him by the end of the night. But ditch that sappy sarong and pop your boobs into my peach sateen tube top. Wear it, and he's guaranteed to kiss you before the party is over."

I wasn't even certain that was my desired outcome. Besides, it was hard to imagine that my chest would be capable of holding up her top given the disparity between our breast sizes.

She resumed shaving her bikini line in our common space. Maybe that was why she had always gotten what she wanted from men.

"Yeah, I agree, Sammy. If you show up tipsy and smoldering, you'll make an impression," Shannon said.

Davis, our fabulous, could-be-gay housemate, called up from the driveway.

"My sweet taffies, the convertible awaits."

We filed out of the house and into our chariot—a sky blue vintage convertible caddy. There was something invigorating about Katy Perry belting out of the speakers as we cruised down a beach-lit drive, confirming that anything was possible, maybe even some fireworks.

We arrived at The Dockside Bar & Grill for a quick cocktail and app, and were greeted by a harried-looking guy belting out Jimmy Buffet. It was hard to tell if he was working there or just a blitzed wannabe. His face looked almost as sun-fried as my father's did by midsummer. It matched the degree that my social life had started to cook.

Davis garnered three rounds of Alabama Slammers for us in mere minutes. He slicked back his hair with my drinking water and pretended to be our waiter. Note to self: don't sip on that water.

"To my favorite ladies, love ya forever."

"Right back at ya, Davis. You're a good egg. I love you too!" I said and shot back my slammer.

And then another, and another. The next thing I knew, Evie tweeted in my ear.

"Shit. I just re-read Buff Boy's text. The party was more of a happy hour thing. We've already missed most of it. We're leaving, now."

Perfect. I'd accomplished her mission of looking "unavailable" by missing the whole damn thing. I wondered if I would ever get to bag the buff, long-haired wonder before summer's end.

"No worries, let's go by the house, anyway. I'm sure somebody is home. Stay positive," Shannon said.

She was always optimistic under the influence. I admired that about her, since I just got sloppy and sad. As we sped down the driveway to Buff Boy's place, things looked low-key, but I prayed that peeps would still be chillaxing by the pool. I stumbled out of the car and Evie followed.

"Remember, open but unavailable," she said.

We approached the house and were confronted with a crooked note tacked to the door.

It read:

You missed the boat, babes. We're gone.

Amazing. This stud had winked at me on paper. I dipped in closer to see the fine print.

For all of you who are man enough to handle it, we've moved the party to Murf's. Go ahead, I dare ya.

Confirmed. Buff Boy had written this note.

"Stop sulking, Sammy. We're not giving up. To Murf's we go, ho, ho, ho," Shannon said.

We sang "Roar," not in unison, the whole way there. We arrived at our destination, and before Davis could bring his buggy to a complete stop, I'd jumped out and ran toward the bar. My loyal posse caught up and we linked our arms as a trio so I could walk a pseudo-straight line. They were excellent wing-women.

I panned the bar from the front door and just missed being shot in the head with a dart. "How could they not be here? They left the note. They dared us."

"Focus on the jukebox," Shannon said. "It always calms you down."

It was a gem all right. So much joy to be had beneath a yellowing sheet of Plexiglas. I adored that thing. My most fulfilling relationship of the summer so far. The raucous scene put me at ease. Coupled with the stench of booze and stale garbage, it reminded me of home.

As I vacillated between song selections, Buff Boy and his entourage emerged. Instead of his usual pussy-footing around, he locked eyes on me and strutted in my direction. I guessed the peach tube top was working. I scratched my nose until my eyes watered. His brother Bob stopped in front of me and offered me a hankie, which prevented me from drawing my own blood. Buff Boy slid up behind me. I stood between them, forming my first ever man-wich. A delicious place to be, and not nearly as unpleasant as the pulled pork sandwich I'd eaten for lunch.

I could see Evie miming behind his back with goofy hand signals. The best I could surmise was she was reminding me to be unavailable yet sexy. She threw her boobs around in circles to demonstrate her preferred approach. Unfortunately, my execution proved not nearly as engaging, since my breasts weren't big enough to twirl.

Buff Boy unpeeled himself from my sweaty back and slid to my side where he outstretched his hand to me and pretended it was the first time we had met. He made extreme eye contact. Hardcore, porn eye contact. I fell to the floor under his spell. Or maybe it was all the alcohol.

"Why, hello there, can I help you up?" he said. It felt like he was panting over me.

"Cake By the Ocean" came on the jukebox. He scooped me up into his arms as if he was going to kiss me but instead swept me into an upright spoon. He thrust his pelvis into my butt to the beat of the music—dirty dancing with a surfer stud. Oh, what a night! I could feel his sweaty pecs and pounding heart against my small and willing frame. As I pondered the possibilities of how best to leverage the situation to my advantage, he dipped me down to the ground where nobody could see us.

"So, how about we make-out right here? What do you say to that?"

Do-me-now came to mind as I allowed myself to fantasize about his likely more-than-ample private parts. While I drifted in wonderment, he remained frozen in our downward dip.

"But it wouldn't mean anything. After tonight, we'd go back to being friends. Are you cool with that?" he said, killing my Alabama slammer buzz.

After nearly two months of cat and mouse, this hook-up scenario was not as enchanting as I'd hoped it would be. I wasn't sure if it was the shots talking or Buff Boy's swaggering hips soldered to mine, but I squeaked out a tentative, "Okay." *Tawdry moron.*

Before I had time to kick some common sense into myself, right there, in front of everybody, he planted a luscious kiss on my throbbing lips. It brought me to my knees, again. Just like my mother, I still couldn't handle my liquor.

My face flushed as I attempted to gain footing, but his deep brown eyes rendered me incapable, so I sat there as the bar and its patrons spun behind me.

"How's it hanging, darlin'?"

Was he mocking me? I was afraid to look down and see if one of my mosquito bites for breasts had popped out of the tube top during my tumble. He resumed the lip smacking before I had a chance to check. I had ended up in the middle of someone else's erotic fantasy, and boy was it tasty.

Thankfully, the smooch-filled reality continued on and off for the next hour. My lips were on the brink of being kissed off. We paused only for brief moments of dirty dancing and drinking in between lip smacks and booze sips. *Keep up that tango and you'll be ousted from the family for good.*

I had no recollection of the ride from the bar to Buff Boy's boudoir because I was too busy necking with him to care. I prayed that my kissing haze would never clear. The bed-rolling aspect wasn't too shabby either. I could live in his room for the rest of the summer, though I had to wonder if it was kosher to cuddle when you were slated to go back to being "friends" tomorrow.

"Babe, I'm dizzy."

How cute. I made a man dizzy. I don't think I've ever had that effect on someone.

"Babe, seriously, do something, I think I have vertigo again."

Vertigo? Who gets that in real life?

"Are you sure?"

"I'm on an all-protein, no-carb diet. Sometimes I get vertigo when I don't eat enough meat."

A downside to being so hot I guess. I should've known this romp was too good to last. It could prove challenging to explain to the girls that I did not fornicate the night away with Buff Boy because he went into a no-carb-induced coma by way of vertigo.

"Can we just stay still and spoon? I'll let you rub my temples. My trainer told me that a forceful rub can help stop the vertigo," he moaned.

Since I hoped to rub much more than his temples, I obliged. I wasn't aware I had such a gift, but apparently I did, since he fell almost instantly asleep under my care. This rendered me unable to sleep, as my untouched nether-regions lay awake and yearning to be stroked. Men were never supposed to be the one to call off a one-night stand; it was unheard of.

As I remained wrapped around his beautiful body, part of me felt relieved that he petered out. As eager as I was to hook-up with him and then pretend like nothing happened, my rational side knew I couldn't have pulled it off. I would have hated myself and then him.

To switch things up, I moved on to his pecs. They looked like they needed some attention. I felt that I should get some satisfaction out of this defunct deal. Massaging his body parts would be well worth the effort, even if it inflamed my carpal tunnel.

As I stroked the goods, two things came into focus. While he had the body of a twenty-year-old, his face was not faring nearly as well. *Fitness* magazine always preached that lifelong tanning was unhealthy. I could see why. It was a pity, because from the neck down he did indeed still look like a college co-ed.

When I thought about things, my decision to smooch him was no smarter than practicing unsafe sun. Who would agree to friendship as a term for canoodling with your crush? *You're an idiot.*

The sun blazed through his shade-less windows and woke me. I had a killer headache, chapped lips, and carpal tunnel from all the temple rubbing. At least I got to accidentally bump into his pee-wee stick last night, when my hands dropped down in defeat after one too many strokes of his forehead. His penis was long and strong, just like I imagined.

Buff woke looking startled to see me. He also sported "friends only" eyes.

"Babe, that was nice last night, but lots of business today. Can I give you a lift back to The Mansion?"

I could be cool and friendly.

"Sure thing, let me find my clothes." *Charming,*

Samantha. Have you no shame?

There were two trends developing this summer: the first being an inability to bounce back after a night of heavy drinking; and second, the older and sexier the man, the more likely he was to *not* want a relationship, yet still command commitment-free sex. The really brazen ones went as far as suggesting moronic deals about post-boinking friendships. The equally moronic women one-upped them by agreeing to such deals.

He yodeled as I searched for my tube top.

"Hey, babe, we need to stop off for breakfast on the way because I won't be able to drive if I don't get some protein in my system."

He drove topless in low-slung jeans for the duration of the ride to Fairway, which made the night and the deal totally worth it.

He gnawed on a pulled pork breakfast sandwich while I nibbled at an egg-white omelet. What was it with men and pork? We barely spoke. I assumed it was so he could inhale as much protein as possible. As "friends," it was understood that silence was bliss. He aborted any could-be romantic fantasies when he burped and didn't bother to do it under his breath. It was a shame we were only going to be friends. I could have liked him, not only for his body, but his table manners.

"Let's hit it. I've got some waves to catch and deals to close," he said.

It was still unclear what he actually did for a living, aside from beach combing. Not that there was anything wrong with that, especially since we were just friends. As we drove back to the house in silence, he flipped his flowing mane in the wind, which made me horny—you've got to love jeeps.

I couldn't imagine how we would end this short-lived fling of ours. While I pondered, he sped to the end of the driveway, stopped the car, planted one last kiss on my cheek, grazed both of my breasts just long enough to make my nipples erect, and then strutted out of the car and over to my side. He flexed his pecs while opening my door, and right when I started to get swept up in the romance of it all, he winked at me.

"Remember the deal, babe."

If he wasn't so damn good-looking, even with all the wrinkles, I would've slapped him across the face and flipped him the bird. Instead, I patted his ass and channeled my sexiest, footloose and fancy "friends" voice.

"You betcha, sweetheart!"

I wagged my butt with sass as I strutted back toward the cottage.

At least he drove down the driveway as opposed to leaving me at the mailbox. He didn't seem worried by the fact that everyone saw his car, and me getting out of it.

I wore my hook-up like a badge of honor as I waved to a few of my housemates who lingered on the deck. It smelled like rain, but nothing would pee on my hook-up parade.

"Morning, guys!" I said with a cheesy smile.

Bagging Buff Boy by temple rub alone was something to be proud of. *Yes, dear, it solidifies your place in life as a tramp.*

My headache moved to the forefront as I crawled

up to the loft. Shannon and Evie looked as hungover as I felt.

"Did you slip him the tongue or what?" Shannon asked.

"That, and then some. I even got to stroke his pecs, while he was sleeping but still."

"Please tell me you did more than that," Evie said.

"Oh totally. You wouldn't believe what I did."

And, of course, they wouldn't. What moron would bed a man and not close the deal? *A Catholic, that's who!*

"He had a spectacular penis. And equally large wrinkles."

Evie looked horrified.

"Face wrinkles, not down there for God's sake."

We laughed so hard. Especially when I told them about the vertigo thing. Life was good.

***

On my way back to the city Sunday night, I passed out on the Jitney until I received a belligerent call from Crazy Molly who interrupted a sensuous dream sequence where Buff Boy and I "penetrated" more than just temples. I tried to follow Jitney law and not answer, but she kept calling.

"Samantha, how can you be so incompetent? You left for the weekend without watering Lisbeth," she said.

"Sorry, Molly, I thought for sure I took care of that right after I sorted and filed two years' worth of client documents."

"Well clearly you didn't, and now her petals are wilted and she's dead! I hold you responsible for her death. You're on notice. You'll have this on your conscience for the rest of your life."

She didn't bother to thank me for covering the office for an entire week during her absence. Nor did she apologize for all of the deranged calls she made to me in the middle of the night and early morning. Despite her above-average intellect, she couldn't manage to figure out the time difference between Europe and New York. Instead, all of my efforts went unrecognized because I forgot to water a flipping plant. Well, flip her! I hung up. Unprofessional, yes, but she ruined a perfectly good fantasy that surely would have ended with Buff Boy and I getting married on a beachside cliff in Capri.

On Monday, I arrived at the office with my happy pants on. My strategy for averting a Molly meltdown.

"How oblivious could you be? I left explicit watering instructions. It's impossible to understand how anybody can be so insensitive to my needs, and then you don't even bother to bring a replacement plant. Didn't your mother teach you anything about manners?" *Believe me, we tried. She's hopeless.*

Christ, how had I forgotten to pick up a stupid flower? This mishap would brand me a looser in Molly's eyes forever and likely result in a pay cut.

"If you respected me and the tranquil office environment I've tried to create, you would have never made such a horrid mistake. Do you even care about this job?"

I was once a highly successful business professional making an imprint on the social media stratosphere. Now I fielded tirades from a bi-polar bitch-on-wheels. I must have missed "plant keeper" in my job description.

The only person more freaked out this morning than Molly was our new intern, Sally, who was getting a crash course on home-office politics. I discovered her hiding in the back bedroom sitting on Molly's treasured cow print ottoman. I quietly suggested she sit elsewhere or risk getting fired. Even the chair looked sacred. I'm sure Sally also missed the fine print warning in the Craigslist ad about a ranting loon of a boss.

"Just so you know, she's not always this crazy. She just..." I whispered so manic Molly wouldn't hear us.

Before I had a chance to elaborate, Molly stood in the entryway of the bedroom carrying the dead lily in her hand, with a pair of scissors. She glared at me and then started to weep.

"Thanks to you, I'm off to my shrink to get some help in mourning the loss of Lisbeth."

Crackpot.

I tried to console Sally while explaining her areas of responsibility. Obviously, I started with the plant procedures. Clearly, I needed a backup in that department.

On her way out, Molly threatened my job one more time. Maybe *I* should go to a shrink to get to the bottom of why I keep engaging in toxic relationships.

To console myself, I took a moment to daydream

about how good Buff Boy might have been in the sack if I'd been given the chance to boink him.

I prayed that three hours with a therapist would help Molly quell her anger. When she bounded into the office carrying two enormous fresh fruit and wine baskets, I thanked God for finally answering one of my goddamned prayers.

Molly stepped up her game. Usually, she followed up tongue-lashings with a miniature bouquet of flowers. I guess a pocket full of posies would have been bad form considering Lisbeth's passing.

"Sammy, I want to hear all about your weekend! Every last detail."

Sure thing, whack job.

I indulged her with the high and lowlights of my night with Buff Boy, in an attempt to avoid another outburst. The sad thing about Crazy Molly was that when she wasn't in the midst of losing it, she was actually fun to be around. Her dating chronicles were legendary; she'd dated many high-profile types back in her day. Even back then, men liked the crazy ones. Maybe I had a chance after all.

"Sammy, don't get sucked into the game he's playing. If a woman is good enough to put out for a man, she deserves more than friendship. That's just common sense. *She has none.* Once you agree to friendship with benefits, there's no turning back. Keep that in mind before you sleep with this man."

As much as I wanted to begrudge her, crazy or not, she had a point. It all came down to self-worth. I should try to get me some of that.

Chapter Twenty-Four

I powered through the doldrums of my weekdays, and lived for the weekends and my return to the Hamptons, bent on conquering my "fling-filled summer" mission.

August was bonus month, so we got the house for two weekends in a row. Evie had been schooling me on how to make the most of the occasion with Buff Boy. Even though I knew we were going to be just friends, I was anxious to see how we would navigate our first post-hookup encounter.

Shannon and I spent Friday afternoon primping for happy hour. I borrowed Evie's plunging purple sundress to optimize my figure, and I drew a larger lip line around my own to make my mouth look lush and seductive, just like the July issue of *Glamour* demonstrated. The way I saw it, the plumper they looked, the more likely that Buff Boy would want to scrap friendship for smooching, and hopefully sex.

We decided on Cyril's despite the trek because, according to Evie, it was otherwise known as the sure-to-score spot. She offered some flirting tips such as walking with equal parts sex and innocence, which I planned to test out.

We took a taxi to the bar so that we could drink as much as we wanted. I got a head start by using the flask my father bought me for Christmas—right before he disowned me, again.

I allowed myself a swig of vanilla vodka when we arrived, and at Shannon's urging, I took one more for good luck, and one for my mother. Evie tugged the V-neck portion of my dress down just a bit further so that my breasts appeared open and available. I didn't bother fighting her—I felt tingly and free.

We bounced out of the car and into the bar where we were greeted by a scrumptious looking bartender.

"Hey, baby, I love your shorts! Can I get two peach mojitos, and a pinch of you on the side?" I said, winking.

A gnat flew into my eye—a moment spoiler yes, but it was August on the East Coast.

Mr. Suave didn't seem to catch my flirt, so I moved on to the next barman. He looked like Zac Efron, washboard abs and all. I licked my lips in an attempt to suck him under my spell, until I saw a sun-drenched Buff Boy sidle up to the other end of the bar. He wore pressed dusty brown surf shorts and no shirt. It looked like he lubed up his pecs with baby oil, flesh fashion at its best. My nearsightedness came in handy, because from afar he looked years younger.

I played coy the entire night, making tipsy chit-chat with the girls, never bothering to wave at him. I did glance over in a sexy way every few minutes though. It was all "friendly." Shannon was not nearly as covert. With each slurp of her mojito, she dispensed love advice.

"It has to come from them, if it is ever going to cum at all," she gurgled.

She sounded like a saucy version of my mother, except Shannon rooted *for* sex and my mother *against.* The more they drank, the more they repeated their sentiments.

Shannon got a pardon because she was right. As long as the man made the move, you were in a safe zone. But when women start making sexual advances, you risked rocking the dating continuum.

As I reflected on her mantra, Buff Boy snuck up behind me and pressed his toned body to mine as he covered my eyes with his big sweaty hands. I could tell it was him by his scent. He smelled like sex, or maybe that was wishful thinking.

"Hey, babe."

I didn't want to be the one to point this out, but his behavior was nothing close to "friendly." His gentle breath on my neck gave every one of my vertebrae the chills.

I remained unfazed on the outside until I accidentally grazed his lips with mine. Good God, what was I doing? I tried to undo it by forcing my cheek his way instead. Cruel, given I had puffed up my lips with Philosophy Red-Hot Cinnamon lip gloss to taunt him, but barely gave him a chance to taste it.

An uncomfortable few minutes of silence

ensued. Evie ditched us for an investment banker who had complimented her on her financial speak as he unapologetically stared at her boobies. She was annoyed with me for the kiss, but I got back on course when I left Buff Boy standing alone with my gloss splattered across his face.

Shannon moved down to the other end of the bar with me, which still left us in eyeshot of him, but just barely. My spot at the bar served great views of the fire-bomb sun that set before us. It reminded me that some love was just too explosive to last. Likely the case between Buff Boy and me; we were just too hedonistic for our own good.

Shannon babbled about letting him come to me until I finally cut her off. Playing hard to get exhausted me, and I needed to step away from the bar before I did something more stupid than the accidental lip graze. We left without saying goodbye to Buff, which was exactly how I wanted to leave things—laced with sexual tension.

The next day, Shannon, Evie, and I headed straight to the beach to sweat off our hangover—a routine that was becoming standard practice for us. I tried to curb my Buff Boy fantasies with wine coolers. When that failed, I conjured up excuses for bailing on the evening's stupid family dinner. Convening with all of our housemates for a meal of overcooked pasta and boxed wine did not sound like the best way to actualize a romantic future. The group dinners reminded me of home-for-the-holidays gatherings, minus the passing of expletives along with the potatoes. The real problem was the Mansion dinners left little time for mingling with

213

eligible men.

"Summer is almost over; we have done our time with these meaningless gatherings," I announced. "We need some real company. Preferably company that kisses back."

"Well, you've got a point. I don't think we committed to group dinners when we joined the house. We've hit our quota and then some," Shannon said.

"Samantha, you have yourself to blame. That public display with Buff Boy set the girls' bitchery in motion. We need to make amends. We need to have a presence," Evie said.

I was sure her topless sunbathing played no role in their annoyance. The women had grown to hate us, but the men loved us. Well, they loved Evie's tits. Between the boobs and her hip-length sateen-black hair, she was package enough for all of us.

"All right, but as soon as the campfire karaoke starts, we are gone, promise?" I said.

There had to be sex somewhere in this God-forsaken beach town, and I was running out of time to find it—the summer was almost over. *Your priorities are once again out of alignment, dear.*

"Here's the plan. As soon as we finish eating that sickeningly sweet peach cobbler, Shannon will announce she has a work function to go to, and she can only bring a couple of us," Evie said. "That's our way out. Deal?"

The heat eased off with the sunset, and we made our way back home to get ready. We soldiered through supper and even sucked down some cobbler. Shannon dropped our exit line and we

214

peeled out. But not before a roundtable guilt session about our early departure, ending things on an identical note as church and every one of my childhood family meals.

***

On the ride from Sag Harbor to South Hampton, for what we hoped would be a killer party, I downed two shots of tequila—to hell with my self-imposed rules. Sometimes you have to just go for it.

Evie parked the car and commanded, "I want everyone to enter the party oozing sex with every step."

I wasn't sure how to make that happen, but I did feel like I was floating. We entered the gargantuan home of some guy named Cass, whose pad trumped ours in every way, starting with gaggles of eligible guys and ending with a plush mauve carpet. I tried to sashay as Evie had demonstrated earlier but it turned into more of a stumble, which caused me to just barely moon someone. Damn Evie and her fashion sense. A micro mini with a thong was not sexy, just stupid. I scooped up my sensible wedge sandal, which had fallen off during my tumble. While I was down there, I noticed a familiar buff ankle. As I tried to conjure up a sultry way to get off the ground, I saw an unfamiliar bronzed foot adorned with a tacky diamond anklet. The owner of said toes, painted electric blue, rubbed up against Buff Boy's.

Was it possible that he offered her the same "friendship" deal? She was probably smart enough to know better than to accept it. Given the Barbie wannabe looks and skanky toe ring, I surmised she was just as stupid as me.

I played things coy yet friendly as I got up off the floor and smoothed my skirt back down to a respectable place. I should have followed my inner voice and worn boy briefs. What was I thinking? *You weren't, like usual.*

I descended from sexy to sloppy when I attempted to squish myself between Buff and Barbie. The fact that I stepped on her perfectly pedicured toe in the process was a bonus. I couldn't be held accountable for my God-given klutziness. This time it worked to my advantage as the maneuver sent her whimpering to the bathroom.

"Hey, what do you sex like party night later?" fell out of my mouth before I had a chance to form a coherent sentence.

After a few more failed attempts at speaking, I opted for silence with a sassy wink. It was hard to ascertain how I ended up on the floor again. Had Buff pushed me or did I merely fall off his lap? Either way, he didn't bother to help me up.

Shannon barreled around the corner, motioning for me to come over and talk to her. Wait a minute, what was she doing with Fritz? The lipstick evidence smeared all over her face became my answer. How did she score slippage before me?

"We're leaving," she said.

"Give me a minute. I'm talking here. Can't you see that?" I said.

"Yeah, Sam, you ought to head out," Buff Boy chimed in.

He wasn't fooling anybody. I'm on to his hard-to-get routine, it's hot. He certainly played it hard, all right. He completely ignored me. I pulled myself up, winked at him again, and followed Shannon out of the party.

I panted over my shoulder, to seduce him from afar.

"Sam, hurry up, Fritz is giving us a lift since none of us can drive," Evie said. "And you're making an ass out of yourself."

This coming from the same girl who went topless at the beach.

***

I must have passed out because I had no recollection of how I got back home. I had faint memories of declining a ride with Evie and Shannon and forcing myself into Buff Boy's car. Perhaps that was why I was riding in the backseat.

He brought the car to a stop, but kept it running as he hopped out of the car to open my door.

"What are you doing?" I said, pulling the door shut. He reopened it. He was a feisty little stud.

"I'm dropping you off."

He must be running low on protein again, hence the terse words.

"I thought we were hanging out tonight."

"Not sure what gave you that idea, but I'm going to bed," he said.

Again with the attitude. Somebody had clearly gotten up on the wrong side of the ocean this morning.

"You need protein, you sexy bad boy, bow, wow, wow."

Tequila made me an excellent seductress. His pecs glistened at me. You gotta love the fact that shirtless was acceptable attire in the Hamptons, even at night. Maybe when he got a glimpse at my hot pink thong he would rescind our "friends" deal for the night. Perhaps Evie did know what the hell she was talking about.

He answered my mating call with a grunt.

"I'll give you some of Sammy's special body protein," I said, and then winked.

I got back into his car after he ushered me out. This time, I sat in the front seat. *Cosmo* said that men like "take charge" women.

"How about we head back to your place for a starlit swim?"

"Whatever waxes your surfboard, babe."

Wow, he was really working me.

Since I refused to get out of the car he drove over to his place. He turned me on with his silent ploy. The Jeep came to an abrupt stop and he got out and walked toward his house. Does this mean he wants me to chase him? Ha! The cat and mouse bit, a classic move on his part.

I stumbled out of the car. Despite what *Vogue says,* wedge shoes are *not* a sensible footwear choice for summertime. I followed him to the pool where his brother and the rest of the entourage were hanging out.

"See ya, Sam," he called out as he slammed the front door shut.

Running out on someone you're hoping to make

love to, seemed like odd behavior, but who was I to judge?

I waved to the other fellas and followed Buff's scent into the house like a bawdy hound in heat. *Elle* magazine said men liked their women primal, so I barked at his bedroom door. I hoped I was at the right room because everything looked the same in the dark. I jiggled the knob. Not sure why his door was locked, not totally inviting.

"I'm feeling easy, Buff. Open up, you sexy beast. I'm ready to rub more than just temples this time."

He did not answer my mating call. I decided to let him rest for a bit and went out to the pool to grill up some pork and hang with his friends. This would prevent me from looking too needy. Plus, my man would be craving protein when he woke up from his late night nap.

Grilling the meat only made me want him more. I devoured my chop and reveled in the spectacular view from the back porch. His house was much nicer than ours, woodsy-rustic, but in a good way. And so close to the water you could smell it.

I alternated between burping and babbling with the boys. I wasn't flirting with anybody, just passing time until Buff woke up.

A couple hours passed and he had yet to join us. I wondered if he had come down with vertigo again. While my patience with his ploy thinned, my animalistic instincts kicked into overdrive. I got up and howled at his window like a coyote.

"Sam, give it a rest. He's not coming down. He's whacked out on that diet. Hang with us or, for fuck sake, shut up," his brother said.

It was hard to tell if it was the sticky air or maybe the tequila wearing off, but a realization washed over me. I had veered off course. I had not played hard to get. Instead, I forced myself over to a guy's house who left me outside while he went to bed. *At last, the light bulb illuminates.*

I should leave. Enough embarrassment for one night. The last thing I needed was for him to wake up in the morning, indulge in a high-carb pancake breakfast, and then find me still in his home.

I moved back over to the pool, grabbed my purse, and tried to slip by unnoticed as I walked down the long winding road toward my house. Brother Bob and his brat pack soon drifted out of earshot.

It shouldn't have been more than a fifteen-minute walk, yet it seemed like hours had passed and I still wasn't home. I dipped in and out of the woods looking for The Mansion. I convinced myself it was safe. It was the Hamptons, for Christ's sake. Nobody but the drunk and disorderly were out at 4:00 a.m. *Exactly.*

My tequila buzz had worn off, leaving me with a dismal portrait of the night. A night that ended with me wandering around in the woods lost, hungover, and barefoot. Not the hot romp with Buff Boy I had envisioned.

"Christ, I will never get home. I'm a total fuck up," I screamed out to nobody through my tears.

I'd never find true love and happiness. This must have been punishment for all of my sinful escapades of the past. *At last, reality is sinking in.* Summer flings were overrated.

Right when I was ready to roll to the ground and sleep in a bush, I heard a car rumbling up behind me. I panicked, thinking it might be the Hamptons' version of Ted Bundy who was out stalking stupid girls who did not wait for men to come to them.

A Jeep stopped and Buff Boy got out and stood before me, topless in his boxers with a chicken drumstick hanging out of his mouth.

It was true what they said about eyes being the windows into someone's soul, because as I looked into his, pity stared back at me. I must have looked worse than I felt based on his expression. It reminded me of the look my father gave me every time I fell short of *his* hopes and dreams for me.

He straightened his rumpled boxers and got back into his Jeep.

"Get in, Sam. I'll take you home."

Even with a greasy skinless chicken bone hanging out of the corner of his chiseled mouth, he was still sexy. I wasn't sure if he came out to find me, or if he just discovered me on his way home from the convenience store.

None of that really mattered because he ended my journey down what would hopefully be my first and last walk of shame.

Chapter Twenty-Five

A therapist might call my walk of shame a defining moment since it got me thinking: how many more of these scenes did I need to put myself through? Candy, Miss Married, was so off the mark with her glorified view of summer flings. Of course all *marrieds* were.

I had endured a long, hot summer, and all I had to show for it was a bruised heart, scraped knees, and a bout of poison ivy. Buff Boy wasn't a bad guy; he was honest about his "friendly" intentions. He didn't pretend to be anything other than what he was: a horny, hot guy with great hair who wanted to hook-up on his own terms with no strings or drama attached.

Clearly he "friended" the wrong woman.

As much as I wanted to, I could not have sex with somebody and not fall for him. Hell, I couldn't even kiss a guy and not fall for him. Maybe this was God's way of not allowing me to ditch my moral high ground. *Please, you have no moral ground, high, low, or otherwise.*

The brisk, soggy weather had seeped in to remind me that it was time to swap my summer infatuation with the Hamptons for a real career.

Crazy Molly would have to do until I could procure one. Luckily, she spent the entire fall season through Christmas overseas, which I took as a holiday bonus. A true blessing, aside from fielding her tirades from afar in the middle of the night because time-change calculations continued to foil her. At least with my boss in Europe, I could put the phone down and let her rant me to sleep.

As I lounged on her bed and wiped my perfumed arms all over her pillow to instigate an allergic reaction when she returned, I had a couple of new revelations. One, I was about to turn thirty; it was time to get serious. Working for Crazy Molly was not getting me to the creative career I yearned for. Two, my love life was a demolition zone. Time to fix that. Incessantly playing Justin Bieber's "Love Yourself" could only get you so far.

One of Oprah's many mantras reminded me that female friendships should always be cherished. Ever since summer had ended, Shannon and I vowed to meet for lunch once a week. Today was our day! Molly would never know I had left the office.

Despite the flipping cold temperatures, Shannon insisted on honoring our tradition of eating outside at the Coffee Shop in Union Square. Rubbing frigid fingertips with one of the wannabe model waiters would be as close to having a date as I'd had in months, which was fine by me. I had exiled myself away from men ever since the Buff Boy debacle.

"Sam, your dating sabbatical has gone on long enough. It's time to get back out there," Shannon said as our Calvin Klein underwear model ushered us to an outdoor table to keep us away from the pretty people. He nodded for us to sit, so we could freeze our asses off while we ate. I prayed that he would eat one day soon, but until then I'd admire his hollowed-out cheeks.

"I'm fine. Men and me don't mix, that's all. I feel blessed to finally understand that. Now I can channel all my love into the banana cream pie. *It* never disappoints."

"Maybe not, but it won't keep you warm at night."

"Neither will sitting outside."

"Anyway. Here's the deal. I'm sick of the pity party. My Christmas present to you this year is to save you from yourself. We're going to Sasha's holiday party tonight. I know you hate Brooklyn, but this will be worth the trek. Free booze and food is within your budget, I presume?"

"Well, I'll go, but you have to promise not to leave me talking to Sasha all night. She never shuts up about how fabulous her life is now that she is in a committed relationship."

"Deal. I will block if she starts coming your way."

After enjoying our catch-up over one too many mojitos and forkfuls of pie, we headed out with plans to meet later on at the Union Square subway stop. Shannon balked at my suggestion of public transportation, but it was the only way she was getting me to a borough other than my own.

***

As soon as we walked into the party, I could have punched Shannon for dragging me out. Everybody was cheerful, and the eggnog far too sweet. Merry f-ing Christmas. I nodded in agreement and stuffed my mouth with bad cookies so I couldn't give bitter responses about my relationship status. Thankfully, Buff Boy had skipped the party. Hopefully, he was hibernating in the Hamptons for the winter since it was too cold out to go shirtless.

After three hours of being grilled about my dating goals for the New Year, I had endured as much as I could take. I gave Shannon the "slit my throat" signal, which marked the end of our tenure at this piss-poor party. She owed me some cheap Irish whiskey back in *my* borough, at Pete's, one of our favorite watering holes—severance for attending this humiliating excuse of a gathering. Nothing like a drunken hottie to soothe my soul. *It'll take a lot more than that to save it.*

"Sasha, what a fantastic night. We really enjoyed watching the complete DVD chronicles of how you and Stan got together," Shannon said without a trace of sarcasm. "But we have to move on to the next party. Busy, busy."

"Oh please!" Sasha said. "What else could you possibly have to do? Aren't you single still? Singles are usually dying for companionship during the holiday season. Stan and I were worried we might have to throw you two out."

Then she snort-laughed at us. F-her. Why was it

that all attached people think every single person had nothing better to do than sit around at stupid couples' parties watching boring videos? If that was what couplehood was all about, screw it. I'd rather relegate myself to a life of spinsterhood.

My desperate need to flee worked in Shannon's favor when I agreed to cab it back to Manhattan. One whiff of the stinky back seat of the gypsy cab (our compromise) made me regret my moment of weakness. I tried some of the deep breathing exercises that *Yoga* magazine recommended for stressful situations. It only intensified the putrid stench of the cab and threatened to make me hurl up one of the several mini-quiches I had devoured at the party.

We walked into the pub after a long, pricy, and stanky ride. Thankfully, we were greeted by two black-and-tan beer concoctions that we downed immediately. My mother would have been proud of my drinking prowess.

We blended into the scene of rowdy hipsters and blitzed Irishmen. I loved the anonymity that pubs offered. Everyone was too drunk to notice you until a certain hour of the night when *everybody* did.

"This unquestionably beats that loser party," I said.

I tossed back a shot of Jameson. It burned its way down my throat. "Who needs men when you've got Uncle Jamey?"

"To us!" Shannon said as she clinked my glass to the brink of breakage.

It was amazing what booze and brews could do for fostering a positive attitude. Oprah should recommend it instead of all her positive self-talk. As I slammed my glass down on the bar and commanded the bartender to pour me another, I noticed a perfectly sculpted pec belonging to an even more perfect body. He was beefy and beautiful even in a shirt. Too bad the bimbo next to him intermittently blocked my view.

"Like, excuse me, like, barkeep, could you, like, get me, like, a sex on the beach shooter, like, right away?" she said as she threw her boobs onto the counter. An annoying, yet impressive, move.

Like, could you please hang me now and like get a real life and vocabulary while you're at it, tramp, I thought to myself, but quickly retracted my inner bitch—I didn't want to risk revealing that wrinkled crease between my eyes that surfaced when I got angry.

She flipped her hair three times, pelting me in the eye every time with her frizzy blonde tresses.

"Excuse me," I quipped as I tried to regain my personal space by sliding my elbow to the bar and knocking her tits off.

Fake ta-tas! Unfortunately, my maneuver forced her mounds of flesh right into Mr. Pecs's sizable hands. He flushed at my faux pas and I cursed myself.

Booby bimbos always made my barely-there rack feel even more minuscule. Thank you, mother, for passing down your surfboard-flat chest.

The way Betty the Bimbo shifted her bosom out of Mr. Pecs's large, shapely hands was impressive because the move simultaneously unbuttoned two more snaps of her already low-cut shirt—a maneuver that inspired me to rally for pancake-chested women everywhere.

"Do you mind? Every time you flip your hair, you're hitting me in the eye. Step back at least."

She thrust her bust into Mr. Pecs's face so that her left tit grazed his chiseled chin and caused *him* to step back. Then she squealed.

"Ah, like, yeah, like, I do, like, totally, like, mind."

Brilliant, she was not. I contemplated if she had the ability to string together two sentences that did not contain the word "like." She retaliated by doing a boob block: a twist turn into a fake faint where she and her boobies fell into Mr. Pecs—the female version of a cock-block.

She even pissed Shannon off with her slutty bravado, which fueled me to continue with my derailment strategy. When Betty the Boob refused to move her gargantuan tits out of my way, I bumped into her. She was dizzy and borderline anorexic, so even though I just barely brushed her, it caused her top-heavy frame to topple to the dingy floor. She had it coming. Mr. Pecs seemed to think so too. When she realized what happened (lying in a puddle of beer must have been the first clue), she fled.

As Shannon and I toasted our success with another beer, Mr. Pecs slid his sexy, sculpted arm out to mine.

"You're funny. I'm Justin."

His words didn't captivate me in that instant, but his body had my attention. I reminded myself that my life was more stable without male entanglements; that I was complete without a man.

Screw stability! I stared politely, sending a vibe of open but unavailable. *Cosmo* said the best way to score a man was to lead him to believe that you're not available.

"Sam, stop overanalyzing and go for it. Suffering through the party earned you this much," Shannon whispered in my ear.

She slipped into wing-woman mode and chatted up his friend, Paddy. Since they were both Irish, they shared an instant moment of drinking and chortling. In five minutes, she managed to get the full download on Justin's vital dating statistics. She motioned to the bathroom, eager to share her insights.

"So, here's the deal. He's an only child, thirty-four, born and raised in South Beach, financially solvent, and never married. And get this, he works in law enforcement," Shannon said.

"And don't forget the wavy strawberry blonde hair and tight butt. I'm tempted to squeeze it," I added.

As I tried to tinkle in the potty, Shannon prattled on with a plan.

"First order of business, another shot. It will chill you out. Second, I'll flirt with Paddy, and you sit still and try to act adorable."

"Got it. I think I might be ready to open my heart to love again. For the right guy. Not that he's it. But…"

"Stop talking now. Just go."

When we got back to the boys, I downed a shot, and then another, just to be safe.

Justin told riveting stories about his life and then sexy, scant details about his work. I did a lot of eyelash batting.

Fueled by whiskey and those beefy pecs, I attempted to look sexy by pouting my lips. Maybe Justin would be different than all the rest—he had to be. *Oh, dear God, here we go. The true definition of insanity: repeating the same thing and expecting something different.*

"Do you guys mind waiting just a minute? We have to pee again. Beer does that," Shannon said.

She threw me down the hall and pulled me into the pisser.

"Oh my God, I love them! Don't you? They are hot and nice and down to earth. I think this is it. We should do it?"

"Do what?"

"*It*," she said. "I haven't had sex since summer. It's time," Shannon said.

"No, it is not time. We can do any number of things, but sex is not one of them. I thought you told me never to be the last person lingering at a party. This night is ending here," I said, channeling my mother's no-sex sentiments.

"I'm begging you. How often do we meet guys like this?"

"Never. That's why we're going to leave them wanting more," I said.

I wanted my loins tended to as much as she did hers, especially since I hadn't had real sex since Frankie. Nobody needed that to be their last defining sexual encounter. But now was not the time. Tomorrow, maybe, but not tonight.

"Fine," she said.

I prayed that I was right. We returned to our men in waiting. I tried to do my sexy walk, hands on my hips, with a swivel step. *Cosmo* said guys liked this sort of thing.

"Hey, ladies, how about we walk you home? We promise, no hanky panky," Justin said.

Despite the dated lingo, he had me at panky. The four of us walked hand in hand, meandering down the snow-kissed East Village street. Hope was not dead, not just yet.

Paddy and Shannon left us as we rounded the corner onto Avenue B, which left Justin and I in the glow of our own company. In one swift motion, with no running start, he leaped over a parking meter and muttered a breathy, "Hey, you."

I stood stupid and speechless. Did he want me to try and clear the meter too? *Say something, you idiot. You can't just stand there and will him to like you.*

"Wow."

Not totally brilliant prose, but the best I could muster between my stomach's incessant flipping all over the place in that whirly-bird way that only happened around boys with potential, like Justin. I tried not to ruin the moment by obsessing over why he jumped over that meter into my life.

He went for my sweaty hand. Was he smirking at me? Damn you, Mother, for not teaching me about the birds and bees until it was too late to matter!

"Justin, where did you learn how to do that parking meter leap?"

"Aw, it was something I picked up at the

academy."

"The police academy?"

"Not exactly."

It turned out the *academy* was the Federal Bureau of Investigations. I had a zillion questions to ask him, such as why he would liaise with me, Simple Samantha, when he spent his days protecting the city and the world from terror?

"Wow," I repeated in rapid succession until, thanks to my internal pleadings with God, Justin walked toward me, wrapped his massive biceps around me, and planted a mouth-numbing kiss to shut me up.

Making out against a parking meter might not be appropriate behavior in the eyes of the Catholic Church, but I saw no problem with it.

When I eventually recovered from a second round of heated street smooching, he looked me in the eyes as if world peace was at stake.

"Sam, is everything okay? You look a little off."

"Oh no, I'm fine, I'm better than…" I rambled until I stopped myself from talking when I threw my body into his with my most potent kiss. This knocked both of us off the meter and onto the street curb, where we continued to make-out.

Hell right, I was off. Or more like wrecked! Over the course of a few minutes, my tightly wound Catholic ass was on fire in the middle of one of New York's most public city streets. I should have been freezing my butt off, but instead, I contemplated stripping down to my skivvies.

I finally got a grip on my raging hormones and peeped, "Wow, I have to head home."

I turned and sprinted down the street. He caught me in a matter of seconds.

"Hey, Sam, hang on. I'll walk you home."

He was a gentleman too, just the type of man I should love but typically repelled. Except this time I didn't.

I felt as if I was in the middle of a movie.

A terrorist-busting boy and a sexually frustrated girl walked hand-in-hand all the way home to an East Side city stoop. Then the beautiful boy dropped off the shaken girl and kissed her so sensually and so lovingly that she had a spontaneous orgasm on the corner of Avenue B and 14th Street.

At the perfect moment, Justin brought things back to reality when he grabbed my hand and grazed it with a heartfelt peck.

I fished clumsily for my keys, turned to him and whispered, "Goodnight."

Chapter Twenty-Six

Thank you, Mother, for ensuring that the Catholic Curse would suppress my desire for sex despite how truly fabulous the man happened to be. Just thinking about Justin brought on that feeling of being a love-struck tween running through the streets during a hot summer rain shower. But maybe I should thank dear old Mom, because not putting out paid. He had courted the hell out of me for four blissful weeks. *Clearly not long enough to stop all the swearing.*

He treated me with respect. Like a princess. Every woman should be in a relationship where her man treated her like royalty. Justin held doors open, called when he said he would, took care of everything, and escorted me down the street, making sure he stayed on the side closest to the street so if a road-raging loon hit the curb, it would be he and not me who would bear the brunt of it. So gallant.

He loved me. The real me. The divorced me. And he played no games that I could detect—a rare case of *what you see is what you get*. I had finally freed myself from the bad boy type, the ones that my mom often reminded me were just "bad news." One month was too soon to mention the "L" word, but it was the only explanation for my feelings. We skipped right through that awkward period of acting silly and unavailable, and opted for honesty instead.

We were laying on my new rose-pink down comforter when things got heated. The flower petals I'd dropped all over the bed stuck to Justin's tanned and sweaty pecs and instead of getting mad, he tickled me. I fantasized about an impromptu fornication session.

"Sam, I want this moment to be perfect, and I want you to be completely at ease with all of this."

Do me now, I thought. I needed me some of those pecs.

Unfortunately, he mistook my wandering mind as a sign to go slower. Part of me loved him for being sensitive to the fact that it might be too soon for sex, but it made me want him to penetrate me, immediately.

He pinned me down by pressing his massive yet sculpted frame into my accepting body, just enough to arouse me but not snap any bones.

"I'm going to contain myself, but next time, I'm just going to take you, no waiting for permission—I'm going to scoop you into my arms and never let go."

Such an honorable man. Yup, I loved him. This relationship bordered on perfection. Candy would be so proud of me. After all the marital and dating mishaps, I was ready to be "taken" and loved by a good man. I deserved happiness, and this was my chance to snag it.

Our relationship mirrored an old school courtship, the kind where you needed to get permission to "see" someone and boys had to work at wooing. A nice counter to today's dating standards where perfect strangers pork each other senseless, particularly in the Hamptons. Sometimes without even wearing condoms, and often over the Internet. Thank God I would never have such worries again, only blissful moments with my very own man of steel.

***

It was New Year's Eve, and luck be a lady, I had a bona fide boyfriend. What a great way to end the year and kick off the new one. So what if I was about to turn thirty in February? I had found true love. Baby was growing up! *Baby was a tramp.*

Justin's ringtone jolted me out of my love-steeped stupor.

"Hey, baby. I've got some bad news."

Oh, Christ. He fell out of love with me already.

"Yes, Sweet Tart?" I prayed to God. He sure as hell better be listening.

"I know this was going to be our first New Year's together, but I have to work, unfortunately. We're back on an orange alert, citywide. But I promise I'll think of you all night as I patrol the beat."

He protected our world from terrorists, so how could I begrudge him? We had a lifetime of New

Year's Eves to spend together. *O* magazine said that women made too much out of this particular holiday.

"No worries, Buttercup. Shannon and I will just dig up something to do, and then I'll wait up for you."

"Copy that, baby."

Oh, how I loved that man. I knew it wasn't in my nature to throw the "L" word around, but I couldn't stop myself. *Get real, dear. Nobody this perfect would ever be interested in you, especially after all of your sinning.*

Spending New Year's Eve in Manhattan easily cost upwards of a few hundred bucks, which just wouldn't fly on my salary. Crazy Molly had cut my pay after the plant watering incident.

My mother raised me to score deals wherever possible, one hand-me-down worth keeping. After some noodling, I reached into the bowels of my remote friendships and reconnected with Pascal, an Asian nightlife guru I had met over the summer at Southampton Social Club. He was short, suave, and plugged-in though hard to understand. This translated into people inviting him to the hottest parties in and outside the city.

He owed me big-time because he put me to work a few months earlier at his *Sex and the City* reunion party, where I ended up peddling scented lubes and condoms. My boss for the night called himself The Lube King. He had left Wall Street to embark on a more respectable business—sexual lubricants. I went hoping to meet Carrie Bradshaw and her once-fabulous gal pals, but in reality, it turned out to be a launch party for a new book about the most sex-inducing spots in town. Oddly, Pascal thought of me. *The King* paid me extra for demonstrating how to apply scented lubricants, which required me to swirl my tongue around test tube shooters. This schooled potential buyers on the key selling points: lubes could be both delectable and functional.

I got sent home early when I did not take him up on his offer to partake in a live "lube job" demo on his "member" during my break. Yes, Pascal owed me.

"Hey, Passy, I need two free tickets to the SoHo Grand's New Year's Eve ball. Can you hook me up?"

When he started to balk, I muttered "lube job" under my breath.

"I see what I can do. Will get back pronto."

He texted me five minutes later to confirm that he had taken care of things. When I called Shannon with the good news, she developed a get-hot-quick strategy. Even though we were "taken" women, we still had to look good.

At a pint-sized nail salon on the Lower East Side, we lapped up the ambiance and allowed ourselves to be pampered. I enjoyed staring at the street riot posters that covered the salon—an odd choice, but it reminded me that things were always looking up. I also enjoyed the sweet and stinky smells of the street meat being cooked outside the shop. Even on the coldest day of the year, those guys were out there slapping together kebabs skewered with unidentifiable meats. *Food and Wine* said that men loved women who ate pork, so I'd tried to incorporate more meat into my diet.

"You know, we are lucky to have bagged such normal hotties in this city, don't you think?" Shannon said.

"Yeah, I mean if anybody would have ever told me that I would be dating an FBI agent and you would be snogging his best friend, I would have growled at them and told them to stop mocking me. Now, I can't stop glowing. We are damn lucky all right."

"May our good fortune never come to an end," Shannon said.

Her dark brown locks were combed to a satin sheen. We conspired on how to usher in a better year than the last.

"Color please, miss?"

"Something saucy. And sexy too. And pink, just not whore-bag pink, sweet sexy girl pink," I said.

"Shut up, Sammy, and answer your phone. Let her do her job."

"What time you want me to pick you up?" Pascal said.

"So not necessary. Shannon and I are going to take the subway to the party. But thanks for the tickets!"

"Color please, miss?"

"Got to go, Passy, later," I said as I hung up and selected a sultry pink shade for my toes. I wanted to look animalistic when Justin slipped into my boudoir late night.

"That's weird. Pascal wanted to pick me up for the party. Probably nothing. Just making up for the lube incident, right?"

"Sam, stop obsessing. Everything is fine. We have great men in our lives, plans for New Year's, and now a fantastic mani-pedi. Just enjoy life, would ya?"

I nodded complacently. My resolution for next year—accept happiness and good fortune. I was worthy. *No, you're not.*

After our nails dried, we trekked through the slushy streets back to Shannon's to get ready together like we used to in the Hamptons.

We shared a block of blue cheese and downed a bottle of champagne. We decided we deserved it. Plus, everything looked better through champagne flutes. Just imagining my late-night liaison with Justin got me hot in all the right places, or maybe it was the bubbly. Who the hell cared!

My "I've Got You Babe" ringtone buzzed. Oh, Justin *had* me all right.

"Baby, guess who got off work tonight? I want to suck your body into mine at the stroke of midnight."

How sweet. Justin and I were on our way to becoming lovers for life. *Don't count on it, dear. I'm sure you'll do something to screw things up.*

"That is so exciting, except Shannon and I already made plans to go to a party, since you were working," I said. "You could always join us, though. I would love that. The only problem is that it's three hundred bucks a ticket. But I'll squeeze into a pink sequined mermaid dress to make it worth your while."

I willed myself to stop babbling but I desperately wanted him to join us.

"No worries, baby. I can't wait. Paddy got off too, so we'll meet you there once I finish up with work. Text me the address, or I can hunt you down, if you prefer." I could feel his biceps bulging through the phone as he hung up.

"Shannon, I love this crime-busting babe. I really do."

"I know, but remember it's all new. Just take it easy. Hey, did you tell them about the dress code?"

"No, but he'll look sexy no matter what," I said.

Justin was usually a tight t-shirt and jeans kind of guy, but I knew he'd conjure up something for our special night. He could show up naked and I wouldn't object. It was preferable actually.

Shannon danced around in the kitchen and then started break-dancing across the checkerboard tile floor. She had it just as bad for Paddy. It was adorable, and so were we. Screw Oprah and her righteous self-help ways. This self is better with a man.

***

It was not until Pascal moved toward me with romantic purpose that I realized he might think we were on a date. I thought I made it vaguely clear that I used him for free tickets to the party, but maybe my communication fell short, as my father often claimed was the case.

I would be cordial, but nothing more. When he approached, I indicated I had to powder my nose. When he threatened to dive in for a hello kiss, I scratched my nose and then picked at it to dissuade

241

him. He released me, untouched, so I darted to the bathroom.

I hid out in there for fifteen minutes, and despite that fact, he stood waiting to greet me when I exited. He placed his sweaty hand on the small of my back and pushed me, rather forcefully, into the party room where techno music boomed so loudly I felt like I had come down with vertigo. Considering the high price tag, I expected something more highbrow, like a swing band. Martha Stewart always said classy, not trashy.

I distanced myself from Pascal when I bumped into an edible sculpture of the Statue of Liberty. I loved Lady Liberty as much as any New Yorker, but seeing her in cheese form felt sacrilegious.

Shannon was hammered on one too many cocktails, so none of my distress signals made an impact. Techno turned even the sanest people into psychos, and Shannon was no exception. She kept throwing her hands up to the sky and down to the ground, in what looked like a full-on body slam with the dance floor. Even for techno, her moves seemed extreme.

She continued to ignore me and guzzled another sparkly drink out of a Chrysler Building goblet. It impressed me how she could dance and balance a drink at the same time, much like my mother.

As I assessed Shannon's performance, my stalking sidekick came in from behind and smacked me on the neck with a slobbering kiss. Then he delivered a sweet nothing in my ear. Maybe the mermaid dress accentuating my minimalist curves was too much for him to handle. How could I explain the curves were for Justin and not him?

"Wow, no, I did not know you worked your way through high school to support your four brothers and sisters. That's admirable. I'm sure your mother is proud."

"Not exactly. She's dead."

"Oh, so sorry to hear that. I bet she's looking down from heaven though and so very proud."

"Doubtful, she too self-centered for that. Not like you. You hot."

My head felt like it could explode for a multitude of reasons, not the least of which included the volume of the music. Did anybody even like techno anymore? I contemplated leaving to end my misery, but then I spotted my beau across the jam-packed room.

Justin had dressed up his usual jeans and tee look with a pec-accentuating denim blazer. He furthered his chances of bedding me by wearing one of those Robert Redford newsboy caps that made any man, even the gangly, handsome. In Justin's case, it made me want to jump him. The fact that everybody else was wearing tuxedos and cocktail dresses didn't even bother me. In fact, I considered snapping a photo and sending it to *GQ,* but thought better of it due to his covert profession. Plus, the last thing I needed was for women everywhere to pleasure themselves in the bathroom while peering at his smoking-hot bod in a magazine.

Staring at him gazing at me from across the room made my heart bounce to the beat. The music shifted down a notch just enough for me to hear Pascal's blubbering.

"Samantha, would you care dance?"

How did I fall into a date with one man on the same night my boyfriend arrived to begin our life together as soulmates? *Face facts, dear, the only one your soul is mating with is the devil.* I was typically dateless, but now I had two.

"Pascal, if you don't mind, I'll pass. I'm not much of a dancer, but thanks anyway. If you'll excuse me, I have to hit the ladies' room."

I needed to ditch him. My terrorist-busting prince charming had arrived, and I didn't want him to get the wrong idea, which was likely the right idea. It would complicate matters if he realized that I was on an accidental date with a party-hopping hound wearing a slick silver tuxedo.

Shannon was plastered and useless. She had stooped to dancing to techno to seduce Paddy. He must love her because it seemed to work.

The main ballroom was dressed up with mini Statue of Liberty sculptures everywhere—the perfect decoys to duck behind as I exited at one end of the room and reentered at the other. I sauntered up behind my sweetie, pressed my body into his, and blew in his ear. *In Touch* said that playing with ears was an instant turn-on for men.

"Hello, you," I said, hoping to sound sexy. *Slutty would be more accurate.*

I felt seductive as our bodies melded together in a perfect upright spoon. Being ensconced within his buff curves was akin to the high I imagined people experienced on ecstasy, but better because Justin was my drug of choice.

"Baby, you look amazing. I can't wait to take

you home," he said.

How lucky was I? I didn't think I had ever had the pleasure of having a man dote on me. It was fabulous. In Justin's presence, all of my insecurities and sexual hang-ups melted away. It was a stupid cliché, but Justin really did complete me.

Shannon continued her seduction routine by gyrating with Paddy to the tunes. Pascal ran toward us, so I pulled Justin up to the dance floor. The music faded into the background and the countdown began.

Justin swept me into his massive arms, twirled me in a circle, and dipped me into the center of the dance floor. The DJ continued, "Three, two, one, Happy…" Justin attacked my lips with a passionate smooch. It lasted for several minutes, I think. I almost passed out from the lack of oxygen.

"Samantha Serrano, I love you," he whispered.

Pascal spit into my other ear, "Two-time whore," and attempted to throw a punch at Justin.

Definitely not the ideal first confession of love.

My man had a heart though because instead of pulverizing Pascal, he let him take another swipe but stopped the punch before it broke any skin. I wanted to sock Pascal myself, but Justin indicated that would not be kind. Such an honorable man, my boyfriend. It was clear that our city and country were much safer with him to protect us. I also knew deep down, if I allowed him, he would protect me from myself.

Chapter Twenty-Seven

Justin took me the moment after we necked our way into my apartment. He led me into the bedroom, which was my living room and also my kitchen, so it made things convenient. He gazed at me lovingly as he unhooked my dress and stripped off his own shirt at the same time. That move would have required three hands on a normal man, but for Justin, it was effortless. His perfect body terrified and turned me on.

He sucked on my nipples to the point of erection—his and mine.

"I love your body. You have the most supple breasts and skin," he said before plunging downward to my nether regions. He grazed them lightly and for once, I liked it. I didn't even attempt to cover up my body—another first. I allowed him to take me in completely, which left me feeling exposed yet coveted.

He knelt down and stroked my inner thighs with his massive knuckles. Then he moved his lips upward until he reached my private parts. I tried not to come, but when he said, "Baby, I need you, I want you, I love you, just let go and enjoy." I exploded inside. With each swath of his tongue, my body reverberated. He pleasured me better than I did myself, which spoke volumes. *You're trampy to do such a thing.*

He straddled me on top of my rose-pink down comforter and smiled. I wanted to stay like that staring up at his engorged penis forever, but Justin had much more in store.

For the next hour, he drank up my body as if it were some sort of magic tonic. And then at the most perfect moment, he entered me. He controlled his penis like a master artist who knew exactly how to command his brush, taunting me as he twirled his wand at the opening of my vagina, which caused me to come again—a feat I never knew was possible outside of soap opera circles. He entered me again as he told me that he loved me. He swaddled me up into his buff body and we spent the rest of the night in each other's arms. I broke my post-coital rules by being able to fall asleep with Justin glued to my backside. I had also broken my own curse by allowing a genuine man to love me, thus disproving my parents' theory that divorcées are unlovable.

Normally, I felt tense and guilty after having "relations," so I stayed awake all night trying to glow and look sexy. This tactic usually backfired because by not sleeping, I would look like a zombie instead of waking with the post-sex afterglow *Cosmo* always talked about. But Justin's calming presence freed me to fall asleep with the assurance that he would still love me in the morning.

I woke feeling panicked over whether or not he would bolt out the door to work out or kill terrorists or something. I prayed that both could wait. *Well, since you didn't bother to wait to bed him, don't expect him to.*

"Shut up. Leave me alone!" I yelled without intending to.

My outburst and thrashing about in bed woke up Justin, and that wasn't the only thing that was "up."

"Morning, sunshine."

He rolled over on top of me, and in one swift movement he draped his body over mine and entered me again—my morning wakeup call. Something I could get used to. He was a gentleman and a marathon man all rolled into one tight, muscle-filled bun.

As I rested in the nook of his sweet-scented armpit, Shannon's ringtone belted me out of bliss.

"Sam, we're downstairs. Do you want to meet us for breakfast?"

I leaned over to my now favorite man in the world.

"Sweetie, are you up for a foursome? Well, of the breakfast variety I mean, not the sex scandal type," I said, willing myself to shut up as soon as the words were out of my mouth.

"Whatever you want, baby. My day is yours," he said.

So, he wasn't going to skedaddle? I needed to get used to the fact that a handsome, respectful, upstanding, and incredibly hot man could love me. It was time. *Time to go to confession and purge yourself of your most recent sin.*

Justin strutted into the bathroom, which gave me a chance to give Shannon an update.

"We *did it.* Multiple times even, because he has the endurance of Superman. We'll meet you there. God, I love him."

I hung up, and while Justin freshened up in the bathroom, I tried to pick out the perfect casual yet sexy outfit. He liked me to show off my minimalist curves, so I settled on skinny jeans and a pink velour turtleneck.

It took him forty-five minutes to shower and get ready which seemed excessive, but his look when he exited was worth it.

It poured rain outside, which normally caused me to sink into a deep depression since I suffered from bouts of seasonal affect disorder, but not even the weather could burst my happy bubble today. We sat for a couple hours at Veselka, the perfect perch for a post-coital binge. The kielbasa platter reminded me of Justin's big-o sausage. The memory made it hard to focus on the food. I tried to converse with everybody to stop myself from daydreaming about our night of love. I also prayed that Justin would not dine and dash. He ate breakfast as if food was going out of fashion. Either his meal was much better than mine, or he was in a hurry to get on with his day without me.

God must have approved, because Justin did not ditch me after breakfast. Instead, he demanded that we spend the entire day together. I hoped that it was code-speak for him wanting to spend the rest of his life with me.

We hit coffee houses and tea shops and even a

double feature at Village East Cinema, an art house theater down the street from my apartment. Despite the daylong rainstorm, my good mood prevailed with Justin by my side. Oprah was right. Love did conquer all. We never unlocked hands the entire day, except for bathroom breaks.

I had to fight the urge to scratch my nose to the point of peeling skin off, but I thought better of that idea. I was worthy of a good man, and not even my bad habits were going to get in the way of keeping him.

Chapter Twenty-Eight

In the days that followed our New Year's Day love-in, Justin and I talked on the phone nightly and spent every weekend together. I never thought it was possible to be involved with somebody and not argue. My parents taught me that a family that argued together, stayed together. If that were true, they would be together forever.

I would never admit this to my parents, but for me, an argument-free relationship was the brass ring, and Justin would get me there. It had taken what felt like a lifetime of screw-ups and missteps to find him, but now that I had, I planned to hang on to him forever. Candy was right again, real love rules.

My romantic reverie was broken when the phone rang. I let it go into voicemail, guessing at this hour it was Crazy Molly.

I couldn't help myself from checking the message.

"Samantha, where are you? It's already 6 a.m. and you're not in the office yet," she said. "I

251

expected you to be here by now with my chai. Since you haven't bothered to show up yet, don't bother. I need you to find a special branch of lavender for a nerve-calming potion. My therapist said it would help calm me down. I will email you the specifics. Hurry up!"

I almost called her back to tell her there's not enough lavender in the world, but I stopped myself because the love of a good man made me more patient. When Justin and I moved in together, none of this would matter anymore. He hadn't asked me yet, but it was bound to happen soon enough.

After hitting eight specialty shops without finding the exact twig of lavender that Crazy Molly required, I knew I should call her to break the news. Oh God, that was probably her ringing again now.

"No, I didn't find it yet, and I know I have let you down again, and for that, I am truly sorry. You're just so crazy. No, I mean, it's such a crazy plant," I said. "Oh, it's you, sweet pea. Love you!"

"Love you too, sugar. Where are you?"

Just the sound of his sexy voice squelched my pissy mood.

"I'm in hell, baby! Hell's Kitchen."

"Perfect. Give me your coordinates and I'll be there in ten."

This was just like him. At a random moment, he would pop up and surprise me. Sometimes he just couldn't make it through the day without seeing me, and I was more than willing to oblige him, in every sense of the word, which sometimes meant "doing it" in his undercover security van. He was always off duty when this happened. He would never put

252

the city in danger because of our hyperactive sex drive.

Before I had a chance to ponder his pecs for too long, Justin sidled up to me and joined me on the curb outside of Amy's Bread. His looks were almost as dizzying as the scent of the cherry chocolate rolls that always smothered the stench of street garbage.

"Kiss me, Pop-Tart."

His kisses could melt Iceland.

Before we had a moment to get caught up in a romantic liaison, he left me as quickly as he arrived. Duty always called. But it didn't diminish the gesture. He put terrorist-busting on hold for a moment just for the chance to see me.

His visit and the sunny haze gave me the strength to return to Molly without the lavender. As I walked to the subway station that was en route to the Upper East Side, I allowed myself to dwell on how much I loved Justin. It worried and wowed me.

We had tentative plans to celebrate our two-month anniversary. Corny, I know, but he knew how to demolish my insecurities. Right when I started to get worried about the relationship, he sensed it and would sweep in and reinforce his commitment to me. Justin's cell stopped me right before I went underground.

"Sugar, come to my apartment right after work, and pack enough stuff for the whole weekend."

"I can't wait! What are we doing?" I said.

"It's a surprise. All you have to do is prepare to be pampered. And it's a clothing optional weekend. Love you."

"Meow! See you soon."

The idea of holing up with Justin in his fabulous apartment was just what I needed to forget my work woes. He had one of those perfectly decorated Pottery Barn type pads that would be how I would style my studio if it were bigger than a thimble.

I loved his place. It was light, airy, and spacious, a perfect romantic hideaway. And his bathroom and the accompanying bath and body products rivaled the Bliss Spa. Sometimes, I wondered if it was normal for a stud like Justin to have a beauty regime that rivaled my own. But one sniff and look at him when he exited the bathroom after one of his hour-long showers and shave routines made up for the length of the cinnamon red-hot scrub.

I returned to the office, sans lavender.

"You are really a disappointment, Samantha," said Crazy Molly, looking at me with wild eyes. "I can't understand why you don't take your responsibilities seriously. When I send you on an errand, don't come back until it's completed. What's your problem?"

Could it be her unstable mental state? I scratched my nose repeatedly while she sipped her chamomile tea and glared at me.

"Forget it, Samantha. Your presence is doing nothing but pissing me off. Please leave and don't come back until you have found the lavender. Are we clear?"

"Crystal. Have a nice weekend, Molly. I will work really hard trying to find it, I promise."

"Don't try, do."

I gathered up my stuff and left before she had a

chance to change her mind. I spent the rest of the afternoon packing my heart-shaped duffle bag with sexy outfits and loungewear.

I arrived in Justin's neighborhood an hour early just to make sure I was on time. The five-degree temperatures made for a nippy walk. I tried to counter the chill factor by doing laps up and down Queens Boulevard. It paled in comparison to a Central Park jog, but Justin was the real attraction. For him, I would lift my moratorium on living in an outer borough. For him, I would move anywhere.

My fingertips were on the brink of frostbite, so I ducked into Justin's favorite diner, The T-Bone. I slurped down three hot cocoas and finally stopped myself before my face got bloated from all the chocolate. Fueled on sugar, I charged out and down the street to meet my man.

He opened the door of his love den with nothing but his FBI credentials dangling around his neck. Not even a terrorist could tackle a hunk like that. I threw my body into his nakedness and tried to neck him to the ground but my earring got caught on his badge. Aside from that, it was my sexiest move yet.

"What's on the agenda for tomorrow?" I asked as I untwined my earring from the lanyard.

"I thought I would take you shopping after we hit the T-Bone for breakfast, but that's nothing compared to what I've got planned for tonight. Devouring you, for starters."

"Meow!"

He yanked off his badge in one fluid motion, which provided an unobstructed view of his tanned, washboard stomach. I could bounce quarters off his buff bod. Tanning and full-on body shaving would not normally be my thing, especially in the middle of winter, but he wore it well. His skin was the smoothest and most sculpted I had ever felt. I guess all his bath products paid off.

Justin swept me up into a fireman shoulder hold and carried me over to his white shag area rug, where he enveloped me in his smooth and silky body. Before I had a chance to catch my breath, all my clothes were off, and he entered me. God, his penis and the way he used it was pitch perfect. I could live with him inside of me for the rest of my life. My boyfriend—the walking orgasm machine.

I relaxed into the luxury of his body for the rest of the night. We made smores by the fireplace, which heated me up, as did Justin's caressing of my nipples. We made love three more times and passed out in the hallway wrapped around each other. Somewhere in the middle of the night, he placed an olive-colored chenille blanket over us. Ever kind, ever color-coordinated.

I woke up with a latte next to my head, made just the way I like it—extra sweet. After a coffee-fueled love-making session, we got up to start our mystery weekend. At the T-Bone we sat hand in hand across from each other, drinking chai tea lattes and eating cappuccino yogurt muffins, our favorite. Justin gazed lovingly at me as I gulped down my treat. Despite the dated décor, this spot oozed romance, or maybe it was Justin.

The geriatric crowd of regulars (all female) came over to say hi. They had likely ogled him in their imaginations, just as I did. They took every opportunity to grab his forearm, pinch his chin, and some even accidentally pulled their hands through has wavy locks.

We finished up, and Justin ushered me out into the elements where it snowed lightly. The moist flakes hadn't even been trampled to a dirty death yet. We browsed in and out of boutiques, some kitschy, others elegant. Justin took me into a few of his favorite jeans and t-shirt shops. A few hours into our jaunt, I was so turned on I contemplated pushing him into an alley and doing him there. *There are not enough words to describe your behavior, but trampy comes to mind.* I thought better of it. We were in public, after all. Instead, I tried to persuade him to take me back home, feigning frosty feet.

"Baby, I have one last store I want to show you."

We glided down the street and he scooted me into a quaint jewelry shop.

"What are you doing, Pop-Tart?" I said. His lover's eyes made me melt.

"I want to buy you something special for our anniversary."

"No, you don't have to. Just having you in my life is present enough. Having you inside of me, even better," I said.

He must have caught the sexual advance, because he moved toward the exit. As we headed out of the store, I spotted a handcrafted double heart ring. It was magnificent in its simplicity.

"I need you, now," I said, pushing him out the door toward home. "You are better than any jewel could ever be."

"Okay, for now. But you have to do me a favor before you head back to my place. I knew you would be exhausted after our day, so I booked you a massage. You deserve a break, on me. Here's the gift certificate and location. You go, relax, and defrost your fingers and toes and then meet me back at the apartment afterwards, where *I'll* heat you up."

"Turnip, you are the best boyfriend ever. Don't you want to join me for a couple's massage?"

"As much as I do, I've got to run to the store to pick up some last bits for dinner," he said.

My undercarriage started to sweat at the thought of him charging down the street, FBI style, to scoop up some produce. He dipped in for one last kiss and was gone.

While my body got the once-over at the spa, I dreamt about Justin putting the rest of my body to work. It really was crazy what a difference a day made. Ever since Justin had hopped over that parking meter into my life, he lifted me into a world that I had never been privy to, a world filled with unconditional love. Having entered that domain, I vowed never to return to the land of misfit lovers ever again. Like Dr. Phil always said, you could never go back, only forward.

I sang my way home and sailed into Justin's apartment feeling sensual with my candy apple red nails, another service he arranged for me. I couldn't tell if it was my nails or his sexual scent, but my private parts throbbed.

In the time since I'd left him, he had transformed his apartment into a love nest peppered with bouquets of tulips and roses, plus a petal trail that led back to his bedroom, where he had built a castle with cinnamon-scented candles, which smelled as red hot as our union.

The rest of his abode smelled of garlic, confirming that Justin had whipped up my favorite—penne a la vodka. A man who could cook in the bedroom and the kitchen. How did I get so lucky? He sauntered out of the kitchen wearing only an apron. I had died and gone to a very non-Catholic heaven where sex before marriage was sassy instead of sinful.

"Happy Anniversary, baby," he said as he draped his barely clothed body around me. Then he pulled my shirt off and handed me a powder-pink pouch. Naked dinner for two, how delightful!

"What's this? You have already done so much. The apartment is amazing. You're amazing. Life is amazing. I could cry."

"Don't do that. You'll get the pasta soggy. Open up your gift."

I ripped open the adorable package. It was the heart-shaped ring from the jewelry store.

"Honey, you shouldn't have…" I started to say, but instead said, "I love it. I love you!"

With the candles burning, the pasta brewing, and my libido on the brink of bubbling over, I realized that for the first time in my life, I was allowing a man to love me. And it felt *amazing*.

Chapter Twenty-Nine

This year Valentine's Day would be monumental. Justin loved me. I didn't need Cupid to stick it to me this year—he would stick his magic dick into me instead. *Not if you don't ditch the trash talk.*

I planned to surprise Justin by arriving two hours early wearing a raunchy two-piece teddy under a trench coat. *Redbook* indicated that a girl had to raise the seduction stakes on Valentine's Day. Plus, I hadn't seen him for two weeks due to what I could only image was terrorist related. My outerwear *almost* protected me from the freezing pellets of rain as I ran the two blocks from the subway station to his place. While my bodice stayed dry, my hair did not. I worried my freshly highlighted bangs would freeze and break right off. But no worries, love would conquer in the end. I tapped on Justin's door.

"Hey, sugar plum! Happy Heart Day!"

I tried to look sexy by leaning on the door, but slipped. Justin caught me before I fell onto the terracotta hallway floor.

I ravished him with kisses to distract attention away from my klutzy maneuver. When that didn't work, I forced myself inside his apartment. When he failed to kiss me back, I threw open my trench coat and pushed him over to his suede, overstuffed olive chair. Something new from Pottery Barn. Then I straddled him as I fed him some of the heart-shaped salted caramel dark chocolates I bought him. My bold moves were impressive, even though it felt like Justin failed to notice. He didn't seem as eager as usual to reciprocate my affection, but perhaps my suggestive behavior had frightened him. Oprah warned that change is never easy.

"Wow, you're here early," he said.

Not exactly the warm welcome I expected.

"I needed you so badly I left early." I shushed him. "I've got plans for the extra time."

I grinned wickedly and forced him up from the chair with my other hand. I led him back to the bedroom. He looked like he might get sick. Had I fed him one too many candies?

I left the room to primp one last time. In the bathroom, I pinched my breasts to make them appear bigger than they were, and sauntered back into the bedroom. He sat on the end of the bed, looking stiff and uncomfortable. I took this as my cue to seduce him further. I pushed him back on the bed and massaged his pecs.

I couldn't tell if he enjoyed it or not. What was going on? I followed *Cosmo's* instructions for relaxing your man with a warm-handed touch. He didn't look relaxed to me. Perhaps I had skipped some crucial step. Stupid, stupid, I knew I should've written the tips on my hand.

Unfortunately, it didn't matter because Justin's privates hadn't gotten hard. This was a first. My maneuvers should have been an aphrodisiac. Was Justin one of those guys that got turned off by Valentine's Day? Some men hated the holiday.

The evening faltered, as did my attempts at initiating lovemaking. He broke the tension by giving me my gifts, which amounted to a package of herbal tea and boxer shorts. Not what I'd call romantic. I didn't even like tea unless it was chai. Boxer shorts weren't even sexy. What man wanted to de-sex a woman's look? I didn't want to offend him, so I put them on anyway.

When I returned from brushing my teeth, Justin was fast asleep and snoring. He never snored.

***

The night passed without incident, and also without intercourse. He was sweet to me, but distant; much more hands-off than usual, but maybe the rainy weather made him sad. *Or perhaps, my dear, your whorish behavior had something to do with it?*

I hoped it was just an off night, but just in case, I decided to take things up a notch by initiating kisses and hand holds. *Redbook* said men liked confident women. But maybe *Redbook* was wrong, because he kept dropping my hand as soon as I held his.

I tried not to think about how weird he was acting as we hauled it all the way to Manhattan to

Gnocco, one of our favorite Italian restaurants, but the meal was unmemorable—aside from the fact that Justin never kissed my hand once during the entire dinner. I ordered the Nutella calzone to go so I could get him back home and seduce him before bedtime, but the dessert and my body went untouched.

In the morning, I could no longer stand his standoffishness. "Hey, J, what's up? You seem distant?"

He looked away from me and sighed—the sigh women hated to hear, the one that said nothing but spoke volumes.

"Why the long face, baby? Are the terrorists getting you down?"

I tried to will my eyes to twinkle because *Glamour* said it's the best way to cut romantic tension. I prayed his distance was terrorist-related. Maybe they were plotting another attack. His ambivalence could be a covert signal for me to flee the city.

He sighed again.

"I didn't want to bring this up on Valentine's weekend, but since you asked...I feel more like roommates than lovers. Do you know what I mean?"

Did I know what he meant? Of course I had no freaking idea what he meant. A couple of weeks ago we were pouring chocolate over each other and licking it off while fornicating all over the place. A week before that, we were having multi-orgasmic sex three times a day. I was not sure what he did with past roommates, but chocolate body painting and porno sex weren't preferred activities in my book.

I tried to ignore his hurtful declaration and attempted to be the bigger person. But I was not a big person. I was small, and according to my father, self-centered. His comments cut like a dagger straight through my heart. I scratched the tip of my nose until it bled and then I cried because it hurt so much. A drop of blood fell onto his white shag rug. He sat there, not cleaning up my mess. I scrubbed at the carpet, which made the stain worse. What the hell was wrong with him, a clean freak unfazed by bodily fluids?

"Um, I don't know what you're talking about. We're totally hot for each other and in love. I'm not sure what roommates have to do with anything other than I feel comfortable enough to cut my toenails in front of you, not that I would ever do that, but, no, I have absolutely no idea what in the hell you're talking about, and I have never in my life had sex with a roommate, so no, I do not understand you," I babbled with increasing hysteria.

Like a skilled FBI agent whose survival relied on an ability to remain emotionless in times of crisis, he uttered flatly, "I'm sorry, Sam. I'm just not attracted to you anymore. I love you, but like a friend. I don't know what to do about that, do you?"

For starters, he could stop saying "friend" and start undressing me with his eyes like he used to. But no, his peeps were cold and calculating, like Bin Laden.

"I thought I'd wait and see if things changed but here we are, having what should be a romantic weekend, and all I feel like doing is playing Scrabble. And maybe we could make some popcorn."

Whatever he said after Scrabble went in my ear and out my mouth, along with breakfast, which I barfed onto his already soiled rug. I knew I shouldn't have thrown up, but I couldn't help it. Nothing could have prepared me for this total relationship about-face.

He started fiddling nervously with his button-fly jeans. Despite his harsh words, it turned me on.

"Hey, you know what, Sam? Why don't we enjoy the rest of the weekend and forget I ever said anything. Okay, baby? I'm sure I didn't mean it."

At least one of us was sure of that point.

There are things in life, which as much as you'd like to pretend you never heard them, were impossible to ignore. Being told you are no longer romantically attractive to your partner was one of them. I willed myself to forget everything he said, but not even my parents' lifelong lessons in the school of denial could deflect my mind away from obsessing on his heart-piercing words.

The rest of the weekend spiraled downward. We watched romantic comedies, played Monopoly, and binged on Cheetos and Fritos. Never once did we have sex. Valentine's Day—the demon holiday from hell.

How in the world could I have missed such a dramatic shift in his feelings toward me? I prided myself on being a realist. *Here's the reality check. It's over!*

Oprah has said that sometimes, to keep someone,

265

the best thing to do is to let them go. Temporarily, I assumed.

When he finally emerged out of his hour and a half-long bathing session, his longest to date, he moved past me and sat on the bed where he refused to look me in the eye.

"You know what, J? Why don't we take the next week to be alone and just think about everything?" I suggested, saying the exact opposite of what I felt. "Things have been too heavy lately, so let's take things light and loose for a bit."

I tried to cheerfully pack up my things as a show of my strength and maturity. Oprah's teachings better be right-on. I prayed that this tactic would make everything better, it had to—I loved this man. And not as a friend.

Justin, despite his big and beefy stature, looked like he might cry, or maybe it was me. He actually looked unmoved. Perhaps he held his tears on the inside, while I blubbered mine all over his muscular shoulder.

He did not hold me tight and tell me everything would be all right. Nor did he balk at my suggestion of "alone" time.

"Maybe you're right. Time apart might help me get out of this funk. I'll miss you," he said.

At least he didn't say, "love you, like a friend," again.

Not even a word about my upcoming birthday. He just leaned over, his massive forearms trembling, and kissed my button nose that he supposedly loved so much. Not enough to prevent him from "friending" me. It was odd how friending in the real world was nothing like being friended on Facebook. Screw Mark Zuckerberg for planting the stupid friending seed in the first place.

As he shuffled out the door to give me some space to finish packing up my stuff, he looked back at me as though we would never see each other again.

Chapter Thirty

The week that followed Valentine's Day rendered me a complete mess. I spent every hour of every day obsessively dissecting our relationship. What had gone wrong? What had I done to make him not love me anymore? Correction. To love me like a friend. *Sleeping with him out of wedlock might have had something to do with it.*

I decided that Justin still loved me even though he never bothered to call me on my thirtieth birthday. I'm the one that offered *him* space. He would not be honoring my dumb boundary if he made contact, I told myself. That would have been un-kosher. Of course he *wanted* to call.

Alone time made people realize what a good thing they had going. At least, that was what *Redbook* said. I hoped they knew what the hell they were talking about.

Even my parents had cared enough to call me and sing a boozy rendition of happy birthday over the telephone. They also invited me to spend the weekend with them in the Catskills. I was hungover from a binge-drinking night with Shannon, so I accepted their offer.

From the moment I arrived under their vacation "roof," as my father liked to refer to their kitschy A-frame cabin, he grilled me about my production job. I updated him that I'd been fired from that post months ago, and my gig with Crazy Molly didn't count as work, because her office was her home. So, in his eyes, I was unemployed.

"Honey, if you get off your high horse and agree to attend the military job fair, you can move back home, temporarily. At least it would show some form of intent on your part to get a real job," my mom said.

I smiled politely and then stared up at the corroded, vaulted ceiling, looking for a God who would deliver me away from this evil. I tried the best I could to block them out, especially when my father launched into a lecture on responsibility, pausing only to take a swig and switch gears to discuss tips on filing taxes as an independent contractor. I wanted to tell him when you earn as little as I do, it's irrelevant. But it was nice of him to care about my finances. His version of *I love you.*

Thankfully, Jimmy and Jackie joined us for the getaway. They deflected some of the attention away from me. Too bad I hadn't realized sooner that my parents had cooked up this weekend as a means for brainwashing me with their threatening career advice.

"Hey, Sam, do you have some pantyliners I could borrow?" Jackie asked.

God bless her. She knew that any mention of

such female business never failed to silence my parents. It was amazing I survived my youth without getting pregnant since my mom was too embarrassed to discuss the birds and bees. Google taught me everything I knew, which could explain Justin's decision to "friend" me.

"I sure do," I said, as my parents pretended not to hear and went to busy themselves in another room.

The cabin's bathroom felt more like an outhouse with its poopy stench and the toilet paper roll hanging from the wall with some twine. The lantern lamp on top of the back of the potty looked out of place. We were in a house, not a tent, though the décor had me wondering.

"Sam, what's wrong with you? You look horrific."

Leave it to Jackie to bust right in with a hefty dose of reality.

"Everything is a mess. Things were amazing with Justin until Valentine's Day. Then he used the words 'friends' and 'not attracted to me' in the same sentence. I offered him space to think, assuming he would never agree, but he did. He couldn't push me out of his apartment fast enough," I wailed.

"Sam, I hate to be the one to break this down for you, but it's over. Giving a man time to think is never a good idea." She looked at me with that married person's pity pout. "You should've talked to me before you did that. Break up with him now. Show yourself some respect."

I wasn't quite sure how to digest her advice, so I

excused myself before I started to cry. Jackie hated crybabies. So did my parents. I snuck out onto the back deck and inhaled as much air as possible. I wanted to dismiss the reality of what she said, but couldn't.

The frigid temps made me choke on my own breath. I ducked down out of sight from what was sure to be a roomful of drunken stares. I dry-heaved until something stopped me. I bowed down.

"Dear Lord, I know it's been awhile, and I'm sure you have a lot more deserving, church-going souls to save, but I'm desperate. I promise if you help me this one last time, I'll, I don't know, I'll start going to church again…" I stared up at the sky waiting for an answer, but got only the icy glint of the Milky Way in return.

"Okay, I'll definitely go back to church. If you're listening, I hope you can help. I met the love of my life, which is hard for me to believe, but I did. Unfortunately, I made a huge blunder."

"What are you doing out there?" my mother shouted out the kitchen window. "It's like you're trying to avoid us. Get in here before your tater tots get cold. A jazz concert is on TV. You know how your father loves jazz."

My father never liked jazz. He listened to it because my mother made him. That apparently made him an aficionado. She slammed the window shut, just like Justin had slammed the door on our love affair.

"Hopefully, you're not in the habit of making people pay for their sins, since I've built up quite a list. Anyway, maybe just this once, you could make

Justin love me again. Amen."

Looking out at the black, cold Catskill abyss, I prayed for some ethereal signal to show me God had heard. I shivered as I waited for a sign that never came.

"Screw you," I said.

Dusting the pine needles off my knees, I stormed into the kitchen, grabbed my parents' box of white zinfandel, and downed three gulps straight out of the spigot. Per Mom's orders, I grabbed a fistful of tater tots and swallowed them whole. I needed power food if I hoped to make it through the night.

"You look like hell. Where have you been?" my father asked when I rejoined the party.

"To church, ha, ha, ha! We should play a fun drinking game, 'Never Have I Ever.' We go around the room sharing tidbits of information, like *never have I ever* gone *without washing my clothes for an entire month.* If you *have* washed your clothes, you take a sip of wine. Does that sound fun?"

It was a tad devilish, appealing to my parents' drunken tendencies, but if it helped distract them from my love life and work situation, it would be worth it.

"Sure," my father replied, already half in the bag.

"I'll start," my mother said, standing for effect. "Never have I ever skipped going to church on Sunday."

I raised my glass until she glared me down. They slurped their wine, clearly not getting the gist of the game. They were devout churchgoers, if nothing else.

"Never have I ever disgraced my family by

living out of wedlock," my father said, waiting for me to imbibe.

"Or disrespected my parents," he continued.

I sat complacently, not drinking, and ruminated on the concept of a non-boozing parental unit. My mother looked ready to attack.

"Dear, please, just drink. You're not fooling anyone. This game is a real kick!" she said, drinking after every word. "Never have I ever disgraced the family by getting divorced like a cheap, sinning hussy."

I had created a monster.

Jimmy and Jackie sat on the sidelines, speechless and sober. They could see where this was headed and they wanted ringside seats for the showdown. It was like a family game of badminton. The box of wine served as the birdie.

I held my mother's gaze. "Never have I ever had sex before marriage," I said, pausing for effect, and then gulped down an entire glass. This game *was* fun.

"Never have I ever had sex for pleasure," I said, watching as horror distorted their faces. With great pride, I cocked the box back, poured myself more wine, and drank it in one smooth swig. Then I belched to nobody in particular and moved onto the burnt orange beanbag chair on the floor. I felt tingly and triumphant, but inexplicably gassy. I burped one more time, and then continued.

"Never have I ever disowned my daughter, repeatedly."

I waited for them to raise a Dixie cup, and then pushed the box to my father, but nothing, so I spoke louder.

"Never have I ever disowned my daughter. Do you not hear me?" I screamed into my father's squinty eyes. "Are you all unable to reach the box?" I got up and lifted the contraption up to his chafed chin. When he failed to start drinking, I filled up his cup until it overflowed, and then moved on to my mother's. I poured wine into her cup until it also spilled over the rim. They flinched away, splashing wine everywhere.

"That should give you both enough to quench your thirst for a few seconds," I said.

"Sam, cut it out," Jimmy interjected. He always took my father's side.

"Show your mother and me some respect. Clean up this mess," my father said, "and while you're at it, why don't you clean up your mess of a life?"

He burped and spit spewed from his mouth. Sweat dripped off his face. His rank breath and BO permeated the room. I almost hurled.

"You have disrupted our jazz, Samantha," my mother said. "Please leave the cabin until you're ready to apologize."

Then *she* belched at me. There was a reason that people over the age of ten should not eat tater tots!

"Ever since you divorced yourself from your husband of barely a year, you have become gross to me," my mother said. "You are so ugly you must take ugly pills."

"Mom, come on. You don't mean that," Jimmy said. It was about damn time he stepped in to mediate this mess.

"Who says that to someone? Take it back," I

wailed.

She took another swig and said, "You drove me to…" and slipped into the puddle of spilled booze on the floor. "Why are you still here?" she cried in her dry heaving/hiccup kind of way.

I went to the kitchen, grabbed a roll of paper towels, and ran back to the family room where I wiped up all of the wine and grabbed the box and slammed it back down on the table in front of my father.

"In case you didn't hear me," I said, "never have I ever disowned my daughter."

I waited for either one of them to chug their wine. I looked for the slightest hand movement toward their cups, but nobody lifted anything. Somebody had to take control of the situation, and from the looks of Jackie and Jimmy, it would have to be me. I picked up the box, opened the spout, and dumped the rest of the wine down my throat, spilling the last sips all over my rose-colored turtleneck. I wore it to give me strength against my family. *Vogue* said red was making a comeback as a power color. I wasn't sure if it was working.

"That drink was on your behalf, Father."

I walked down the hall to grab my iPhone and lingered as I passed by the entrance of the "family" room. Ours was anything but.

Dipping my head back into the room, I said, "Your wine tastes like asshole. Fitting, considering the company."

I didn't bother waiting for a response. I walked out and slammed the rickety door behind me as I started down the dark dirt path leading to who knew where. I paused for a moment to look through the window. Everybody looked so peaceful without me, lounging around the fireplace sipping wine as if nothing had happened.

***

After a stumbling walk through the woods, I hit the main road and landed at the only bar in town. It stank like raw sewage and beer, but I felt at peace for the first time since Justin "friended" me. It was somehow fitting that I was most comfortable surrounded by fellow degenerates, all of whom appeared to want nothing more than a cold, wet drink, or in my case, three Alabama Slammers. Like Mama always said, alcohol could cure anything.

"Do you think I appear lovable?" I asked the outdoorsy-looking bartender. He wore his red flannel shirt well. It made *him* look powerful. He just smiled.

"Have you ever been disowned by your family and sort of dumped by your boyfriend, all in the same week?"

"Wow, that's rough. How can you be sort of dumped? Either you are or you aren't. I don't think there's a gray area when it comes to breakups. I'm Tomas," he said.

I felt like throwing my shooter at his chiseled face, but I thought better of it. Never insult the barkeep, my father always said. Tomas sure was a looker. His square, shapely hands reminded me of Justin's.

"Well, what would you call it when the love of

your life says he likes you like a roommate and is no longer attracted to you? That's a pseudo-breakup, don't you think?

"Maybe."

"Then I offered him space, alone time. Do you think I did the right thing?"

He looked away awkwardly. I slurped down the rest of my shooter, pounded my shot glass on the bar, and then flipped it upside down to ensure he understood it was empty.

"That is a bad week. I don't recommend giving a guy space. We find way too many things to do to pass the time, if you know what I mean," he said.

Unfortunately, I knew exactly what he meant.

"Well, flip that. I'm not going to wait around for him to break up with me. You know what? He can come back to me all he wants. It won't matter. Sammy's sex shop is closed for business. Roommate? What the fuck," I said, burping up more tater tots. *Jesus Christ, what is wrong with you? Your mouth is ugly and so are you.*

"I divorce him! Two more shots, Tomas. Ha, that rhymes. Doesn't it?"

"Wait a second, you're married?" he asked, taking me too literally. "You didn't tell me that. You know, you may want to think twice. My mother always says divorce is not the answer."

Figures. Tomas was just another guilt-ridden Catholic masquerading as a bartender. He was no longer cute.

"Can you just get me another shot?"

He left and I bumbled back to the ladies' room to practice my breakup speech.

"Screw sensible speak!" I said to the women in the stall next to me, and then I dialed.

"Hello, Just-friends Justin, is that you? No, no stupid voicemail. Whatever, you'll hear this eventually. It's your girlfriend, the one you love, like a roommate."

I hung up and slouched against the stall door, trying to collect my jumbled thoughts and quell my nausea. I went to the sink to splash water on my face. Some stupid girl named Sally had scrawled *love rules and so does Jules,* all over the bathroom wall. I hope Jules one day "friends" Sally—her handwriting is crap. The trash can overflowed with tampons, and the stench made me gag. I did some deep puffs, just like *Shape* had depicted in last month's issue. I redialed.

"And yes, you judgmental man-boob, I'm drinking and loving every minute of it. How could you do this to me after all we shared, after the memories, and the sex? The sultry, stupid sex, I knew it was evil. Well, stuff it."

I continued to rant as I peed. "And no, I do not want to be your friend or roommate, you loser. I can't take your girly bath and body products any longer. Friends, for fuck sake, you overgrown, over polished man-boy. We were in love. People don't float seamlessly from love to friendship and for fuck sake, roommates. They're just people to share rent with. By the way, your voicemail message is fruity. So, take this, you buff, muscled freak. I am no longer in love with you. Stick it!"

I contemplated hanging up, but was unable to stop myself. As I exited the stall, a plump redhead tried to squeeze her way in front of me at the sink. I blocked her and continued my rant.

"And, by the way, Mr. Fancy Pants, you're not kidding anyone. You're obviously gay because what hetero man pays that much attention to grooming details and keeps the entire Bath and Body Works lotion and gel collection in their medicine chest? You're supposed to be an FBI agent for Christ's sake. Why don't you grow a pair?"

I waved my fired-up hands toward the sink, indicating to the redhead that my work there was done.

On a tell-off high, I continued my dialing diatribe by ringing Crazy Molly's office.

"Hello, Molly's goofy-dopy phone message. Even though you are a communications maven, you blow. Couldn't you come up with a better greeting than that? And you know what else? You're bonkers. You can take your stupid job and your ridiculous plants and stuff them down your Botoxed pie-hole! And, by the way, just because you send amazing wine baskets after berating people, it does not make up for your bitchery. Suck it, bitch!"

Wow, I felt invigorated. If only I had known of the buzz and balls you can grow by drinking boxed wine, I would have adopted it into my drinking repertoire years ago.

The bathroom started to spin, making me do my sexy dance into the bar. Everyone, including my now estranged bartender, stared at me. They just wished they had half the balls I did. I should break up with perfectly sculpted men more often. It felt fabulous. I sat back on my bar stool and dialed Justin's number again. It went straight to voicemail. Where the hell was he?

"And just so were clear, ha, this is one hell of a voicemail, ain't it? Just know this. I'm divorcing myself from our relationship. Seriously, who wants to be having sex with a gay man-friend? Aside from the obvious AIDS and genital warts issues, it's just stupid. Men and women can never be just friends. You should know that since you've seen *When Harry Met Sally* at least a million times. Sex is always going to get in the way, except for you because I have turned you gay, and you probably like anal sex with men. Have a good life, goodnight, and good luck! You're so ugly with those bulging muscles, you must take ugly pills. Wait, no that's me, whatever, beat it."

I flicked my phone off, and returned to my barstool.

"Wow, I feel so much better. You were right, dude. If you're the breaker-upper, it is so much better."

"Huh?" Tomas said.

"Whatever, it's all good. Do you know where I could catch a lift back to the city? This mountain air is making me want to vomit."

Charming, dear, this is why your husband divorced you.

"Look, just hang out here. You can't head out on your own. I'll find someone to cover for me, and give you a ride to the train station," he said, and then he winked.

***

I woke up the next morning on the floor of my apartment, not sure how I got there, but with a new understanding of why cheap wine and making out with cute bartenders didn't mix. Note to self: boycott boxed wine. Its after-effects could explain why my parents were always so cranky and plagued by chronic diarrhea.

I finally made it off the floor and fetched my phone. There were voicemails. See, somebody does love me, Mother, no matter how ugly I am to you. I swathed my forehead with a cool cloth as I played back the messages. I felt barf brimming.

Message 1: "Hey, baby, it's me. I've been thinking about you all week. You were right. I just needed a little time. In the past, I've had a tendency to run from commitment when things get too close, but I love you more than ever, and I'm ready to really do this, for good this time. I need to make love to you up and down my new sheepskin rug. I'm rock hard for you, always have been. Roommates, seriously, what was I thinking? I will love you always, promise."

Gulp.

"I love you too, baby!" I shouted out the window, and then ran to the bathroom to puke.

As I stood hunched over my toilet, a disturbing string of flashbacks played in my mind. Cheap wine, parental showdown, more wine, dive bar, Alabama slammers, drunk dials, oh my. What have I done? *Well, you've once again made a mess of things. You're like relationship repellant.*

Message two: "Samantha, just so you understand us, because you can be slow on the uptake at times, you are not welcome in our home or lives. P.S. Your father also agrees."

Delete.

Message three: "Just got your messages, baby. Wow, I'm sorry I hurt you. I need to see you. How about Friday night at eight? You know the place. I love you."

Repeat message. Repeat, and fall to the toilet bowl. Damn, I was an idiot. Note to self two: must stop drinking someday soon.

How was it possible that despite everything I did, this man still loved me? Clearly, he must be atoning for some horrible sin.

Could it be true? Somebody finally loved me, drunk-dialing, ugly pills, and all.

Chapter Thirty-One

I was super excited to see Justin, but also super sick. Like vomit sick, and no, I had not been drinking this time. I had been resting, cradled in my bed, ever since the Catskills. Lovesick, I guess. But tonight was our reunion, so I had to rally.

At seven o'clock, I willed my body to get up but couldn't move. Then my phone rang, forcing the issue.

"Hello."

"Samantha, we do not want you to say anything. Just sit there and listen. We are on our way to see the priest to figure out how to excommunicate you out of the church and our family, for good."

Yet they continued to call me.

Besides, I wasn't even sure that was possible, but the Catholics *were* experts at excommunications. Whatever, I was about to leave that behind and meet my non-gay, dreamboat boyfriend. I deserved true love just like everyone else. *Well, that's debatable. You are more unlovable than ever.*

I really could turn devastation into destiny when

I put my mind to it; I could also look fetching when reclaiming my man is the mission. Who cared if those people disowned me? I could just start a family of my own—with Justin. I took one last peek in the mirror, primped myself, and dashed out of my apartment.

***

As I entered Rue B, Justin's lips met mine at the door. His muscles, among other things, appeared to be throbbing.

Before I had ample time to soak it all in, a jazz trio started playing a soulful rendition of "Have I Told You Lately That I Love You." Justin fumbled in his shirt pocket, causing his muscles to bulge even more. This seemed to go on for an inordinate amount of time, until *it* fumbled out. And then *it* continued to bounce gingerly to the floor where *it* just sat, staring and sparkling at me, like only the finest diamond could do.

Marriage? I panicked at the prospect, puking, first on his beautifully exposed forearm, and then all over the diamond ring. Without any attempt to wipe my barf off him or the ring, I darted out of the restaurant and down the block. I stopped just long enough to see Justin standing on the corner.

It could have been bad eyesight, but even from afar, Justin's beautiful eyes were glistening—and not a joyous glisten, more like weeping. I started to make a move back in his direction. *Go after him. This is your best shot at redemption!* But something stopped me. I turned and ran in the other direction,

284

never once looking back until I hit the 14th Street subway stop. I tumbled down into the station and leaped into the waiting subway car. *Oh, you moronic loser, what have you done?*

Chapter Thirty-Two

I peered out the window and accepted there was no turning back. I was stuck on a 747, jetting across the Atlantic. I tried to quell my urge to purge. Vomiting at the aerial view of Lady Liberty would not be a good way to start an eight-hour flight to Rome. Even though barfing at all the wrong times and places had become my thing lately, plane puking seemed like a fate to be avoided. Nobody wants to be seated next to a barf bagger.

Despite no longer being a legit Catholic due to the supposed excommunication, I found myself drawn to some of the trappings of the religion, like going to church for solace, and confession for forgiveness. *It's a little late to start saving your soul, dear. It has already been damned to hell.* My sins were so plentiful a power-confession session at the Vatican seemed like the only option for me.

I swear I wasn't running from my life. I always wanted to make the pilgrimage to Rome, City of God, Homeland of the Catholic Church, Land of the Lord. It wasn't Justin's proposal either. I'd had enough of New York. Sure, it was the city of dreams, and destiny, and whatever other crap the media used to market the town, but it was also the city of terrorists, gigantic rats, stinky sewage, and minuscule overpriced apartments. I was over it.

Marriage didn't seem like the right move. Not for me. Especially since I'd skipped the annulment, and as such, in the world according to Catholicism, I was technically still married. Plus, Justin's pecs dwarfed my less than ample bosoms. No woman should ever marry a guy that had bigger boobs than her own, even if his were all muscle.

Determined in my new mission, I popped an Ambien, closed the window shade, and blocked out New York, along with everyone and everything that went with it.

***

The Italian public transport system was not nearly as unreliable as *Lonely Planet* claimed it to be, especially coming down off of an Ambien hangover. It was blissful. As were the Italian people. I paced around the cobblestone streets of Vatican City for two hours until a pauper girl barked at me in terse Italian. I let her meanness slide, and defying *Lonely Planet's* orders, I slid her one American dollar in hopes of placating her enough to not rob me.

I jostled through the crowds that swarmed the metropolis, eventually ending up at the steps of the church. The massive nature of the building within the walled confines of the most religious city in the universe caused me to suddenly sob.

Now that you've finally made it to church, buck up and get inside. It might take you a lifetime to be absolved of your sins, and you ain't getting any younger.

Once I'd cried myself dry, I shuffled awkwardly inside the cathedral to ask for God's forgiveness. I'd flown across the goddamn globe for this moment—my sins deserved absolution.

The church was mobbed inside, even more so than around its periphery. The gigantic ceilings threatened to scare me right out—but I persevered. The ethereal stained glass windows were the only things that showed weakness. I stopped short at a pyramid of candles. In a Catholic church, this was where you're supposed to drop money in a bin, light a candle, and pray for someone in need of redemption. My mother had been lighting candles on my behalf ever since I hit puberty. Instead of wasting my wishes on another, I decided to pray for the strength to confess my own sins.

Making the sign of the cross in rapid succession, I stopped long enough to throw twenty euros into the bin. Would buying your way out of Hell be frowned upon? This generous gift on my part caused me to cry a little more forcefully, until the little Italian woman next to me stared so intensely I felt guilty for occupying the space. I couldn't be certain, but I thought she gestured with her head in the direction of the confessional, as if to prod me toward the booth.

What the hell, I thought. *I might as well get it over with so that I could begin to enjoy my life abroad.* Sweat engulfed my armpits. *Oh shit, just step up for once in your life.* I walked toward the confessional and tried to organize my thoughts to determine which of my screw-ups were most significant. Despite overthinking my confession strategy all the way from New York to Rome, I still hadn't decided if I should go in worst-to-not-so-bad order, or start with an alphabetized list.

I ended up in the line for a face-to-face confession but worried if that would be too close. The priest might be able to catch me in a lie if my eye twitched. Not that I would do that...but just to be safe, I moved to another confessional line where the Italian elder in front of me proceeded to glare.

"Sorry I ended up in the wrong place," I mumbled, looking down. "I need a partitioned confessional. Sorry, I forgot my glasses. God bless." If you tell white lies while inside the church, did that count as a true sin, or a means of survival?

In choosing this option, the priest would know I wasn't tough enough to go face-to-face, but it was worth not having to make eye contact with him.

I stood in the wimp's line for nearly an hour where I contemplated getting the hell out of the blessed fossil of a church. *For the love of God, would someone stop her from leaving?*

As I peeled out of line, a wobbly old man opened up another confessional and invited me in. Oh, for shit's sake. It would probably be a sin to deny a priest's beckon. I walked forward.

"Inglés, do you speak Inglés?"

He nodded.

"Hello, sir, and thank you for opening this up for

me. You really didn't need to, I swear I would have come back. I just needed to get a gelato. It is so hot in here. Don't you think it's hot? I mean, I could go get gelato for both of us. Yes, that's what I'll do. I'll be right back."

"Gelato is not necessary, my child. Let's continue," he said and nodded at me in that condescending way that only a priest can conjure. *Oh, would you just shut up, you moron, and confess.* "Okay, well if you insist, I guess I'll save the gelato for later."

"All right then, why don't you step in here next to me. Face-to-face confessions are more productive and intimate."

Mind? Of course I minded, you bloody old geezer! Isn't intimacy in inappropriate places what got priests into trouble in the first place? Sinning is not supposed to be about intimacy, unless you have committed various forms of adultery, which okay, I guess in the right situations it could be intimate. *Shut up, you idiot, and get in there!* Feeling pressured, I walked into the confessional and sat right across from the priest.

"Whenever you are ready, you can begin."

"Well, hum, you know, I'm not totally comfortable in here. It's, well, you know, disturbingly quiet, and I really wouldn't want the neighboring confessor to hear what I have to say, because, truth be told, Father, I'm a wreck. I just turned thirty, and I've been sinning a lot more than I ever thought was possible. Oh shit, do you have any idea what I mean? Hopefully you hear this all the time. Well, not the cursing. Sorry about that. I meant the sinning part." *Profanities are a sin, you bozo. Most people are not stupid enough to actually commit more sins while confessing. Can't you do anything right?*

"Why don't we start with the basics? How about we discuss the last time you went to church? Just breathe, you can rest assured nothing will surprise me. I'm a very old man."

Breathe? Breathing, for Christ's sake! Why was it that everybody kept telling me to breathe, as if that would end all the troubles in life, and just cause everything to "poof" and disappear? Like breathing was anything different than what we do every goddamn day. I mean, we do it to stay alive, so it was condescending, in some ways, telling someone to breathe. Wasn't that a given, and our God-given right as humans?

"Well, church attendance probably isn't the best place to start considering my record, but okay," I began, overcoming my reservations in the interest of getting this over faster. "Forgive me, Father, for I have sinned. I have not been to church in a couple of months." *Please, stop with the lies.* "Okay, several months. I try to go every year at Christmas, not last year, but the one before that. Is that bad? I mean, well never mind, of course it's bad, because as Catholics, we're supposed to go to church every week, but I'm not sure how that is possible. I am single, alone, divorced, and trying to support myself. Plus, I'm a whore whose been kicked out of my own family. But why get caught up on these technicalities? Trust me, there are much worse things for me to confess, I promise. Wow, this is

291

really nerve-wracking. I tend to babble when I'm nervous, and sometimes I even throw up, but I'll try to keep both to a minimum. Has anyone else ever done that? Hurled in here? That would be embarrassing and probably hard to clean off these old floors. Sorry, I'll stop talking now. Is there a restroom nearby, in case the urge to purge becomes too much to handle?"

Why was it that everything "Catholic" was a struggle? Is this really what Jesus Christ had in mind when he suffered and died on the cross for our salvation?

"Remember, dear, just breathe," the geezer said. "Are you ready to continue? There is no need to worry, you can skip to the big stuff if you prefer."

I nervously panned the coffin-like confessional, squashed next to a priest who may or may not be perverted and have a tendency to fiddle with innocent little boys. Who knew what to believe these days? I knew I was supposed to be breathing away my problems, but decided to screw breathing—I just needed to confess and get a gelato.

"Well, I alluded to the whorish behavior, but I guess I should be more specific. I inadvertently engaged in an adulterous affair. It bears mentioning that I did not know it was adultery at the time, because he was supposed to be getting divorced. Maybe that means it doesn't count. But then I did come to learn that he wasn't divorced. But it was too late. I was already porking him, and in love with him. But the adulterous intent was not there initially. One could argue that maybe it didn't count, right?"

"You might be missing the higher issue."

"Really?"

"Were *you* married when this entanglement transpired?"

"No, of course not, absolutely not. I was already divorced by that time. Long since divorced. Did you mean the whole sex before marriage thing? We did do that. Does that still really apply nowadays? Because it just seems like…well, it's not socially acceptable to withhold sex until marriage. Believe me, I tried for a really long time, and then it was looking like I was coming dangerously close to dying a very young spinster."

"Oh, so you were once married and then divorced? Was your marriage annulled?"

Here we go. Talk about digging myself into a ditch, or more realistically, my own tomb. What could I have been thinking, coming here?

"Well, no, not technically…" I rationalized. "I just couldn't handle the added pressure at the time. The guilt over my affair had stifled me. Ending my marriage over it made things even worse. So an annulment seemed more than I would've been able to handle…" I trailed off before resuming my babble with renewed gusto. "I guess, in that instance, it was most definitely adultery because I was married to Sheldon, even though he left me for dead out in Colorado." *Oh, would you listen to yourself? You're disgusting.* "Holy shit, I'm disgusting. I've had two affairs. And you know what? I cuss all the time and I never go to church, I lied before, I don't even go at Christmas. And you wanna know what else? I hate my ex-husband and

293

my parents for driving me to do all of this. And I know that I am not supposed to hate anybody, but I do. My parents, you know what they do? What their version of unconditional love is? It's excommunication. That's what it is! They kept kicking me out of their house whenever I did something they didn't approve of. And when I became too old to get thrown out of their home, they kicked me out of the family instead. I can understand being angry or disappointed, but are you really supposed to dislike your children to such a degree that you excommunicate them? Is that even possible? Oh, fuck. Look who I'm asking—you people invented the sport!"

"If you don't mind, I'm going to have to ask you to keep your voice down; this is a place of worship," the priest said kindly but firmly. "I am here to help you reach redemption, but you need to control yourself. Would you like a tissue?"

A tissue? These people are always trying to cover up something, whether it was sobbing sinners or altar-boy molestation—who was kidding who?

"Sorry, but I just needed to say it. I hate my parents, and I hate this church, and I hate myself. I make myself sick; that's how much I hate myself." *Don't worry, dear, we echo the sentiment.* "Don't look so worried, I'm not going to puke, I'm too angry," I said. "But you know who I don't hate? Justin. Oh shit. What have I done? He is a wonderful man who miraculously seems to love me despite all of my screw-ups. He only temporarily stopped loving me that one time, but then he rebounded and wanted to marry me. And I left him," I shouted through the tears. *Pull yourself together, you pussy. You're at church.*

With one quick grab for a hankie, I blew my nose, made a sign of the cross, excused myself from the confessional, and ran out of the church. I cried like my mother with dry heaves so violent that I vomited all over the steps of the Vatican. I had arrived.

***

One would think that after all the physical and mental purging, I would be ready to enjoy my trip and grab some gelato. Instead, I sat paralyzed on the steps of the Vatican.

Sitting on the godly stoop, I caught the eye of a little old man who stared at me, and then made the sign of the cross at me. What the fuck? *Clearly, neither the grand stature of the church, nor your embarrassing confession, has done anything to curtail your gutter mouth.*

Complete and total strangers could tell I needed redemption just by looking at me. The man continued to stare and make the sign of the cross. Who was this goon?

"No speaky Italiano!" I screamed at him.

He made another sign of the cross and flicked his head as if to direct me back into the church.

I ran back inside, pushing down the aisle through the throngs of pilgrims, tourists, and Romans, ending up in one of the pews at the front of the church. A larger-than-life-sized statue of the Virgin Mary and Jesus Christ stood before me. The fake

Christ's eyes leered down at me. Talk about stone-faced.

My body bobbled so much I hit my head on the pew, which at least stopped my aggressive dry heaves. The last time I cried this hard was at my wedding.

Sucking back my urge to keep crying, I stared up to Heaven, folded my sweaty hands together, and began to speak out loud. "My life is beyond my own control. My misguided steps and indiscretions are countless. I have torched every job and romantic relationship in my life, and the only time I seem to be able to cry is in a goddam church. I don't know what the hell that is all about, but it's certainly ill-timed. Sorry. I can't seem to stop cursing either. No matter how hard I try, the screw-ups just keep coming. It's my own fault. I hate my life and everybody in it, and as much as I want to get things together, I can't seem to figure out what keeps getting in my way..." *Perhaps it's your cheap, tawdry, ways.* I tried to stop myself, but couldn't. "I know that I'm a good person, but I keep fucking things up. Sorry, I mean screwing up. Everything I have tried to avoid in my life, I've ended up doing in spades, including my divorce and a landslide of adulterous affairs. I need an answer and I need one quick, because I have run out of places to hide. For the love of God, can't you help me? For Christ's sake, can't anybody up there help me? I need some mother-fucking help! Hello, God, are you listening to me? I need a sign that you hear me and are open to forgiving me! Hello?"

"Excuse me, miss, but I'm going to have to ask

you to leave. This is a place of worship and peace," said the nun who appeared at my pew.

It was official. I had been officially kicked out of the church. Finally, I was successful at something. This should make my parents happy and maybe even make them love me again.

***

I stood at the exit gates of Vatican City, looking back at the most striking church I had ever seen— massive and wistful in its old age. I was not welcome.

Running with the speed of a cougar, I screeched through the gateway and continued hauling down the cobbled streets of Rome. I ran for miles it seemed, until I hit Trevi Fountain, thick with crowds of obnoxious tourists who clicked their cameras and clacked in stupid faux-Italian accents. The nakedness and offensive nature of the statues, all connected by water, glared at me.

Why was it that all Italian sculptures involved naked men? It wasn't very holy. My *Lonely Planet* guidebook said that if you threw one coin in the fountain, it ensured that you would return to Rome. Two coins meant you would find romance, and three guaranteed you would marry or divorce. Having committed it all plus multiple counts of adultery, it was hard to determine where I fit into the equation.

Screw *Lonely Planet*. Just because we read their books didn't mean we were destined for a lifelong sentence of loneliness. I tossed a coin in the fountain, and then another and another. As each landed with a dull plunk, I shed a tear. I couldn't stop myself from crying or coin tossing until I took the entire contents of my travel purse and dumped it into the holy water. Then I bawled and heaved so loudly and with such force I fell over onto the marble landing of the fountain, with my sundress flying up over my head and my face inches from the pool filled with global currencies. Maybe it was time to start eating carbs again.

I felt the leers of seedy tourists everywhere staring down and judging me. *They're not judging. They're laughing at you.*

Laying at the foot of the fountain with my tattered Strawberry Shortcake underwear exposed, I felt someone tap my shoulder and then assist me by pulling my dress down to an appropriate level.

"Are you okay?" asked an oddly familiar voice. "Jesus, Sam, is that you?" It was unmistakably the voice of my ex, Sheldon.

Holy God. I sat there stunned, unable to process his presence in this place. I looked at the nerdy tourists with their khaki shorts, knee-high white tube socks, and sneakers, and then back at Sheldon. Yep, he was definitely still there; I hadn't imagined it. Then I saw that stupid old man from the Vatican. He made the sign of the cross at me again. What in God's name was he doing here? Or, more to the point, what was Sheldon doing here? He hated traveling. And Rome was the city of romance, religion, and history; all things he deplored. And who was he here with? He never took me to Italy.

"Sam, let me help you up. You've got to be

uncomfortable down there."

Well, that was profound. I was sitting on the ground in children's print undies that were ripped and slightly soiled, since I was traveling light and re-wearing underwear inside out to economize space. And now they were stained further by the ancient puddle slop of Trevi Fountain water.

Sheldon reached out his hand to me and for a minute my mind raced back to a scene from our wedding when he had extended his hand out to me, guiding me away from my family's debauchery. Now, after all this time, here he stood framed between the ancient rocks of the fountain. I willed him to help me up off the ground and whisk me to safety, despite everything I had done to him.

I realized that I should say something but couldn't conjure the appropriate words, so I just said, "Okay." And then I stared at him with a solo tear trickling down my sunburned cheek. As I gathered my words, out of the corner of my eye I saw the stupid Vatican man again, who made another sign of the cross at me.

"What are you staring at, bozo?" I shrieked, as if the coin throwing and sundress peepshow wasn't enough to draw attention.

"Sorry, Sheldon, I didn't mean to scream in your ear. Who are you doing it here with? Sorry, I mean, what are you doing here? Fancy meeting you here at church. Well, close to a church. A big, honking church. Never mind, you get what I mean, right? Well, I'm not even sure I know what I mean, so how could I expect you to understand anything about me…"

"Sam, just breathe."

Again with the bloody breathing.

"I think you might be in shock from the fall."

"Yeah, I guess you're right, but sorry, it's just weird."

I still could not stop staring at Vatican man, who was bobbing in the background, trying to hijack my attention back toward my sins.

"Sam, I hate to leave you like this. But I'm running late for the conference," Sheldon said. "I'm on a speaker symposium panel about event security in a time of crisis. But maybe we could meet up later in the week for lunch or something? It would be nice to catch up with you, if you're up for it."

I stared at him, and then prayed to God silently. *You ought to be doing a lot more than praying. Get back to church and try to get confession right this time.*

I prayed for the strength to say something appropriate. Tears welled up in my eyes as Vatican Man circled like a vulture and continued to make signs of the cross at me.

"Well gee, maybe," I said.

"Whatever you feel comfortable with. I just thought with us both being here, in Rome of all places, we should take it as some sort of sign that maybe it's time to talk."

Gulp.

"Well, why don't you just think on it?" he said. "It's really good to see you. Here's the number for the hotel where I'm staying. It would mean a lot if we were able to get together."

Ha, I knew it. He did learn something from me

after all—the Catholic guilt trip.

All I could do was nod in his general direction as I struggled to hold back tears. He looked at me with the innocence of a school boy, then turned abruptly and left me at the very spot where he had picked me up out of a puddle only a few minutes ago.

As I watched Sheldon peel away from the crowd, I could also see Vatican Man following him, until he turned in my direction and made an exaggerated sign of the cross. I blinked my eyes to flush away the tears. When I could see clearly again, both of them were gone.

Chapter Thirty-Three

I composed myself enough to walk away from the fountain and made it to a rickety old bench under a gnarly olive tree. My hands trembled but I steadied them so I could fetch my cell phone, which I'd stowed in my bra for safe keeping. *Lonely Planet* said to keep electronics out of the sight of pickpockets while traveling. Thankfully I listened, so my phone did not share the same soggy fate as my purse when it went airborne into the fountain.

I took three deep breaths, just like the priest had ordered, and in between sniffles, dialed. Thank God I had opted for the international calling plan.

"Oh, Christ, just bloody pick up. Oh, sorry about that, Dad. I didn't notice you'd answered."

"Of course you didn't, because even after that failed attempt at a career in the tech industry, you still can't manage to operate a cell phone correctly. No wonder you lost that job."

He hadn't changed.

"I didn't lose it, Dad. The company never went public, and as a result, I was downsized. It's not the same. I got stock options as part of the deal."

"Whatever. What do you want, Samantha? In case you've forgotten, we weeded you out of the family," he said.

"Well, I just thought I would say hi. You know, see how you guys were doing since it's been a while."

"What do you need?"

"Nothing really, I just...well, is Mom there? I sort of wanted to talk to her."

"Oh, Christ, what have you done? Did you go and get yourself knocked up? Susan, get on the phone. Your daughter is on the line. We're on speaker. Spit it out. Anyway, where are you? This connection is lousy."

I heard the sound of my mother picking up the phone.

"What do you want, dear?" she asked.

"Just to clarify, I am not knocked up, so you can rest another night," I said. When no one spoke, I continued. "I just, well the craziest thing just happened. I was at church going to confession—did you hear that, Mom? The Vatican really is as beautiful as you said. And you will never guess who I ran into!"

"Would you just get to the point, dear?" my mother said.

"Sheldon. Can you believe that?" I said, trying to inspire interest.

"What did you just say?" my father asked.

Finally, I had someone's attention.

"Sheldon, my husband—well, ex-husband. After all this time, isn't that wild?"

303

"Where did you say you were? It sure as hell sounded like you said the Vatican," Dad said.

"That's in Rome, dear," my mother added.

"Yes, I know that. I'm not a moron, Susan. That's reserved for your daughter."

"That's where I am; I'm in Rome," I assured them. "I went to confession, Mom. I thought you'd want to know. And that's where I ran into Sheldon—well, not in the confessional, but here in Rome. He wants to have lunch with me. I don't know if I should go, you know, dredging up all those old memories…and, well, I'm not sure if spending time with him is the healthiest thing for me at this point in my life."

"What exactly are you doing with your life, dear?" my mother said, ignoring my subtle plea for help. "First, you want this man, who, in case you've forgotten, we didn't recommend you marrying in the first place. Then, as if that wasn't bad enough, you divorce him. Did you get an annulment when you were at church at least?"

"Shut up, Susan, that's beside the point."

Apparently, my father managed to find a way to get sauced over the course of this five-minute conversation.

"I thought we made ourselves clear," my father said, commanding the airwaves. "We are no longer interested in having you in this family. I'm not sure what you expected to gain by calling us, but the deal stands. We're done with you and the lunacy of your love life."

Click.

Dick.

My mind raced between thoughts of my parents, the consummate assholes, and at Sheldon for stepping into my life all over again. In Europe, for God's sake—how was that even possible? I scooped up my soggy purse from the bench and sprinted down the rocky road.

***

No one was more surprised than me when I found myself back on the steps of the Vatican. I chalked it up to a bizarre calling of sorts, to make up for lost church time perhaps. I entered the building and swam through the crowds until I got to the front of the church. I maneuvered into a pew.

Man, it was bloody hot. Get with the times, people. This was the age of climate control. Christ could handle it back in the day because he was outfitted in scraps of cloth, but now we lived by higher standards.

A Japanese couple hovered overhead in the pew behind me, talking in a foreign tongue, pointing and gesturing—just two of many gawking tourists—all likely making fun of me.

"Shhhhh, I'm trying to concentrate," I whispered, looking back at them briefly.

They ignored me and continued to babble while pointing and clicking their stupid oversized camera in my direction, like reporters eager to pounce on a story. They looked equally fascinated and horrified, as if they'd just caught a nun in the midst of a sexual act. Maybe they had.

"Beat it! Where I come from, it's rude to stare at

people and ruder still to click pictures at someone who is obviously upset. Plus, no snapshots in church for Christ's sake!" And then, as if by magic, Vatican Man appeared wearing nothing more than a Jesus-style loin cloth. Guess he couldn't take the heat either. I tried to ignore him.

My trip was not going at all like I had hoped. A failed confession, kicked out of the Vatican, falling at the foot of a famous fountain, running into my ex-husband at said fountain with my underwear fanning the crowd, being taunted and followed by a lunatic, and then being kicked out of my family— again. Not what one would call a stellar start to a new life.

Foreign tongues continued to bark all around me. Were services starting? Or maybe I just hoped they would so I could get the hell out of the church. My head felt like it could erupt at any moment, so I knelt down, bowed my head, and began the deep-breathing exercises I learned from *Yoga* magazine. Yes, I guess the priest and Sheldon had been right— it did always come back to simply breathing. Kneeling proved painful due to the scrapes from my tumble at the fountain. Apparently, the Vatican was too holier-than-thou to opt for padded kneelers.

I tried to escape the crowds in the back by moving up to the row closest to the altar. Not many souls would be brave enough to sit here. Being right next to all the godliness haunted me. Tourists lurked in hidden corners, I could feel them.

Focus, Samantha, breathe, breathe, breathe.

Wow! That did help—thanks, *Yoga* magazine. I continued heaving big, long, deep breaths, visualizing breathing away my problems: my parents, Sheldon, mean nuns, crazy old men, tourists, and even Justin and his oddball proposal.

The next thing I knew, my head snapped forward, jolting me awake. Yikes, had I actually fallen asleep? That deep breathing was powerful stuff. I dipped into my bag to grab a Kleenex to wipe the drool off my forearm. It had all but disintegrated yet it was still functional. I rooted around for my shawl. The Catholics didn't want anyone entering a church in Rome without covering their shoulders. I had been busted on that earlier. I continued to rummage through my soggy bag, but no luck. What the hell?

Holy shit! No shawl. Or wallet. I was certain I'd grabbed everything when I scooped my purse out of Trevi Fountain. Could someone have snatched it while I sleep-prayed? That would surely be a sin. Frantic, I dumped out the entire contents of my purse onto the pew in front of me, some stuff still wet from earlier. Nope, no wallet. I gathered everything back into my bag, made a sign of the cross, and excused myself out of the row.

"Hail Mary," I said.

I pushed past the crowds tripping again, though this time I refrained from flashing my underwear at people, and ran out of the church, stopping only when I reached the front steps. Masses of people were scattered all over God's front yard.

In the distance, I saw a nun scamper toward the exit of Vatican City. She threw a sharp sneer at me and picked up speed as she parted the crowd. From the steps, I watched as she tossed off her habit headpiece and pushed people out of her way, gaining even more speed. With each step, she looked less like a nun and more like a person who had just scored a life savings...wait, she had—mine. Why hadn't I converted my cash into traveler's checks like *Travel + Leisure* magazine recommended? I watched the gypsy-posing-as-a-nun flee the blessed city.

Had these thieves no shame? Not one bloody magazine article bothered to warn tourists about falling asleep inside the church. The world assumed that the Vatican would be sacred ground, free of pillage and robbery, but apparently not.

And then as if God transported someone to answer me, Vatican Man reappeared. He just shook his head, not even bothering to make the sign of the cross anymore. I guess I was no longer worthy of even a senile old man's attention.

"What are you looking at? Go back to your own country," I shouted to a pack of sneaker-clad tourists who were being led into the church by an underage Italian tour guide.

"Watch your bags, people. Nothing is safe in this town!"

A nun, hopefully a real one, appeared before me as if to deliver me from evil. Instead, she shooed me off the steps.

"What? I'm not looking glamorous enough for you? I'm sorry. I was just robbed," I yelled.

Just like the nuns of my youth, she showed me no mercy. She pointed at a bible and shooed me away from the entrance. I was not worthy of redemption.

"What, is looking unkempt a mortal sin too? What ails you people? Eve ate the bloody apple already, so clearly we are not meant to be perfect!"

She pushed me aside.

"Whatever."

I clutched my empty purse and tried to get away from the church as fast as I could. Due to the crowds that grew thicker with each step, it took me far too long. When I finally reached the edge of Vatican City, I looked back at the grand dame of a church and shouted, "Screw you, Jesus Christ!" and flipped nobody in particular the bird.

How much more could one person take? Let alone on what was supposed to be a leisurely romp through Rome? The last few years of my life replayed in my mind like a horror movie.

As if on cue, Vatican Man reappeared. What was this guy's problem?

"Go find some other soul to save, mister, mine is unsalvageable," I said. Then I flipped him the bird too.

I pulled out my phone, the only thing that the thief did not steal since it was still stuck to my tit, and dialed as fast as my flipping middle finger could fly.

"Hello?" my dad said.

"Hello, Father, I would like to have a word with you, I hope I'm not interrupting your cocktail hour. Ha, who am I kidding? Every hour is happy hour with you people," I said as I giggled wickedly.

"What could you possibly have to say to me other than an apology, which could take a while. Susan, get me a beer," Dad commanded, ever the

309

gentleman. "Your ex-daughter has graced us with another phone call. Two times in one day, not sure what in the hell we did wrong to deserve this."

I took three breaths, made an abrupt sign of the cross to Vatican Man, and began.

"Well, as a matter of fact, my damning parents from hell, I do have something to say. I am no longer equipped to deal with you people. During every major milestone in my life, you have done nothing but denigrate and disown me. This is not good Catholic behavior. Don't you remember the commandments? *Love thy neighbor like thyself?* Only I'm not your neighbor; I am your god damned motherfucking daughter, for Christ's sake! Well, try this on for size, geezers. *I'm* firing *you* from the family. So take that and stuff it up your tightly wound, bad-practicing Catholic asses! And, by the way, you drink too much, use incorrect English, and are incapable of making eye contact. Didn't the Bible ever teach you people anything?"

Free at last.

Chapter Thirty-Four

The triumph of firing my family fizzled when I realized I had no idea where I was. I'd paced around for a few hours trying to get as far away as possible from the Vatican. Never again would I buy a cheap travel phone. This one didn't even have a maps app.

I needed to get inside before sundown, since *Lonely Planet* warned against blondish women traveling alone in Italy. The last thing I needed was to get mugged. But instead of feeling scared, I felt empowered—weightless in a way, having released myself from the talons of my parents' lifelong grip.

If I had known that issuing my family a pink slip would have felt this liberating, I would have done it years ago. Now I could be whoever I wanted to be—Catholic, heathen, or maybe just happy for a change. We all made mistakes, granted some of us much bigger ones than others, but I'd done the best I could.

A few minutes later, I stumbled upon a café, the Italians' rendition of an Irish pub, but more brightly lit. This place felt extra welcoming because it was airy and free of beer stank. Instead, coffee, liqueurs, and sweet-scented pastries wafted out the windows.

I entered, made my way up to the bar, and sat atop a lonesome stool, prepared to enjoy the serenity of this quaint little spot.

"*Bella*, welcome, you're not from a here, are you?" a portly balding barista greeted me.

"No, no I'm not, and if you don't mind, I don't feel much like being entertained with anecdotal stories about Rome. Can you just pour me three shots of grappa and leave me alone please? Wait. Make that three shots of espresso instead. *Grazie*."

"Whatever the beautiful lady wishes," he said as he bowed and withdrew.

As I waited somewhat impatiently for my coffee shots, I took in my surroundings and realized I was the only American in the place. Not even a nun or Vatican Man to be found, thank God. I should have felt awkward and nervous, yet instead, I felt strong and safe. Perhaps it was the marble counter and mahogany tables that surrounded me—symbols of strength.

I found it impossible not to obsess over what Sheldon was doing in Rome. What were the odds? I couldn't imagine what we would have to talk about after all this time. Maybe I could regale him with my family firing. He would surely share in some of the delight of my bold move. My parents were never kind to poor Sheldon. The countless times they called him a gigolo-hussy never sat well with him. Or me.

The barista finally returned with three dainty cups of espresso that he set down with a flourish in front of me. He started spewing something about the grind of the beans and flavor profile. I blocked out his babble and that of the people sitting next to me by tossing back the first shot of caffeine. It burnt the back of my throat as I swallowed, but damn, did it taste good on the way down. As thoughts about a potential lunch with Sheldon cluttered my mind, I sucked down the next shot with ease. *Sheldon be gone*, I thought.

As I let the coffee flavor linger on my lips, I did a double take when an Italian stallion, whose build made me think of Justin, sauntered into the bar. He had icy blue eyes, olive skin, and sleek, dark hair. I had to admit, he looked striking. His biceps matched Justin's in stature and girth.

As he walked toward the bar, I felt him mentally undress me with each step. Every blink of his gigantic eyes reminded me of Justin and his proposal. The memory of Justin's adorable eyes staring back at me from the street corner was a painful one. Remembering me charging down the street away from him the last time I saw him wasn't any better. Running and ultimately fleeing the country had to be one of the worst ways to not answer someone's proposal of marriage. A simple "no" might have sufficed.

I stared for a minute longer at the beautiful Italian man and his perfectly sculpted chest that was exposed more than any American could ever pull off in a public place. He continued to walk toward me, forcing me to gulp down my final coffee shot. I gagged at the exact moment he took the seat next to me.

Without words, he began to stroke my hair, and then he pulled a cocktail napkin from the bar, and ever so gently began to wipe away the espresso that had spewed out of the corner of my mouth. He continued to move up to my eyes where he wiped away the train of tears that had begun to fall without my knowledge. He parted the hair out of my eyes, and spoke softly in Italian, none of which I understood.

I gazed into his eyes, but all I could see looking back at me was Justin. The stallion gently kissed each of my eyelids, as if to grant them permission to stay closed. He moved away from my lids, down to the cheeks, eventually landing on my lips. The next thing I knew, we were in a tender and loving embrace coupled with soft kisses, and then an ever so slight slide of his tongue up to the roof of my mouth.

Something jolted me out of this sensual experience—namely the fact that as much as I wanted him to be, this man was not Justin. He was just a random person who I allowed to try to mend my broken heart in what I imagined was the Italian way—drowning devastation in kisses. This was no longer an acceptable means of coping. As if another meaningless sexual tryst would help me forget what I had done, or melt away my fears of a normal life. *You are right. You deserve better than this. Now is your chance to heal.*

"I'm sorry, sir. I appreciate your kindness, and while I certainly enjoyed your supple lips and looking at your shapely ass—I mean buttocks, sorry, I'm trying to stop cursing. Anyway, I can't keep doing this. I left a man, a very good man, a very sweet man, in the middle of a Manhattan street with my engagement ring, because I didn't feel ready to accept his love, so this just wouldn't be right. Thank you, but no thank you."

Without thinking, I pulled out the scrap of paper where Sheldon had scribbled his phone number and dialed. He answered.

"Hey, you, hope you had a nice conference," I said. "I've had a chance to breathe, as you suggested, and I was thinking it would be nice to meet for lunch, if you're still open to the idea."

"Yeah, it's time, Sam. It really is. Let's meet back at the fountain. Tomorrow at noon?"

As I hung up my phone and reached for my wallet to pay for the espressos, I realized that I had no wallet thanks to the local talent. Before I had a chance to panic, though, stallion winked and said something in Italian, which I understood to mean he had taken care of things for me.

I hugged him and left the café, feeling much lighter than when I entered. I strolled down the cobblestone street trying to find the best route back to my hotel. The street was strangely barren except for one person I saw up ahead. I picked up my pace trying to catch up, curious who it was—and saw Vatican Man. Something was different though…he didn't look nearly as scary anymore. In fact, he actually smiled at me. And then he kept on walking, as did I, until all the craziness of the day—and a lifetime—melted away, right along with him.

Chapter Thirty-Five

I paced around my hotel room and obsessed over the facts. I had been married, divorced, fired, disowned, and almost excommunicated by a meddling nun. But at least I was alive. Hard to know if I should count that as a blessing or a curse, but I opted for the former. Now it was all about my come-to-Jesus meeting with Sheldon, fitting considering my proximity to the religious capital of the world. *You can do this. It will be okay.*

I stressed for two hours trying to pick the perfect outfit, one that would strike a balance of looking cute and sassy but not too overdone. I landed on my favorite pair of pink jeans and a fitted baby tee. I paused to check my look in the mirror. It worked. I continued to stare at my reflection, looking for a sign that I was not about to embark on one of the bigger mistakes of my life. *You can do this.*

The thought of seeing Sheldon again petrified me, but something propelled me to leave my hotel.

As I walked back toward the fountain, I felt like I was about to jump off a cliff. All sorts of crazy things ran through my mind. Would Sheldon spit in my face and berate me for all the sins of my past? Did he somehow find out about the affair that led to the dissolution of our marriage and want to call me out on it? I wondered if he would ever be willing to forgive me.

This scene from my overly active imagination played out. Sheldon ambushed me at Trevi Fountain and threw me in. As I flailed in the dirty water, unable to swim, tourists tossed large coins at me while he attacked me with barbs that detailed all the ways I had ruined his life. Was this lunch just a setup?

I continued to walk, committed to facing my fears like a grown up. What had he been up to all these years? Had his workaholic ways paid off, did he ever remarry, and most of all, did he hate me or still love me just a little—all things that would soon be answered.

My phone jangled me out of the turbulent trance.

"Hey, Sam, I'm wrapping things up at the conference. Are we still on for lunch?" Sheldon asked.

"Yep, I'm on my way. See you soon."

As the city streets streamed by, so did a filmstrip of memories and disturbing feelings toward my family, but the closer I got to Trevi, the slower the home movie rolled. Maybe it was the gravity of the situation I was about to embark upon, or perhaps just the godly streets of Rome, but the horror movie version of my life stopped playing. I picked up my pace to a gallop, making my way through alleyways and bumping people out of my path without even tripping. Progress. The thick crowds indicated that I must be getting close.

Beads of sweat fell to the cobbled streets beneath me as I ran, anger dissipating with each step. It was time to stop blaming God and everybody else for my problems. What if it had been me all along?

I glanced up to the sky and prayed—it was Rome, after all. I prayed for the courage to make it through lunch. I prayed for the strength to not cry. I prayed for Sheldon's forgiveness, or maybe more than anything, my own.

The ground was damp from the kids splashing water out of the fountain so I almost lost my footing, but stopped myself from slipping this time. I didn't want Sheldon to have to fetch me out of the fountain again.

I steadied myself just in time to notice him standing by the famous edifice. Despite the passage of time, he looked the same—better, actually. And God help me, I was still upright and dry. Not even a single tear flowed this time, only the water that ran through the fountain, ebbing rhythmically. Everything in life, ancient marks of history, even me, eventually moved forward. *You are strong. You can do this.*

As I approached, Sheldon went first for a handshake and then a hug.

"Sammy, it's good to see you, I'm really glad you decided to come. You look great," said a much softer Sheldon than I remembered.

"You too," I said, gasping for breath.

We found a ledge nearby and sat for several minutes surrounded by tourists, yet I felt as if we were the only two people in the city.

As the minutes and then hours progressed, we swapped stories about where our lives had taken us. I left out the parts about Frankie and Superstar and the countless family feuds. It felt like another lifetime ago and irrelevant to where I now found myself.

As we talked about the different paths we had taken to bring us to this moment, I realized we had both actually turned out okay. Better than okay. Sheldon had built a security empire. The Super Bowl gig gave him the experience and exposure that eventually led to an opportunity to staff and manage a multitude of sports complexes and arenas throughout the country. All of Sheldon's sweat equity had finally paid off.

We had moved on in our lives, or in my case fumbled along, but when nobody was looking, it seemed we might have even forgiven ourselves and each other for being the kind of people who did the kinds of things that we did way back when.

Our behavior wasn't always pretty, our actions— okay, more accurately, my actions—were often not acceptable, and none of it was ever planned, but that was then. It was time to move past all that now.

Sheldon pulled my hands into his, and with that one gesture, he settled my racing mind. I looked at him directly, for the first time without guilt or pain. Despite the swarm of tourists, I stayed present in our joint gaze. We exchanged what felt like decades of memories in the glances between us. Meaningful eye contact turned out to be not nearly as scary as I'd once thought. He looked at me kindly. Maybe I wasn't that bad after all. Just a normal woman who had fought hard to break away from her family's vision of her and finally won. I might have lost Justin, but maybe it had been worth it to get to this place of peace.

Sheldon and I walked off together, strolling until he stopped at a craggy little house rich with cracks, a caving wall, and a sunken roof—but amidst the flaws and remnants of a storied past, there were modern touches tucked between the old. Like a rebirth in the making.

He stared at me and then hugged me as if it were the last time I would ever see him. I felt a solo tear welling up, so I willed it to stop. *You are okay, you can handle this.*

"Don't worry, Sammy. We're all good, you and I," he said. "If you ever need anything, I'm here for you. I always will be, just like I'll always remember you exactly as you are right now."

And with a dry-eyed yet heartfelt goodbye, he walked off with one last look at the rickety home that I suspected was destined for a comeback, just like me. He glanced back a final time and mouthed what looked like, *I forgive you.*

Chapter Thirty-Six

I landed at JFK stinky and jetlagged, but it felt good to be back. Europe was as great as the next place, but there were things in America that just couldn't be beat, like soft, non-abrasive toilet tissue, for starters.

Shannon agreed to meet me at the airport so we could catch up and she could kvetch about my choice to, as she put it, "run around Rome without her and my engagement ring."

She honked the horn of her jalopy so loudly I wondered if she had accidently fallen asleep on the steering wheel.

"Sammy, I'm so happy to see you! And don't you ever pull a stunt like that again. I was so worried about you," she shouted, bear hugging me as I climbed into the passenger seat.

"I know. It all happened so quickly. I just had to get out of the city and reckon with my religion. God seemed to be working against me instead of for me."

"How did that turn out for you?" Shannon asked.

"Well, I fell into a fountain, got tossed out of the Vatican, bumped into Sheldon, and…no, never mind the lowlights. I'm not gonna do the sob stories anymore. I've wasted too much time on that stuff. The highlights—Sheldon and I got closure, and you know what?"

"No, I'm still processing that you bumped into him. That's nuts."

"He doesn't hate me. I think he might have even forgiven me. And I decided to forgive myself, right after I fired my family."

"You did what?" Shannon asked.

"I finally stood up to them. Oprah was right. Boundaries are key. I can't tell you how amazing I feel. Like, I've got a chance to start over without all the negativity sniping in my ear. And I'm going to Al-Anon."

"It's about damn time," she said.

"And after being asked to leave the Vatican, I decided to take religion into my own hands. I trust that there is a kinder God up there looking out for me. All I need to do is get out of his way so he can do his job without the hazard of me getting in the way of myself."

"Well, I take back all of the tough love emails I sent you. If you needed to go all the way to Rome to find this stuff out, so be it. I'm just glad you're back. So now what?"

"No booze for me."

She laughed. "No, really. Where should we go out? I think all this good news calls for shots."

"Seriously, I'm done with all of that. A Serrano without a drinking problem…imagine the possibilities. As far as the rest of my life, I wish I knew."

Chapter Thirty-Seven

I walked down the street toward my new office. My very own business based in Alphabet City, whose seedy past, much like my own, was over. I decorated the trendy tenement building loft space with lots of retro furniture and pink accents.

When I got back from Italy, I had been bombarded with frivolous, easy-to-delete voicemails, except for one from Babs, of all people. She told me to get my ass back in the country because NetSocial had finally gone public. Her voicemail will stay in my archives forever.

"You're fucking rich, Sammy. Come have fun with me!"

In a matter of months, I took my earnings and transformed them into a solo endeavor called *Sammy Can!*—a one-stop event planning and promotions company catering to anybody who needed help—a concept I could have benefited from in the past.

My tenure with Crazy Molly ended with a few perks that I worked to my own advantage. The first one was that I had mastered the art of working with difficult people, which came in handy as a sole proprietor, as clients could be uber-demanding (and on bad days even a bit crazy). Many of my initial customers came as a result of my work with Molly. Some felt that if I could work with her, I could manage any high-stress situation, and they were right. She was a nutcase, but her client contacts were A-list all the way. When she retired after a breakdown, Molly directed most of her customers to me—but not before chiding me one last time, about the drunken voicemail I had left her from the Catskills. I sent her an obnoxiously oversized wine and fruit basket that, while pricey, made everything better between us.

I offered a full range of services, from public relations to event planning, which included throwing saucy parties for the most discriminating, and in some cases, famous clients. People liked my tough yet friendly approach to business along with my ability to hyper-focus on their needs. *Yes, you've become a skilled professional.*

To generate some positive buzz for my company, I hosted a high-profile party for a client who launched a new jewelry line crafted from baubles confiscated during drug kingpin arrests. My client transformed the gems into one-of-a-kind sparkly works of art. I oversaw the auction for the line, which donated a percentage of the proceeds to Catholic charity foundations around the globe.

***

On a sultry, hot spring morning, I was celebrating the success of the party over a cappuccino yogurt muffin and an iced latte when the front door of my office jingled and swung open. The visitor balanced a tower of boxes, flashing his badge beneath them, not bothering to look up.

"Official FBI business," he said.

I peered past the parcels to check him out. When he looked up, our gazes intersected. Despite the longer mane of wavy strawberry blonde hair, there was no denying it was Justin. I would recognize those muscles anywhere.

"Wow. How are you? I mean, well, I'm sure you're fine, better off, actually," I stammered.

He looked at me flatly, and I felt as if he were staring right through my newly redeemed soul.

"I thought you ran off to Europe," he said.

I tried not to read too much into the biting tone.

"You're not too far off with the running part. I wasn't totally prepared to deal with, well, you know." Of course he knew. It was all over his face. *It's okay to tell him you made a mistake.*

"I hope you found what you were looking for," he said. "I had no idea you were behind this jewelry program. It's gotta make your mom happy, giving back to the Catholics."

He winked at me. Was it possible he still cared?

"I hope she's glad. She and the Catholics mean well, even if they're a bit antiquated in their approach," I said. "And guess what? I fired my family when I was in Rome. It seemed fitting after all the times they'd tossed me out of their lives. It was time to return the favor," I said, and then giggled nervously, remembering how close I felt to him but not sure it was appropriate anymore.

This moment was about Justin, not my family. How did one come up with the right words when you wronged someone so deeply? *Speak your heart, and those worthy of it will listen.*

"Maybe now you'll be ready to find a way to repair things…maybe," he said, looking equally apprehensive and awkward.

Was it possible he was speaking more about us than my relationship with my family? Or maybe that was just wishful thinking. *You'll never know unless you take the risk.* I paced around the office, dusting my pink orchids as he followed me with his eyes.

"I really wish things worked out differently for us," I said. "There hasn't been a day that I haven't thought of you."

I prayed for him to hear me.

"I got to get back out there," he said. "The terrorists never sleep, ya know."

And just like that, he left. No wink this time.

I waited for him to look back, but he never did; he just crossed the street and ran down toward the neighboring alley. After all this time, he still looked both stealthy and studly. I wondered why one of us always seemed to be running away. I contemplated what it would mean to run *to* someone instead of *away* from them.

So what if Justin didn't look back? Maybe I needed to give him a reason to do so. I opened one of the boxes he left, grabbed a handful of confiscated jewels, stuffed them in my purse, and ran out. Morning commuters peppered the streets, but it didn't stop me from picking up speed as I charged toward Union Square. I felt like Super Woman tearing through the streets, knocking over flower pots, jumping over fire hydrants and small dogs.

"Oh God, please let me find him," I chanted as I hit the street corner and stopped, waiting impatiently for the light to change.

I looked across the street and saw Justin, speaking into his shirt's pec pocket. The FBI thing still did it for me.

I sprinted toward him, screaming his name and flailing my arms. He looked alarmed, but I didn't stop. Then I spotted it—a parking meter!

As I approached the metal pole, I made a sign of the cross, crouched, and then leapt as high as I could, flapping my hands as if they were wings. I went semi-airborne, but instead of clearing the meter with grace as Justin had done on the night we met, my pink bubble skirt got caught on my way up and I flopped to the ground. Fashion and flapping arm-wings could only get you so far, especially when you're as short as I am. Justin laughed, though I couldn't be certain if it was *at* me or *with* me. It didn't really matter.

The cement was sticky with ice cream, but not even a stained frock could derail my mission. I pulled my skirt back over my underwear (some things will never change) and tried to straighten myself out. One of the confiscated baubles fell out of my purse. Sweat poured off my brows and I felt like I could vomit. But I stopped myself—I had been learning to quell this tendency to expel. I picked up a honking huge platinum ring that formed two mating flies, clutched it firmly, and rose to my knees. I looked up to God and sucked in a big breath.

"I'm sorry that I'm stinky and sweaty, and that you had to see my underwear in this particular light," I said. "I'm also sorry I couldn't clear the parking meter like you taught me, but what I'm most sorry for is running away from you when you proposed."

I waited for him to say something. He spoke not a word, yet a tiny smile twitched over his lips.

"I have loved you from the moment I saw you and your pinch-worthy pecs at Pete's," I said. "I have never stopped, not even when we took that break. I want to spend the rest of my life with you, or die trying."

He looked at me, and then cocked his head. Did he feel sorry for me or enamored? It was hard to tell from my vantage point.

"Sam," he said.

"Okay. Wait, no! I want you to understand me. I love you, and me and you, and heck, maybe I even love my parents for putting me on this earth so I could find you!" I yelled.

"Yes," he said.

"Yes, what? You love me too, or you love my parents, which would be totally weird considering you never met them and have only heard my horror stories."

"Okay, I guess I'm gonna have to break this down for you," he said, his eyes softening back to the familiar gaze I adored. "Yes, I love you, and yes, I love your parents because they are a part of you, and yes, I want to spend the rest of my life with you."

He picked me up and placed me on top of the parking meter, then kissed me right off that thing until we were both kissing and laughing our way around the street corner.

Somebody—the right person—finally loved me. And I vowed, this time, to let them.

***

I bustled around my office stacking files and rearranging potted tulip plants in between daydreaming out the window. This is what content people in love do on sun-kissed spring afternoons. I am not totally sure why my luck finally changed for the better, but who was I to question it?

My telephone rang with the "I've Got You Babe" ringtone. Corny, maybe, but second time around, love did that to people.

"Hey, baby, how are things coming along? Do you need me to haul anything to the park?" Justin asked.

"Nope, I've got it covered. But I love you for asking," I said. "This is my deal. Remember, that was the agreement. Just meet me at the boat pond at two pm sharp. I can't wait!"

I hung up the phone and finished the last of my wedding preparations. Justin agreed to legitimize our relationship in the middle of Central Park, just a small gathering with a wedding officiate, my brother and his brood, Shannon, Candy, Paddy and a few of Justin's mysterious work associates.

I dressed simply in a vintage light pink chiffon cocktail dress. A quick peek into the full-length mirror that was stashed back in my file room made me giggle. I looked like one of the wives on *Mad Men*, except I wasn't smoking or swilling drinks, at least not anymore. And as I lingered on the thought of retro women cocktailing in the middle of the afternoon, I thought of my mother. Then I cried ever so slightly. *Go ahead. You are ready.* I breathed in deeply, and because I was still a Catholic at heart, I prayed that maybe now things would be different.

I picked up the phone, fingers trembling, and dialed. Midway through the digits I started to hang up, but with one glance at an adorable phone-side photo of Justin and me posed next to a parking meter, I grounded myself.

"Hey, Mom, how are you?" I said.

"Samantha, is that you? Where are you? I hope you finally came back home. Get up here, Sal! Your daughter is on the line."

God, help me.

"Samantha?" my dad said.

"Oh good, you're both there. Before you say anything, I just wanted to say that I'm sorry. And I love you both."

Dead silence—a "pregnant with twins" type of pause. And then, I heard what sounded awfully close to a dry heave of some sort, and then some muffled sniffles.

"It's okay, Mom, you don't need to say anything.

I just wanted you to know that I'm back in the states. And I am doing okay now. Actually, I'm amazing. And I know you probably won't approve of this because I never went through with the annulment, but I'm going to Central Park today to marry Justin. He loves me, and I love him. I'm ready this time. I hope you can find a way to be happy for me."

My father grumbled in the background. I wasn't sure if he was swilling a beer or sneezing, but it really didn't matter.

"Well," he said, and then I could hear my mother smack him on the back.

"I guess that's okay. It's good you found someone finally," he said.

My mother smacked him again.

"We do love you, Samantha. We always have. Emotions have never been easy for me. You know that." And finally, I did.

"What we are trying to say is, we're happy for you." And then she dry-heave cried into the phone. Some things would never change, and that was okay.

"All righty then. You guys take care. I love you."

I looked at my watch and realized it was time, my time. In a fit of excitement, I touched up my make-up, smoothed my up-do into place, and ran out the door. As I gazed out over Manhattan, on the most magnificent first day of the rest of my life, I looked up to the sky, made a subtle sign of the cross, and said, "Thank you."

Acknowledgements

This book would never have been possible without the tireless support from head cheerleaders Candy Jackson and Shawna Parks, who flat out refused to let me give up on this dream. I am forever grateful. Candy, you wore far too many hats to count, some of which included fangirl, beta reader, marketer, fashion consultant, tear wiper, ego plumper—the list is endless—but most importantly, friend. You have been a part of every major milestone in my life, the highs, the lows, and everything in between. This book (and my sanity) would not exist without your love and encouragement. Thank you.

Eileen Lydon, your friendship and support are immeasurable. We have shared so many incredible moments over the years. I have you to blame for making my time in Manhattan some of the most amazing (and raucous) times of my life, in all the gnarly and beautiful glory that was our thirties. Though life would eventually pit us on opposing coasts, nothing could or ever will stand in the way of our friendship.

To my readers, my fabulous readers. Thank you, thank you, thank you! If it weren't for you, this story would have remained nothing more than a closed book. Thank you for taking the time to get to know me through these words. Your support means the world to me.

To the tireless team at Limitless Publishing, thank you for taking a chance on an unknown author and supporting me every step of the way. I couldn't ask for a more committed group of professionals to lead the charge. Laura Kemmerer, thank you for your attention to detail and insightful edits. This book is the best it can be thanks to your work.

To Ann-Marie Nieves, Laurel Hilton, and Rick and Amy Miles. You "got it" and made sure the rest of the world would not only know about this book but read it. Thank you for taking all my crazy ideas and running with them, and for knowing when to kibosh a few of the really out-there ideas. You are all brilliant at what you do.

Robin Madell, you dropped into my life at the precise moment I was about to give up. Your belief in my work gave me the courage to carry on when I needed it the most. You became the first professional champion of this story, and I couldn't have asked for a better advocate. Your eagle-eye editorial insights brought a welcome and crucial perspective. Thank you for the role you played in getting this book out into the world. It would have never happened without you.

Thank you to Lauren Patrice Nadler, my first beta reader. I remember that night when I showed up with my beloved brand new (old) rescue pooch Cari-Anne. You came barreling in with a gigantic dog-eared first draft of my manuscript, with ideas out the wazoo on how to make it sing. Some of your notes went on to shape the very fabric and heart of this story. It's come a long way since then, in part due to your input early on. To my critique partners and fellow writers Patsy Ann Taylor, Barbara Toboni, Amber Lea Starfire, Kate Reeves, and Ana

Manwaring, you offered critical feedback early on, when I desperately needed an outside perspective.

To my brother, Joey, who slogged through a very early draft, and made it to the finish line despite what you like to refer to as "all the penis talk." You have been a beacon of support and encouragement my entire life and for that, I am oh so grateful. To my sister-in-law Debra, who wiped away the tears and celebrated the triumphs, and thankfully, convinced me to move to the Napa Valley, where at long last I would actualize this dream of a writer's life. Mom and Dad, you brought me into this world and showed me what it means to live life to the extreme. You also taught me to never, under any circumstances, take no for an answer. Thank god I listened to you for once!

To my husband, Derek, and our heart-melting twins Cindy and Dakota. You all are my rock, my salvation, my everything. Your love and support are what make this life possible and worthwhile.

And finally, to all the *other* men who came in and out of my life. Without you and your daring, loving, and at times deplorable behavior, none of this would have been possible.

About the Author

Christina Julian writes snarky rom-coms that celebrate the underdog and live to make people laugh. She adores dysfunctional leading ladies and the tangled twisty lives they lead. She adamantly believes there is nothing in life that can't be conquered with a bodacious wine, strong cup of coffee, or a generously iced cupcake. When she is not tapping out her next novel or wrangling her 3-year-old twins, she can be found swilling and swirling in the name of research as a wine and food columnist in Napa Valley. She strives always to live her life to the extreme.

Christina's work has appeared in the *San Francisco Chronicle, Wine Enthusiast, Weddings California, California Home + Design, 7×7, Napa Valley Register, Napa Valley Life, Bohemian, Weekly Calistogan, NorthBay Biz* and beyond. Connect at christinajulian.com.

Facebook:
http://facebook.com/ChristinaJulianAuthor

Twitter:
https://twitter.com/christin_julian

Goodreads:
http://www.goodreads.com/Christina_Julian

Made in the USA
Columbia, SC
27 August 2017